Chennaivaasi

T.S.Tirumurti is Joint Secretary in the Ministry of External Affairs, New Delhi. He joined the Indian Foreign Service in 1985 and has since served in Indian Missions in Cairo, Geneva, Gaza, Washington, D.C. and Jakarta. He is the author of a travelogue, *Kissing the Heavens: The Kailash Manasarovar Yatra*, and a novel, *Clive Avenue*. This is his second novel.

Chennaivaasi

T.S. TIRUMURTI

HarperCollins *Publishers* India
a joint venture with

New Delhi

First published in India in 2012 by
HarperCollins *Publishers* India
a joint venture with
The India Today Group

Copyright © T.S. Tirumurti 2012

ISBN: 978-93-5029-101-6

2 4 6 8 10 9 7 5 3 1

T.S. Tirumurti asserts the moral right
to be identified as the author of this work.

This is a work of fiction and all characters and incidents
described in this book are the product of the author's imagination.
Any resemblance to actual persons, living or dead, is entirely coincidental.

HarperCollins *Publishers*
A-53, Sector 57, Noida, Uttar Pradesh 201301, India
77-85 Fulham Palace Road, London W6 8JB, United Kingdom
Hazelton Lanes, 55 Avenue Road, Suite 2900, Toronto, Ontario M5R 3L2
and 1995 Markham Road, Scarborough, Ontario M1B 5M8, Canada
25 Ryde Road, Pymble, Sydney, NSW 2073, Australia
31 View Road, Glenfield, Auckland 10, New Zealand
10 East 53rd Street, New York NY 10022, USA

Typeset in 11/14 ITC New Baskerville
InoSoft Systems Noida

Printed and bound at
Thomson Press (India) Ltd.

To my wife Gowri

Prologue

She sat outside.

It was almost six-thirty in the morning and the light coolness of night still hung in the air. She had wrapped herself in a thin shawl. Chennai was not always like this. In fact, for eleven months of the year, it wasn't like this at all. Usually, the day started warm, became hot and stayed hot. Without respite. Day after day. Sweaty. Sultry. Sapping the strength of man and animal and bird. But this was the season for cool mornings. Cool, even chilly mornings.

She sat patiently on an ancient wooden bench on one side of the open verandah. There were two other people sitting next to her. She had been the first to come. She had pretended that she was going to a temple, told her daughters-in-law not to get up, and left through the back door so as not to disturb her husband. The road was narrow and the driver had taken his time to negotiate it. It wasn't too difficult to locate the building, an old one with a sloping tiled roof. But it was only when she saw the shy name board outside that she realized she had reached.

Agastya Naadi Josium, it said in Tamil and was almost buried in the foliage.

The receptionist was already there, an old man, looking fresh and sprightly with streaks of white vibuthi across his forehead. A fresh incense stick was stuck in front of a large picture of Ganesha mounted on his vahanam, the mouse. The picture dwarfed him in the tiny room. But that was what gods were supposed to do. Dwarf men. The room smelled of hibiscus.

It was nearly seven when she saw a couple of middle-aged persons clothed in white starched veshtis go into the building and guessed that they must be the Naadi astrologers. By now, others had joined her on the wooden bench. The receptionist came out and took her into the prayer room. He brought out a sheaf of small white square papers and a stamp-ink box.

'Could you dip your finger into this and imprint it on this paper?' he asked.

She did as she was told.

'Do you want me to write my name behind the paper?' she asked.

'No, no, Amma,' he said, sounding alarmed. 'We don't need your name at all nor do we ask for it. We just need your fingerprint. Now please wait outside, Amma, while we locate your palm leaves. It may take some time. Maybe another half an hour. You could have your breakfast and come back…'

'No, it's all right. I will wait.'

Less than twenty minutes later, another person dressed in a similar white veshti motioned for her to come in. She was led into a small room. It was empty apart from a table with two chairs on either side. A bundle of palm leaves bound in cloth had been placed on the table. She sat on one chair and he took the other.

'Amma, my name is Keshavan. I am going to read your Naadi palm leaves today. I have tried to locate your leaves by using your fingerprint and have brought some bundles here. I will read out the first few lines from each bundle. If it pertains to you, tell me. I don't want to know your name or anything else. If what I read is about you, tell me. If not, say no. We will move on to the next one.'

She nodded.

The Naadi astrologer carefully untied the knot of the top bundle and took out a palm leaf. It was in old Tamil, the grammar and intonation quaint. At first she strained to understand. He explained it in simpler Tamil.

'… as the only child of Swaminathan avargal and…' he read out, and she quickly interrupted him: 'No, it's not mine. I am not an only child, I have a brother.'

He put the bundle away and picked up another. '… grace of god to be born as the only daughter of Thiruvengadam and Kamalambal—'

She shook her head. 'My father's name is not Thiruvengadam nor is my mother Kamalambal…'

He carefully wrapped it, put it away and opened another. That wasn't for her either. Neither was the next. It was only after he had read out eight more that it came.

'Hailing from the banks of the Cauvery, you were born to Ramamurthi and Kamakshi and have one brother by the name of Narayanan. You birth star is pooradam and your husband's name…'

'Yes, that's mine,' she said, a quiet excitement creeping up her spine.

'Amma, now let me show this palm leaf to you so that you can read it for yourself.'

'No, no,' she protested. 'I don't doubt you.'

'No, Amma. That's not the point. You will enjoy reading it and see for yourself how this had been written several thousand years ago during the time of the great sage Agastya!

All written thousands of years ago, for this day when you will come to have your future read!'

He placed the open palm leaf in front of her. It was dry and looked firm, if old. She didn't touch it. It was Tamil all right. The words were joined to each other so that they formed one long string of letters without a break—like a string of pearls. The handwriting was beautiful.

'See, your name is here and your parents' names are here,' he pointed out.

Yes, she could see now, clearly. She read the lines carefully. The time of her birth was mentioned as well as the place. *You have three sons and one daughter*, it said, and it even mentioned their names. She could barely contain her excitement but felt it would be undignified to show it.

'Read it to me,' she said.

'Amma, I will now take this bundle inside and transcribe it into simpler Tamil so that you can understand it better and it can also serve as a record for the future. It will take me about an hour to write it down. You could probably go have some breakfast and then come back. There is a good restaurant doun the road. He makes most of his money from the people who come here.' The Naadi astrologer chuckled.

She looked at him thoughtfully and then said, 'I don't need a record. What will I do with it? In any case, I am not going to share this with anyone. You could read it out to me right now and translate as you read. That will do.'

He looked at her and nodded. 'If that is your wish. I will first read the general part, which will give you an overview of your past and future.'

'Even the past?'

'Yes, everything. You see, Naadi astrology works on the principle that everything is preordained. It even tells you when you will come to read this Naadi. You are destined to read this Naadi only today. Not yesterday. Not tomorrow. Here, Amma…' He pointed to the second palm leaf and read out: 'You will come to read this Naadi on the second day of the week in the month of…'

She sat back, stunned. She hadn't quite expected this.

He read out the Naadi. It started with the invocation of Shiva, the Lord of Chidambaram, and with Agastya's prayer to Shiva. It described the contours of her fingerprint from which the palm leaves were identified. The Tamil month of her birth and her star; where Saturn and Ketu were located at the time of her birth. She was of Brahmin birth, second born in the family. Her name and her husband's name. Their three sons and daughter.

'Due to graha dosham and sins from your previous life, you are facing some family difficulties. Things may not happen as you desire. There is much confusion and consternation in the family. All your efforts seem to end in failure. Both you and your husband are deeply affected. There is also a separation of one of your children from the family.'

Her past. Her previous birth. She had been the wife of a wealthy landowner in Orissa. She had been a pious person. Her only regret before her death had been that her son had not married and she could never see a daughter-in-law in her house.

Back to the present. Her last child—a son—was successful in his education and work. But this boy had relations with a lady not from the country of his birth and this was causing distress to the family. The family might be in danger of breaking up.

'You may feel that your efforts are not helping. But you still try your best and invoke all the Ishta deities you do puja to daily. It is your steadfast prayer and all the good deeds you and your husband have accumulated from your past that stand your family in good stead during this period,' said the palm leaves.

And stopped.

For a few seconds, there was silence. She waited for more.

'What about the future?'

The Naadi astrologer looked perplexed. He took the cloth in his hands and tried to see whether he had left out any leaves. There was none.

'It usually does tell you about the future, Amma,' he said, quickly regaining his composure. 'But sometimes we are unable to locate it. I don't think you should let this bother you. Maybe if you read the other parts, there will be further detail…'

Her face fell. She had come all this way, braving her husband's wrath and children's displeasure. They would not have approved of her trying to learn about the future. 'Come on, Amma. I don't know why you keep believing in this junk,' her children would have said. She had just come to find the answers to some questions, answers that had evaded her so far. She had always wanted to consult the Naadi palm leaves but never felt the need to—till today.

She left the *Agastya Naadi Josium* building.

She had to find the answers to her future herself.

The answer came the next day.

She died in her sleep.

Part 1

1

She heard the gate open and the car enter. It was her husband returning from the Kapaleeshwarar temple. She could hear the door being opened. And shut. Footsteps climbing the steps. A pause in the verandah—that was Appa removing his chappals. The sound of the chappals sliding to one corner of the verandah.

Amma was prepared. She had been rehearsing what to tell Appa. She had to try and break the news gently—if that was at all possible.

Their third son Ravi had finally returned from America. That was good news. But he had come back with his American girlfriend Deborah.

'Ravi was here an hour ago,' she said when Appa came in. She looked away to avoid eye contact. God only knew how Appa would react.

Appa stopped in his tracks for a brief second.

'That good-for-nothing! When did he come to Madras?' he asked as he walked towards the bedroom.

'Yesterday.'

'What brings him here? I thought he had decided to stay in the US with his darling girlfriend!'

'You know he was returning to take up a job here.'

'He can go to hell.'

Amma kept quiet. Appa went into the bedroom, took off his shirt and pant and exchanged them for a veshti and banian. Amma followed him into the room and opened the wardrobe, pretending to look for something.

There was silence.

'Has he come with his white woman or come alone?' Appa asked finally.

'He has come with her.'

'What? Did he come to our house with her?'

'No… not to this house… he came here alone. They flew down to Chennai together yesterday and are staying in a hotel.'

'I hope you told him I don't want to see his face or the face of that wretched woman in my life?'

'Yes.'

'In so many words?'

'Yes, in so many words.'

'That porukki will not step into this house. He—'

'This is no way to speak about your son.'

'I'll call him this and more for the way he has behaved. That porukki thaazhi. He is a disgrace. He has ruined this family's reputation. We are the laughing stock of our friends and relatives. After the way I brought up my sons and daughter, this idiot has gone and ruined everything. Everyone is asking me what happened to all those wonderful values that I taught my children. With what face can I go out now? Who will respect us? All because of your favourite son.'

'He was as much your favourite,' she said gently.

'He is no more my son, let me tell you that. Once he went to America, he started thinking he knew it all. Like those upstarts. Not worth even a quarter-anna, going around with whores and picking up American habits! I never expected Ravi would be like this, that madayan.'

'Well, what's happened has happened. How long are we going to—'

'As long as I live,' Appa cut her short. 'He is not coming back to this house and he is not getting a single paisa from me.'

'What if he asks for his share of the house? After all, this is an ancestral property. He has a right to a one-sixth share…'

'He can go to hell, that madayan.'

'Let's not provoke him to do something silly. A case filed by the son against the father will become a soap opera. That's the last thing—'

'The goings-on in our house are already a soap opera because of that madayan. Anyway, let him do what he wants. I don't want to see him or have anything to do with him.'

'He may come back here to—'

'If he comes here again, I'll break his legs.'

The previous day, when the plane touched down at Anna International Airport in Chennai, Ravi and Deborah dismounted gratefully. Their backs were stiff, their legs wobbly. It had been a gruelling journey involving two transit halts.

The airport seemed friendly enough. It was no comparison to any international airport, not even as good as the one in Delhi, but the Chennaivaasis had to make do with it. Anna International Airport was named after the famous son of Tamil Nadu—Annadurai. Ravi remembered how small it used to be before, almost as if the city had no time for air travellers. Small and crowded.

On the other hand, visits to the train stations in Chennai—whether Madras Central or Egmore—were grand occasions.

Madras Central Railway Station was a particularly impressive structure. It was an 1873 Gothic revival-style structure that punctuated the Chennai skyline with an imposing clock tower. You had to fight to get platform tickets from the dark, tiny counter. You shoved your hand in with the money and got a ticket in return, dished out by the unseen ghostly figure sitting inside. When you entered the platform, the diesel smell and the farting of trains and steam engines made you giddy. Rows and rows of compartments bursting at the seams, filled with hawkers selling hot coffee, chai or paneer soda; coolies dressed in rust-red shirts and white veshtis weaving their way through the crowd with a pile of suitcases on their turbaned heads; a circle of waitlisted passengers accosting the ticket-collector to convince him that they desperately needed the last vacant seat on the train; mounds of brown gunny sacks, carrying anything from fruit to army rations, lying unattended on the platform, waiting for the goods train which always seemed to be stuck at Basin Bridge to let more important passenger trains pass through; a family of beggars arrogating a corner of the station for themselves near the public toilets; the excitement of trying to locate your relatives and friends through the windows even as the train streamed onto the platform; and the smell of railway dust wafting out of every compartment when the door opened—Madras Central was a busy station. Ravi loved it.

Holding his father's right hand—he must have been about five then—he marvelled at how just one engine could drag so many compartments. He dreaded the prospect of Appa losing the platform tickets and not being allowed to leave the station.

Father and son had their own favourite beggar, who sat just before the main exit on a torn gunny bag spread out over a flattened cardboard carton on the ground. Appa usually tossed him a four-anna coin before they left. There were other beggars outside, some afflicted with leprosy. The worst affected sat in a cart while the others dragged him around, holding out their stumps, the sores open and raw. Ravi would watch them in horrified fascination while his father shouted at them to go to a government hospital to get free treatment instead of begging. Appa did not favour giving beggars money, though he was a generous person otherwise. Begging has substituted daily wages, he warned. The more you encourage, the less you are helping them to become productive citizens. Look at some of these able-bodied beggars. They deserve to be whipped. But given the high unemployment rate, it was better to beg with open sores and fill the stomach than to starve with cured leprosy. And so these beggars persisted in their profession day after day till they withered away and died.

Appa always stopped in front of the station bookshop and bought Ravi *Amar Chitra Katha* comics. Mythology, epics, pictures and colours all merged into one another. It was worth going to the train station just for that.

Anna International Airport certainly had none of this excitement. You couldn't even see the planes take off. Now and then you could hear a plane thunder past, but that was useless. There wasn't any *Amar Chitra Katha* in the bookshop either. Even the beggars were shooed off by the police. It was useless to go to the airport. It just wasn't worth the journey.

Ravi and Deborah got their luggage. The four monstrous suitcases contained all they wanted to start a new life in Chennai. They collected it, told the disbelieving customs official that they didn't have anything to declare, and walked into the night.

It was a strange feeling for Ravi. He had always been met at the airport. Usually it was his father who landed up religiously and waited in the car, reading a book. Sometimes the car came alone with just the driver. But those were rare occasions when Appa was travelling. Today, there was no one. No Appa. Not even a car.

Well, there was always a first time. Ravi and Deborah took a taxi. Beyond the portals of the airport, the only thing they were sure of was their hotel booking. And their jobs. Very little else.

And, of course, their determination to make things work. To make Ravi's father agree to their marriage.

Appa held the key.

Amma sat quietly on the bed, pretending to stitch back a button that had come loose on Appa's shirt.

'Which company has he joined?' Appa asked.

'I don't know. But it pays him very well.'

'Obviously, all these American companies pay well.'

Ravi had told her that he would be soon shifting to Kamala athai's house. Along with Deborah, of course. Kamala athai was Appa's younger sister and lived in Gandhi Nagar, close to the Adyar river.

'That Kamala…' Appa shouted as soon as Amma told him. 'She's so gullible. Ravi must have given her a sob story. I thought my sister had better sense than to let my son and that thevidiya into her house. Tell her she is being naïve and foolish by letting that madayan stay with her. Her reputation will be ruined.'

'I'm not going to say any such thing. You tell her if you want. If you don't want him here, that's one thing. But let Kamala decide what she wants to do.'

'He can stay in the whorehouses of Kodambakkam, for all I care.'

Amma let that comment pass.

'Kamala has asked me to visit when I get the time,' she said.

'If you visit Ravi, don't come back to this house.'

Amma kept quiet. She had hardly expected him to bless her visit to Ravi but it was important that Appa know she was planning to go. With or without his permission, Amma was determined to see Ravi. That much she owed her son.

When Ravi's exhausted body woke up the next morning, he left behind a sleeping Deborah and headed out alone. Straight to the house at No.1 Vedaranyam Street. That was the first and only logical thing to do. He was sure of a welcome, even if it was not a very warm one. If no one else, Amma would be there, he thought.

The house-behind-the-row-of-Ashoka-trees was just as he had left it a couple of years earlier. Sprawling and huge, unchanging through good and bad weather. The paint on the walls was peeling and the garden was big and unkempt. The bougainvillea crept up the wall, as unruly as ever. The tulasi plant in the tulasi madam in the corner had grown to look more like a tree. Rainwater continued to leave dark streaks on the walls. A new makeshift garage had come up to hold the four new cars. The house was lovely with all its flaws. With all its warts. With all its wrinkles. Ravi had grown up within these walls. They formed a part of him.

He stood for a second near the gate, admiring the house. There was something graceful about a home even if it had been made with concrete and bricks. But he hadn't come all the way to admire his house, he reminded himself. He had other things to do.

2

The ancestral home at No.1 Vedaranyam Street was all of fourteen grounds. Appa had christened it 'Sundari' after his stepmother.

Sundari—the House of Extraordinary Beauty.

The house lived up to its name. It was imposing and grand but had a soft grace. There was a time when several families lived in the house. Appa had been head of this large family for as long as Ravi could remember, which at various times consisted of Amma and their four children, Appa's younger sister Kamala, her husband and son, his uncle's unemployed son who came to look for a job and stayed on endlessly, a retinue of servants, the watchman Varadarajulu and the cook Nagarajan. Some—like his brother's wife and their daughter, or his close friend Nallamuthu Gownder's son from Udumalpet who had come to the city for the first time to get admission into Presidency College and stayed on in Sundari till he found a hostel, or Bhavani manni who came for her medical treatment—came in and out of the house for periods ranging between one and six months. Others of indifferent pedigree, calling themselves athaan manni, ammaanji manni or naathanaar, came and stayed for shorter durations and acted as if the house belonged to them. When you entered Sundari, it was like entering a wedding house. You never got any privacy, but you didn't really mind.

Amma was the fulcrum around which every activity in the house revolved. Food was not cooked in small pans but in large andaas. Chips were stored in larger bins, and sweets, especially theratti paal, were kept in the bell-metal uruli. All savouries were stored in huge aluminum drums. Pickles were stored in endless rows of large porcelain jars—avakka pickle, manga thokku from the mango tree in the garden, vadu manga and green pepper pickle. Coffee powder was freshly ground, not in grams but in kilos. Sweets and savouries were made regularly—murukku, naada pakoda, gulab jamun, badaam halwa, Mysore pak and, Amma's speciality, rasagulla. An arukanchetti was used to churn whey from milk to make rasagullas. How a Bengali dish became her speciality was a mystery to most. She was one of the few who recognized the importance of copyright when it came to recipes. Her recipe book, where every recipe was penned in her neat calligraphic handwriting, contained the name of the person she got each recipe from—Lakshmi's Penang Sauce, Gowri's Adai and Bhavani's Badaam Poori.

There was no dearth of food.

Sundari—the House of Really Good Food.

It was a wonder Appa could afford to maintain the whole lot. He occupied the first room on the left on the ground floor and kept an eye on all those who came in and out. The room adjacent was his study where he kept all his books: British and American fiction, engineering textbooks, *Reader's Digest* issues stacked in a neat pile and sorted according to year of publication, Tamil classics like *Ponniyan Selvan* and *Parthiban Kanavu*. Appa had a habit of signing his name as soon as he bought a book, believing that others would be deterred from borrowing it, or at least make sure to return it when they saw his signature sprawled inside. He was wrong on both counts.

To all those who frequented the street—the night duty policeman Pandurangan, the ironing man John Arul and the cobbler Muthu—and to those who frequented the potti kadai at the corner of Vedaranyam Street, Sundari was not just any bungalow. It was a landmark.

The watchman Varadarajulu was the first to spot Ravi. He rushed out and grasped Ravi with both arms. 'Chinnadorai, when did you come?' he said affectionately. Ravi greeted him with equal warmth. When Varadarajulu ran around to the boot of the taxi to take out the suitcases, Ravi told him he was staying in a hotel. The boot was empty.

'Why?' Varadarajulu exclaimed. This was a question Ravi himself had been contemplating.

'I'll tell you in good time, Varada,' he muttered. He walked down the gravelled driveway and up the steps into the open verandah.

Amma was at home. Appa was out. So were his two elder brothers, Anand and Arjun.

That suited Ravi fine.

Amma emerged from the kitchen, wiping her face with a dirty towel, the one she usually tucked into the folds of her sari near the waist when she was in the kitchen and used to wipe her perspiring face or the occasional splatter of hot oil leaping from the vessel onto her hands. She looked just as she had a year earlier, when Ravi saw her last. Her face was still young, her sparkling diamond nose ring and seven-stone Belgian-cut diamond earrings glittered like stars. Ravi couldn't imagine her without those earrings. Amma wore a thin cotton sari—It's too hot to wear anything else in this damn city, she would complain.

'Enna da, you're finally back?' she asked, half smiling half anxious. She glanced nervously at the doorway and seemed relieved to see no one else there.

'Why do you spend so much time in the kitchen even now?' Ravi asked as she mopped her sweaty face with a towel. 'Give the cook a chance!'

'What do you mean even now? If I don't do this, I will have nothing to do in life and Alzheimer's will set in.'

'Alzheimer's! Where did you pick that up?'

'Why have you grown so thin?' she asked, predictably. 'You were extolling the virtues of all the different canteens in Cornell, and you come back so thin—like a neem stick.'

'I was busy with my new job, Amma. I didn't have time to breathe.'

'You even stopped writing to me.'

'It is the new job, Amma.'

'Everything is work, work, work. What's this new job?'

Ravi described it to her. 'I've returned to Chennai for good.'

'Good. How much does it pay?'

He told her.

'So much! It's nearly as much as your father! Are you sure they are not overpaying you by mistake?'

Ravi laughed. Amma didn't.

'Have lunch. I've made your favourite murungukka sambhar. Someone sent a bundle of murungukkas yesterday.'

'No, Amma. I've just had a heavy breakfast.'

'Just have the sambhar. Your tongue must be dead by now without tasting murungukka or vethakozhambu for a whole year.'

'No, Amma. I'm fine.'

There was a pause. All questions had been asked.

Ravi looked around the drawing room.

It was a massive room stuffed with furniture. Nothing in the house was small. His room upstairs was large enough to accommodate all his stuff. And more. Even a wife, he thought. That was why joint families survived for so long in Chennai. The houses were big and everyone could squeeze in comfortably without treading on each other's toes. He could have hidden a girlfriend in his room for weeks without someone noticing.

The sofas, chairs and curtains had the same old rust-and-beige upholstery. But the paintings and artefacts had changed. The old Ganesha Tanjore now hung between the two large windows and a large warli painting hung over the sofa. Two new glass showcases had been placed in the corners and several crystals, small artefacts and woodcarvings were displayed, no doubt collected by his brothers during their visits abroad. Tube lights had been replaced by ornate light fittings with bulbs and that was a welcome change. Appa could never understand why several small bulbs were needed when one good tube light would suffice. There was even a Bohemian ashtray on the centre table, though with Appa around, Ravi was sure no one would dare light up a cigarette.

'Is she going to stay with you?' she asked finally, avoiding his eyes.

'Yes, She has found a job in the same firm.'

And then Amma—who had been struggling all along to remain firm and composed—broke down.

'Ravi, you have brought great unhappiness to our lives,' she wept.

Amma sat down on the sofa and buried her face in her thalappu. Ravi sighed and sat next to her. He gently put his arms around her.

'Amma, don't cry.'

'How can you do this to us?'

'Amma, don't get upset please. We have discussed this before. Don't start all over again, I beg you.'

'Then what am I supposed to do?'

'You're being unreasonable.'

'Me? Unreasonable? Do you have any idea what anguish you have caused us? We had dreams for you...'

'I have dreams for myself, Amma,' he said quietly.

'And your father... he did so much for you.'

'Yes, he has done a lot for me. I'm indebted to him for that. But that doesn't mean that he gets a veto over my life.'

'Veto? We are not asking for veto, Ravi. But you have had no consideration for our sentiments. No consideration at all. That is what has given us so much pain.'

Her voice choked.

'Just because I want to marry someone doesn't mean I lack consideration, Amma. Don't I deserve some consideration from you?'

'Don't talk about consideration. Do you know how much money your father spent to send you to America? It's not cheap to study there. But he still sent you. Why? For your future! For you to study hard and succeed in life. Not for you to get married to a vellakkaari.'

'But I studied well and am determined to succeed, Amma.'

'Do you know how much hope he had for you after your return? Do you know how much pride he had in you?' she asked, raising her voice.

'I know, Amma, and I'm really grateful,' he said. 'But I have the right to live my life the way I want and decide what is good for me. Why can't you both take pride in what I am and what I plan to do? Isn't this what you have prepared me for? To find my own path?'

'Go ahead. Lead your own life. Don't please us. But don't say we didn't do our duty as parents.'

'Of course not. You and Appa have done everything possible for me and I acknowledge that.'

'I am not asking for acknowledgement. I'm trying to tell you what's good for you.'

'I understand. But…'

'What but? I even sent you the horoscopes of Brahmin girls from very good families who were studying in Cornell itself. Even Ramamoorthy's daughter Vidya's horoscope was sent to you and you kept saying no…'

'Amma, this long-distance matchmaking was going a bit too far. You ended up recommending girls you had no idea about.'

'Perhaps. But you could have taken the effort to find out something about them since you were already there.'

'I did.'

'So what was wrong with Ramamoorthy's daughter?'

'There was a problem—a big problem.'

'With you or with her?'

'With her.'

It had been a moment for rejoicing in the Sundari household when Anand was born. The first child in the family. That too a son. Appa was particularly happy—and relieved that the firstborn was a boy.

'So you have got an heir,' people said.

'To inherit the family wealth.'

'Congratulations. You both can rest in peace now. This boy will protect you till the end.'

'This boy is going to double your wealth, just watch.'

Both parents soon got into the first-child syndrome. They were in awe of everything the child did. Whatever it did was new. Whatever it said was new. And whatever they did to the child was new. When their second child was a boy, Appa was happy. Daughters got married and became part of their husband's household. Even their gothrams changed. But sons remained forever. Amma was disappointed. She had wanted a girl. When these two grow up, they will become ruffians; only a girl can bring softness and gentleness into a family, she told Appa. They called the boy Arjun. After several years they had another child. It was a girl. Amma's life lit up. Appa doted on the baby. She had prayed to both Kanchi Kamakshi and Sringeri Sharada and when a girl was born, she was convinced that she would embody the virtues of both the goddesses. They called her Jayalakshmi. Anand and Arjun were fascinated with their little sister.

Ravi happened almost as an afterthought. His birth didn't create any excitement in the house and everyone received the news with equanimity. Ravi grew up hidden in the shadow of his brothers and clothed in their hand-them-downs. Only Jaya was close to his age and she became his best friend.

Ravi was always full of life, full of stubbornness. He never gave in to anything until he was totally convinced of it. Appa realized early on that Ravi was different from his other two sons. Anand and Arjun could be ordered around and they listened. But not Ravi.

Once Ravi, barely eight years old, came home with his friends from a round of cricket to have lunch, with every intention of gulping it down and returning to the match.

'Have you finished your homework?' Appa asked him.

'No, I will finish it at night. It's not much,' said Ravi.

'I have told you not to put things off till the last minute,' Appa shouted.

'Appa, I have to go. I am batting and my team has to win.'

'I don't care. Finish your homework and then go.'

'I have to go now, Appa, or my team will lose,' Ravi pleaded.

'No. First do your homework.'

'I have to go.' Ravi held his ground.

'You can't go out.'

'Just for half an hour. I can finish my homework in ten minutes.'

'If you have to go, then get out and don't come back into this house,' Appa exclaimed furiously and went into his study.

Ravi waited for a minute and then left the house.

An hour passed, with no sign of Ravi.

Two hours, and still no sign.

It was only when his friends came looking for Ravi that Appa and Amma realized that Ravi had not gone to play with his friends. They began to hunt for him everywhere but Ravi was not to be found.

The perennial residents of Sundari and some others, who rushed over as soon they heard the news, kept the parents company. Amma chided Appa for being so harsh on the poor child and Appa blamed her for being indulgent with Ravi, making him completely disobedient. He went into the puja room and prayed to all the gods he could think of. I will offer a hundred and eight coconuts to you if he returns safely, he prayed fervently to Ganesha.

When it was about to turn dark, Ravi entered the house, almost as if he had just come back from a casual stroll in the neighbourhood, went up to his mother and asked for dinner.

'Where were you all this while?' Amma asked anxiously before Appa could start shouting.

'Right here,' was Ravi's cryptic answer.

'Where?'

'Here, in the house. Appa asked me not to go out.'

'But you were not in the house. We searched everywhere and you were not here.'

'I was sitting on the compound wall behind those bushes in the garden.'

For seven hours, Ravi had been sitting silently on the compound wall, hidden from the house by the bushes and from the road by the Ashoka trees.

The next day, Appa went to the Pillayar temple to offer one hundred and eight coconuts.

Ravi went to Vidya Mandir School and then to Vivekananda College—both institutions dedicated to high achievers and good pedigree. That pretty much defined his Brahminical upbringing. His father had taken every opportunity to sensitize his children—all four of them—to the values and traditions of Hinduism and the Tamil culture. Ravi was, one might say, a well-rounded TamBram boy.

Ravi loved to travel. He got into every moving vehicle as long as it went somewhere. He went to temple towns and cities in and around Tamil Nadu, and later visited Assam, Kashmir, Varanasi, Bhubaneshwar, Imphal, Mount Abu and many other places. That was when he became a non-vegetarian. To look for curd rice and sambhar in Amritsar was silly so he began to eat butter chicken. Later, in Panihati, he graduated to maachher jhol—the Bengali fish curry. And finally, on the beaches of Goa, to chouricos—the fresh Goan sausages—mixed with feni and pressed in an earthenware pot for twenty-four hours. Ravi had arrived.

But whenever Ravi stepped into Sundari, he became a good TamBram. Not just because he was afraid of Appa but because he genuinely believed in the power of the Gayathri Mantram and his poonal. He was one of the few, at least when compared to his two brothers, who took pains to understand why all Brahmin boys were initiated into the poonal ceremony and what the Gayathri Mantram meant. 'Om bhoor-bhuva-svaha, thath-savitur…' he meditated and knew exactly what it meant. ' … May we receive Thy supreme sin-destroying light; May Thou guide our intellect in the right direction…'

But Ravi didn't like to pray. That was a pity and Appa resented it. 'Why can't you spend just a couple of minutes every day in the puja room?' Appa kept asking.

It was not that Ravi didn't believe in god. He did. But he didn't think god had to be prayed to and appeased. God wasn't going to judge Ravi by how he prayed. He also didn't think that being a non-vegetarian made him any less Brahmin. Even when he ate spicy Goan tongue of beef, he didn't feel guilty. God wasn't going to judge him by what he ate.

So Ravi led this double life until he finally decided to come clean and tell his parents—which essentially meant Appa—

that he was not the epitome of Brahminical correctness, at least as far as his eating habits were concerned. With this confession, Ravi felt a burden lift from his shoulders. But he soon realized that he had merely succeeded in shifting the burden from his own shoulder to his father's.

His confession shattered Appa. His own son a non-vegetarian? It was unacceptable. He stopped talking to Ravi for months and asked Amma to cook separately for Ravi even if it was vegetarian food. Ravi was quite happy to eat alone without Appa around and the point was totally lost on him. An uneasy truce was finally struck with Amma's help and neither of them raised the issue again. But in Appa's eyes, Ravi had fallen from grace. Appa blamed himself for it. He had a shastrigal come home and perform a homam to prevent the sin from descending on Ravi and the whole family. Just when Appa had started taking pride in his boys being different from the meat-eating, alcohol-drinking atheists who called themselves Brahmins, Ravi had blown the dream away.

Ravi—the less-than-Brahmin boy.

3

One afternoon, there was a letter waiting for Ravi when he went back to his room at Cornell. It was from Amma. She had touched upon the topic of Ravi's marriage earlier, but this time she had a concrete proposal. She had managed to locate a girl in Cornell, whose parents lived in Chennai. Vidya was in her third year in computer science. Her parents were originally from Coimbatore.

Why don't you both meet and see if you like each other? Your horoscopes match. We have discussed it with her parents, who have promised to write to her about you. She is supposed to be a bright, intelligent girl, doing very well in her studies. Both of you are graduating at the same time. Do tell me what you think. Amma.

Ravi's first instinct was to tear up the letter and throw it away.

'My mom's silly,' he told his room-mate Bob. 'She wants me to meet this girl who's studying here and see whether it works.'

'When did your mom start setting you up on blind dates,' Bob said without looking up from the TV. There was a basketball game on. Bulls vs Grizzlies. 'Is it anyone we know?'

'Some girl called Vidya. She's supposed to be majoring in computer science.'

'Not Tom's girlfriend?'

'Tom?'

'Yeah, that nerd with the long hair. He's in computer science. I think that Indian girl lives with him.'

'Are you sure?'

'I'm never sure. When the fuck am I sure? But that's what I heard. I think they're into coke and stuff. Check it out with Chris. He hangs out with those freaks.' Bob went back to the TV.

When Chris came in that night, he confirmed what Bob had said. 'She looks nerdy and her eyes are always glassy,' he concluded.

'My mom has no bloody idea what she is doing.'

Ravi was furious. He took a pen and wrote out a scathing reply to his mother's letter. *Why are you getting into this matchmaking?* he scribbled furiously. *Do you have any idea what's happening here? Without knowing anything, you have already started discussing it with Vidya's parents.* After he had vented his anger, he read the letter and realized that he wasn't being fair to Vidya. What she did with her life was her business. Her parents probably had no idea what she was up to, but that was their problem. Amma's letter was Ravi's problem. He tore up the letter and wrote another one. *I'm not in the mood to marry now,* he wrote simply. *Please don't pursue the Vidya option any more.*

He didn't know Vidya had written a similar note to her parents.

Don't pursue the Ravi option any more.

Amma listened to Ravi in horror. She had heard of such stories from others. She even had a friend whose sister's son had married a girl from Stanford. The girl left him a week after the wedding because she was already living with another man. Amma closed her eyes and sat still for a second.

'Shiva, Shiva. Spare me these stories. Thank god you didn't meet her.'

'I'm not someone who does things behind your back. That's why I've brought Deborah here. I have come to ask your permission to marry her.'

'*Marry* her!'

'I want you to agree first before we—'

'Have you gone mad?'

'Amma, I want your consent. I really like her.'

'If you marry a white woman, there'll be no one to continue our family name!'

'What family name, Amma? Which world do you live in? Anyway, you have two other sons who will continue your family name.'

'Appa was so sure that our family tradition would be carried forward by you. You have always been brighter than the other two. You have hurt Appa deeply.'

'Amma, I don't understand this family name business. What has falling in love with a foreigner got to do with defiling the family name? I'm not committing a crime. Why don't you just meet Deborah?'

'I can't do it.'

'You will like her when you meet her. At least agree to meet her.'

Amma merely shook her head and broke down again.

'I know Appa will not agree. But you can meet her.'

'Why should I meet her? Who is she that I should meet her?' Amma flared up suddenly.

'At least you can decide for yourself whether you—'

'I have already decided for myself. Don't think that Appa

is the only one who is upset with you. All of us are. I'm very upset. I don't want to meet her.'

The conversation had ground to a stop. Amma sat, her face streaked with tears, her head buried in her thalappu. Ravi sat quietly, wondering what to say, when he heard footsteps coming down the stairs. They were his brothers' wives. They must have heard Amma's sobs. Perhaps they were eavesdropping. After all, who wouldn't like to hear the story of an American girl and a TamBram boy? They went straight to Amma and held her up gently. Amma protested at first and asked them to go away. 'No, no, leave me alone,' she said. But her strength had ebbed. She let herself be led away. The wives didn't look at Ravi. Not even a word of acknowledgement. Ravi took that as a sign not to follow them.

As he stood alone in the living room, he wasn't sure if he should venture into the house at all. Was he allowed to do that? Did he have their permission to wander about his own home?

And thus, without so much as a goodbye, he left the house quietly. He had come expecting to be treated like a son, but slipped out like a thief.

Deborah's parents agreed to let her go to India with Ravi. Very reluctantly.

When Deborah had delicately broached the subject of Ravi—if at all such a subject could be delicately broached—it was a shock for them. What will you do with an Indian, that too a Hindu? they had asked. What is wrong with all the Jewish boys you meet? They had hoped she would marry a Jew. She could have easily found herself a handsome Jew. She was a smart, good-looking girl. But an Indian? And a Hindu at that? Her parents couldn't believe it.

Before she talked to her parents, she decided to talk to someone else—her favourite uncle. Her father's uncle, to be precise, another Schonfeld. He had a laidback approach to these things. He had seen half his family disappear into the jungle of non-Jews. Sitting in a cane chair in one corner of the room, a pipe clenched between his brittle teeth and dry lips, puffing hard to provoke some life into the tobacco, he asked, 'Does he have a funny hat and beard and drive a cab in New York?'

'No, he isn't Sikh,' she explained.

That seemed to satisfy him.

'Which school did he go to?'

'Cornell.'

'Does he have a job?'

'Yes, he's just joined a multibillion-dollar IT firm,' she said, emphasizing the multibillion.

'Then go for him, Debbie. He's as good as any Jewish boy!'

When Deborah confided in her best buddy, Diana, her friend was quite categorical. 'As long as he fucks well, you shouldn't worry. It'll be a pity if you marry him for love and don't get fucked properly. You may as well marry a Jew then.' Diana had a knack for getting to the bottom of a problem quickly.

'Debs, they burn their brides.'

'Don't be silly, dad.'

'What if he burns you with kerosene? We can't do a damn thing sitting here in Norfolk.'

'Honestly, dad, Ravi's not going to burn me.'

'You don't know his family yet.'

'I'm not getting married to his family.'

'You might have to live with them.'

'They're not the bride-burning type.'

'How do bride-burning types look, darling? I suppose they look like you and me. Or Ravi. Perfectly normal.'

Deborah shook her head in despair.

'Everyone will speak Hindu,' her father warned her.

'Hindu is a religion, dad, not a language. In any case, Ravi's family speaks English, probably better than we do.'

'Whatever… I hear they don't wipe their backsides but only water them like plants.'

Her father was the easier of the two to tackle. Her mother went into a permanent sulk. Deborah could sense the sudden stillness that had crept into their relationship. One day she would be all sunshine and smiles; the next, quiet, tranquil, like the eye of a storm. Her mother tried to reason with her, dissuade her, gave her the silent treatment. Quiet disapproval followed by open disapproval. Emotional outbursts timed to make the maximum impact. Even the family rabbi was brought to counsel her. But Deborah's mind was made up.

At least her mother wasn't like one of those Jewish parents who, when their daughter or son married a non-Jew, cut off their links completely with their child. Some even went to the extent of pretending their child was dead.

'What are you doing this week?'

'We are sitting *shiva*. Our daughter is dead. She has just married a Hindu.'

No. Her mother wasn't like that. She was just afraid that the Jewish pedigree of the family was being diluted. She had nothing against Ravi except his not being a Jew. Maybe the fact that she came from a refugee family from Europe and faced prejudices even in the US had something to do with it.

'I must tell you what happened when I went to Israel for the first time—in fact it was the first time for both your dad and me,' her mother told her one day. 'When the flight touched down at Ben Gurion, your dad and I were so excited. On our first night in Jerusalem I could hardly sleep. I was so wound up. With the first ray of the sun, we walked to Kotel—the Western Wall. To see the original wall of the demolished Second Temple, still standing after all these years… it was unbelievable. Your dad broke down, so did I. We rushed up to the wall and touched it, felt it and wiped our tears on it. We prayed and stuffed our Tzetel—those pieces of paper with our prayers written on them—into the cracks in the wall. We had also carried Tzetel from our friends here. The cracks were stuffed with millions of prayers. We stood there for god knows how long, staring at the wall, not willing to let go. Men and women came to see it by the busload. There were Jews in long black Hassidic coats and hats, swaying in prayer. There were many Bar Mitzvahs going on side by side around the periphery of the wall—young boys in the traditional garb, parents and relatives in their yarmulkyes and prayer shawls, the rabbis smiling and preparing for the important event. It was a sight to die for. We had come to Israel for Kotel and nothing else mattered.'

She stopped to wipe a tear. Deborah listened silently. Her mother had always been the more religious of the two.

'Even after all these years, I can't help crying when I think of that moment. It is said that when the Second Temple was destroyed, all the gates to heaven were shut but one—the gate of tears. But I haven't come to your room to cry. I wanted to tell you something else. As your father and I stood there that day, all of a sudden there was a hail of stones from above. Just out of the blue. One nearly hit your dad. Suddenly, everyone started running all over the place, towards the gate or to the steps behind us. We ran too. The stones were from the dome above, where the Al Aksa mosque was. The Palestinians did it. A few Muslim worshippers had gathered on top of the wall and decided to rain stones on the Jewish worshippers below. It lasted just a few minutes before the Israeli guards cordoned off the place. But it was scary. One minute we were worshippers in the divine presence of god, the next we were being hounded like thieves. As I looked up at the Golden Dome, I was furious about the way we and hundreds of worshippers were being treated—as trespassers to our own temple. I was a stranger to Israel but not a stranger to the stories I had heard from our friends in Israel—in Jerusalem, Haifa, Rishon LeZion and other places. Their children being attacked, their life constantly in danger. The Jewish teenagers who do their time with the army put themselves directly in the line of fire of these fanatics every day, it's horrible even to think of it. The wives said goodbye to their husbands every day in the fear that they might not return home. When I went back to the hotel that evening, it was with disgust and not with the overpowering love I had experienced that morning in the presence of the wall.'

Her mother sighed.

'I know you are wondering why I am telling you this, that too after all these years. We Jews were born for greater things, Debbie. We are special because we have endured persecution over the centuries and survived. And with our culture, religion, identity and dignity intact. Don't forget that you lost your great-grandfather to Auschwitz. But we never gave in. We sought refuge among strangers. And now we don't hesitate to extend a hand of friendship even to those who seek to destroy us. You are young, beautiful, intelligent and have a bright future. You deserve happiness.'

She bent over and kissed Deb's forehead.

'For Jews, our very existence is spiritual. That's what makes us Jewish. It makes us special. We are also aware of the dangers our religion faces. You will face that everywhere. That is what makes our religion different. That is why I know in my heart that you can find true happiness only if you marry someone who can understand your Jewishness. Not someone who is a stranger to our religion. Ravi's religion is not a religion of the book. God knows what these Hindus will do to you. You will find happiness only—'

'Mom, I love him.'

Sitting over several chilly evenings by the Potomac, down Wisconsin Avenue, Deborah and Ravi made their plans.

Soon, her parents stopped making any reference to Ravi.

The issue of Indians watering their backsides like a plant did not crop up again either.

4

Kamala athai was the youngest of Appa's sisters.

Kamala was younger to Appa by nearly nine years. This large age gap only increased Appa's fondness for her. He was more a father to her than a stepbrother. Kamala was also the naughtiest of Appa's siblings, and had spent much of her childhood teasing Appa. She hid his pen, scribbled in his college notebooks, took away his erasers, and even put a live cockroach inside his bag once. She refused to call her elder brother 'anna', and insisted on calling him by name. Sometimes she even called him 'da'. Once Appa chased her around the house because she had called him 'da'. The chase finally ended when Kamala tripped and fell and chipped a tooth. That day Appa swore never to be aggressive with her again.

In August 1981, the Tamil Nadu Express she was travelling on capsized near Kagaznagar. Her coach turned over and her leg was crushed under the fallen plank of the seat above. Many people lost their lives and it was a miracle she survived. She was extricated from the overturned compartment and rushed to the general hospital. One look at her leg and the doctor knew it couldn't be saved. Her right leg had become practically useless.

Ravi was fond of Kamala athai. He had spent many a childhood holiday at her house in Kumbakonam, where he had watched the world amble past as he sat with his cousin Vignesh in straw-covered bullock carts, visited temples where he was made to recite all the shlokas he had been taught, and jostled with the teeming crowd to take part in the ritual dip at the Mahamaham tank when the Mahamaham festival took place every twelve years. When he returned to Chennai with Deborah, he hoped Kamala athai would recreate that same magic for Deborah.

Knowing that Kamala athai's house was small, Ravi had hesitated to ask her to take him and Deborah in. But Kamala athai insisted.

'So what if my brother doesn't let you and Deborah into Vedaranyam Street? I will take you both into my home. You are like my son and she is my daughter-in-law.'

'No, no, athai, I don't want give you any trouble…'

'Why? Is our house too small for you?'

'No, of course not…'

'Are you afraid Deborah will not be comfortable here?'

'Not at all. I just don't want to come and dump ourselves—'

'Shut up, Ravi. Don't you remember how many years your athimber and I spent at Vedaranyam Street? I didn't ask your father's permission then and he didn't even dream of asking me to leave. In fact, he sat and cried when your uncle and I left for Delhi. You youngsters go for two years to America and suddenly start becoming formal.'

'No, no, athai, there is no formality or dakshinyam. I just don't want your relations with Appa and Amma to get strained.'

'So that's what's bugging you, is it? Look here, Ravi. I know my brother very well. I happen to be the only person in the family who can tell him off. He may not agree with me but he will never shoo me away. That's the kind of relationship we have. So, don't worry, I can handle your father.'

'But you will have to make many adjustments for our sake…'

'What adjustments? The only thing you have to decide is whether Deborah will like it. In America, people are used to living separately and she may find it hard to live with all of us around. But you needn't worry too much. You know your athimber, he will go his own way and speak very little. Vignesh just visits once a week. And I promise I'll keep my talking to a minimum. Of course, in a hotel, she would live in five-star comfort…'

'Athai, that's not the issue at all. In fact, if we can stay with you even for a few days, Deborah will get properly introduced to the family.'

'That's settled then,' Kamala athai declared. 'The two of you will move in tomorrow.'

Ravi and Deborah shifted the following week into her house, and found that it was the most sensible thing they could have done.

Kamala athai enjoyed Deborah's company and made Deborah feel welcome. She didn't have to be on her best behaviour all the time, which in itself was a relief. She wasn't being judged all the time, which was a greater relief. The greatest relief was that Kamala athai gave them the space they wanted. Though they stayed only for a month, it was their best time in Chennai.

'Whats's Ravi's dad like?' Deborah asked one day.

'Stubborn,' said Kamala athai.

'Stubborn? I thought Ravi was the stubborn one in his family.'

'They are cut from the same cloth, father and son. His father means well. He wants the best for everyone but thinks he knows what's best for them. That's the problem.'

'Even if he dislikes me, I wish he wouldn't shun Ravi.'

'It's not about you. He doesn't even know you, kanne. This is about Ravi not listening to him. That hurts his pride. He can't stand it and is taking it out on the poor boy.'

5

Ravi was in Washington, D.C. for a summer internship. He was excited that he had been selected for the job even though he was on an F-1 visa. He had assumed that his American classmates would get it. But the United States recognized merit, unlike Tamil Nadu where you had to be of the right caste, and certainly not a Brahmin.

In D.C., Ravi stayed with his friend Gopal. V.R. Gopalakrishnan had been a year senior to Ravi at Vivekananda College and had come to the US to do a master's in computer science. Gopal shared the three-bedroom flat with two others—Bala and Senthil. All three were delighted to find another Tamilian in D.C. and readily agreed to let Ravi stay. Ravi quickly became friends with their friends—Sam, Harry, Monty, Jane and Anuradha. Their real names, of course, were Shanmugam, Harvinder, Mohinder, Janani and Anuradha, but they had changed them so that the Americans could pronounce them correctly.

Gopal and Ravi had enough time to reminisce about the good old days and the not-so-good old days at Vivekananda. Like the time Gopal was caught smoking by one of the Ramakrishna Mission swamijis. That too when he was in Mani Kadai, the shop outside the college premises, where generations of students had regularly gathered between classes to enjoy a quiet puff and a sip of coffee. Barely bigger than a tin shed with only enough standing space for one, Mani Kadai was an institution for all youngsters inducted into Vivekananda College. The owner, Mani, sold all brands of cigarettes, betel nuts, and saunf to hide the cigarette smell; cool drinks, hot drinks and all that was necessary for making that transition from childhood to adolescence.

'Swamiji, I'm not a kid,' Gopal pleaded. 'And I'm not even inside the college premises.'

'No, Gopal, you cannot smoke,' the swamiji insisted.

'But look around you, swamiji, many others are also smoking. Why are you singling me out?'

'Because you are from a good Brahmin family. Smoking is not for good Brahmin boys.'

I am a bad Brahmin boy, for heaven's sake, Gopal was tempted to say, but refrained. 'This is discrimination, swamiji! I didn't know caste determines who smokes and who doesn't,' he said in anguish.

The irate swami promptly wrote a letter to Gopal's parents. There ended the smoking career of Gopal, the Brahmin boy.

Ravi and Gopal were products of Vivekananda College. The results spoke for themselves. Some of the finest students passed through its portals. Straddling a whole block right in the middle of the city in Mylapore, the college was hemmed in by a high compound wall. The Ramakrishna Mission Road, onto which it opened out, was busy through the day except on those days when the Student's Union went on strike. The students were pulled out from their classes by the Union leaders and some threw stones at nothing in particular. Without stones a strike was never complete, but being students of Vivekananda College, they made sure the stones didn't hit anyone. A sea of cycles and mopeds went in and out every day and soon the parking area had to be expanded. A few cars of students from privileged families could also be seen parked. Since the college, its administration and the swamijis of Ramakrishna Mission believed in spartan living and the undivided pursuit of knowledge, those who came in cars were almost apologetic that their parents were rich and could afford to buy them cars. They slinked in and out sheepishly.

Vivekananda College was all about simple living and high thinking. Both of which Ravi possessed, though occasionally his thinking aimed a bit lower.

Ravi was very excited. It was his first day in office. Ravi wore the only suit he had got stitched in Madras—a jet-black one—and the polka-dot burgundy tie Anand had brought for him from France. The rest of his formal wear included a couple of navy-blue blazers from his school days, a light grey coat that once belonged to Arjun and a brand-new brown tweed jacket he had bought in Cornell. He had all of six trousers, eight shirts and seven ties—one from each trip his brothers had made abroad.

That morning, Ravi wanted to look his best. He kept looking into the mirror as he got dressed. He dabbed some aftershave on his face. He had inherited his mother's looks and his father's strong chin. He wasn't dark or fair. Not stocky but well-built with a little muscle on his biceps. And he was taller than his father's five-foot-nine.

Ravi applied some more aftershave and then walked up to the small idol of Ganesha by the bed. The idol came with his suitcase. It was an idol meant for a suitcase. There were idols for every place—for puja, for the drawing room, for car dashboards, for travel, and for suitcases. When he left for Cornell from Chennai, Amma placed it in his suitcase along with a small book of prayers. 'Don't take these out. Let them remain here. They will ensure a safe journey,' she told him. Much as he didn't like to pray, he believed in god. Dai Ravi, Amma often said, what do you lose by praying? Maybe he should pray once in a while—just in case. Why should he screw up his job for want of a silly prayer?

So Ravi went to the idol and prayed.

'*Vaakundaam, nalla manamundaam, maamanaraal nokkundaam...*'

'Clarity of mind and speech, and Saraswati's blessing are bestowed by Ganesha...'

Ravi hailed a cab. The first day was important. He didn't want to experiment with the subway and land up late. His tie felt like a noose around his neck and he kept adjusting it right until the cab stopped in front of his new office. He went up in the lift and emerged in front of the receptionist.

'I am an intern. I have come for—'

'Cathy,' she announced into the intercom. 'There's a handsome young man looking for you.' And waving to Ravi, she said, 'This way, darling. Second room on the left.'

'Who am I meeting?'

'Cathy, the admin officer.'

Ravi straightened his tie and walked down to the second room on the left. The only other occupant of the room was the blonde girl he had seen during the interview. His eyes widened. It was the same girl he had called a bimbo.

When the three boys had been called for the interview earlier that month, there were three girls waiting for the same interview. One of them was a pretty young blonde, with thin lips and high cheekbones.

'That sexy blonde bomb is getting it, wanna bet?' Ravi had whispered and they had laughed out loud. 'All bimbos get it. Again and again.'

When her turn came, the boys came to know that she was called Deborah. 'Debbie baby will get it!'

Now Debbie baby sat there with her legs crossed. She looked away when she saw him enter.

'Hi, have you seen Cathy?' Ravi asked nervously.

She looked at him with cold eyes. 'Cathy's in the next room.' She paused briefly, then added, 'I'm the bimbo you saw in Richmond.'

At lunch, Ravi sat alone in one corner, eating his chicken and blue cheese salad. How was he going to make up with Deborah? What an ass he had been! He kept an eye on the door but Deborah didn't appear. He looked at his watch. Another ten minutes before he had to go back to work. He gave up, dumped the plate and had almost reached the door when she entered the cafeteria. He walked up to her.

'Deborah, I have been waiting all morning to apologize to you.'

'You have to wait longer, I'm afraid,' she said coldly, walking away.

'I just need a second,' Ravi pleaded.

'I'm in a rush.' She grabbed a salad bowl, some hash browns and a Diet Coke, paid the cashier and sat down at the nearest table. Ravi sat down opposite her.

'I just wanted to talk to you for a moment. All I was—'

'I don't have time.'

'Just one second. All I was joking about to my friend Bob was that girls had an unfair advantage. I wasn't—'

'That's not what I heard,' she cut him short.

'Okay, I called you a bimbo. But I didn't mean it. Honest. I mean, I don't even know you.'

'All the more reason you should've kept your bloody mouth shut.'

'You are taking this too seriously.'

'I'm not.'

'I was just using the word as a cliché.'

'Bimbo is not a cliché,' she said without looking up.

Ravi wasn't getting anywhere. 'Deborah, I'm sorry,' he sighed. 'Will you let me make it up to you? I will show you that I am not the guy you think I am.'

'I don't care what you are, frankly.'

'We have to work together for the next couple of months.'

'I hope not.'

'Just give me one chance, okay?'

She didn't answer. She was almost done with her salad. She gulped down the rest of her Coke and choked on it, coughing violently.

'Bless you,' Ravi said automatically.

'You don't bless someone who is choking, damn it!' Deborah said and coughed some more.

Ravi smiled. Then he laughed. Silently at first but after a while he couldn't control himself. It was too funny. He put his right palm over his mouth and tried to stifle the laughter but he couldn't.

'I'm sorry, that's too funny,' Ravi gasped before bursting into laughter again. 'Don't choke,' he pleaded. 'I wouldn't know how to save you if you got asphyxiated.'

'Gopal, how do I soften up this girl, Deborah?'

'Ask Bala.'

Bala was one of the three roommates. Bala was different from the rest. He was on an H-1B. He didn't need the job or the money. He had both in India, and in the US as well. He had completed his master's in hotel management and was quickly absorbed into a hotel. But what truly set him apart was that his sole objective in life was to take a different woman to bed every weekend. It wasn't the loftiest of aims but it was one that Bala managed to achieve with surprising ease. 'My charm works all the time, machchi,' Bala boasted.

'Bala, tell me what I should do,' Ravi asked him.

'Are you fucking her?'

'No, we're just friends.'

'Then just apologize and make peace.'

'I have apologized, sort of.'

'That's enough for someone you're not sleeping with.'

'But I want to know her better.'

'That means you want to fuck her. Take her to the best Italian restaurant you can find. Then take her to bed.'

Ravi got his chance rather unexpectedly. Deborah got violently sick one night and had to be hospitalized. He decided to visit her the next morning and go to work a little late.

Deborah was sleeping when he got to the hospital, so he waited in the visitors' room. Ravi soon discovered that if one wasn't sick or dead, the best place to relax was in a hospital. For one thing, there wasn't much to do, since all the attention was devoted to the patients. The magazines were months old and unreadable, cell-phones had to be switched off. So Ravi sat like a zombie, sipping the same cup of coffee till it was completely cold or nibbling a cookie until it crumbled and fell into his lap as fine cocoa sand. He remained there until they finally took him to see Deborah.

He gave her a hastily arranged bunch of roses.

'You actually came to look me up?'

'No, I got sick too and am occupying the bed next to you.'

Deborah noticed that Ravi had chosen one of the best restaurants in Washington, D.C. He would soften her, placate her, tell her how sorry he was, how he hadn't meant what he had said that day. She decided to enjoy it. It was not every day she was treated like this by a boy.

Choosing a good restaurant wasn't easy in D.C. Unlike New York, which believed in itself even if it didn't take itself seriously, Washington, D.C. took itself seriously even if it didn't believe in itself. It didn't quite believe it could be a first-rate cosmopolitan city but took itself seriously as a capital city. The White House, Capitol and Pentagon loomed large over visitors and residents and the city was satisfied with second-rate restaurants, cinema theatres and other cultural hubs. The food was so prosaic that the cutlery was referred to as 'the implements' and the food was 'worked' upon. What the restaurants lacked by way of quality, they made up for with quantity, dishing out huge portions of barely tolerable food—rich in fat and cholesterol—which the Washingtonians ate without a murmur.

The ambience was perfect. They sat outdoors. A table for two in a corner, a wooden hearth next to them providing a ringside view of the breads. It was a lovely summer evening and Dupont Circle was teeming with shoppers, diners, loafers, chess wizards and a lone jazz player belting out old tunes.

Ravi ordered an expensive Barolo. The wine wasn't too old but it was good. He ordered Tuscan skewers of sausage, chicken, veal and roasted vegetables. She commented wryly that he was overdoing it and ordered spaghetti tossed with shrimps.

The evening had begun well.

Coffee and no dessert.

It was dark when Ravi and Deborah left the restaurant. She felt like walking back to Georgetown. 'I love the fresh air,' she said. 'Walk down with me.'

'Isn't it a little late for that?' Ravi asked. 'I'm not sure you should risk it.'

'I should,' Deborah replied. Her pale hair glowed under the street lamps. 'M Street is not even a block away.'

A couple of noisy boys in shorts, CD players around their waists, earphones and pink hair, ran down M, throwing a football to each other. One of them had a big steel hoop for an earring.

Ravi looked at Deborah to see if she was fully sober. Yes, she looked sober. And she was good-looking—smooth skin, high cheekbones, shining brown eyes. And that lovely blonde hair.

The crowd thinned as they walked down M Street. Broad sidewalks, glass showcases and closed shutters greeted them. They passed 20th.

'Back to work tomorrow?' Deborah asked.

'Yeah, I have to face my asshole of a boss again.'

'Shit. Maybe we should prolong today and forget about tomorrow.'

'You have already done that, Debbie! You finished a Barolo all by yourself.'

'How about one last drink for the road? Tomorrow is Friday and I have to head back to Norfolk to spend the weekend with my parents.'

'Well, okay. Where?'

'At Brickskeller.'

'Brick what?'

'Brickskeller. If you haven't been there yet, you should. Come on, it's not far.' She took Ravi's hand in hers and ran across Hampshire. Her hand was soft and gentle, but the grip was firm. Ravi loved it.

'Let's take this shortcut. It will take us to 22nd.'

Ravi took one look at the alley and his heart sank. *Ward Pl.,* the sign said. It was everything an alley should be—dark, gloomy, forbidding. The streetlights were designed to give minimum light and confidence to a pedestrian. There wasn't a soul in sight.

Washington was remarkable for its isolated oases of intense activity—M Street, pockets on Connecticut Avenue or Wisconsin or Adams Morgan. People walked in and out of restaurants constantly. Youngsters held hands or sucked face on the sidewalks. They cracked loud jokes. But when you turned into the next street, you encountered a different world, as silent and still as the eye of a cyclone.

So it was in Ward Place. An eerie stillness greeted them. Deborah walked down the alley as if she had done it hundreds of times. Ravi hesitated for a moment and then followed her. He could hear their shoes clicking on the tar below.

'Debbie, I hope you know what you are doing.'

'Darling, I've done this several times.'

'You may have done this several times, but there's always a first time,' he muttered.

They heard footsteps behind them. Ravi looked around anxiously and quickened his pace. So did Deborah, to keep up. They didn't notice the postal vans parked in the shadows.

22nd was barely a few metres ahead. The footsteps were nearing. One of the men walked past them and in one swift motion, swivelled around on his heel and blocked their path. Ravi gasped. He turned around quickly to see another man standing right behind them, his hands in his pockets.

'Where the hell d'ya think you're goin'?' He grinned at them. 'Let's go fuck somewhere, you little white ho.'

For a brief second, both Deborah and Ravi stood rooted to the spot. Both the exits seemed covered.

But things happened with blinding swiftness. Just as the first man reached for Deborah's bag, she rammed herself into his ribs. He staggered and fell and hit his head against the sidewalk.

'Come on,' Deborah screamed, and they started running. They had no idea where the other man was nor did they want to know.

They turned into 22nd and ran for their lives. Darkness enveloped them. The streets became longer and longer. They felt the trees converging on them and expected the thugs to block their paths at any moment. After what seemed an eternity, they saw the bright lights of P Street and 22nd in the distance. There were people about and a few cars passed by. Still hand in hand, they ran across the intersection.

'I don't think they are following us,' Ravi hissed, stopping to catch his breath. He looked up. They were right in front of Brickskeller.

When they parted after their internship, after more than two months together in the firm, Deborah and Ravi promised to visit each other.

'You'll come to Cornell?' he asked.

'Wait and see,' she smiled.

While he was in D.C., Ravi received a letter from his mother. It had a US postage stamp. Obviously handed over to someone who was traveling to the US and posted here.

Amma had a style of writing that was unique. Her handwriting was almost calligraphic. For a moment, Ravi sat quietly without reading it, just gazing at the curved letters. He had not read Tamil in some time. Her last few letters to him had been in English.

It had been Amma who had instilled in her children the urge to learn Tamil. She sat with them during their homework, and made sure they enjoyed the language. All four of them studied Tamil right through school in preference to high-scoring language subjects like Sanskrit and French. She read out the *Silappadikaaram* to them, making the smells and sights of Madurai come alive with the sound of her voice. Ravi opened the letter. There was good news from Madras.

Sri Rama Jayam
Vedaranyam Street
Madras

Dear Ravi,
I hope this letter finds you well. We are fine here.
I write to share some good news with you. Our prayers to Lord Venkateshwara for a suitable boy for Jaya have finally been answered. We have decided to get Jaya married to V. Mahesh. By god's grace, the engagement ceremony will be on the twenty-eighth of next month. The wedding date will be fixed in consultation with the priests.
Mahesh is the son of T.R. Venugopal, the well-known industrialist. They are originally from Tirunelveli but are now settled in Bangalore. Mahesh has completed his BE in Electronics

from IIT Delhi and is now working as R&D manager in his father's company. He is a little dark but he is tall and soft-spoken. Jaya and Mahesh met last week in our house, where we had a very dignified girl-seeing ceremony with both families present. The astrologer, our Venkatramaiyer, had already compared the horoscopes and found them fully compatible.

Mahesh's parents acted with humility even though they are a big name in the business world. Appa liked them too, though he was slightly unhappy that Mahesh's father did not even offer to meet part of the expenses for the wedding. I reminded your father that the responsibility of conducting the wedding is always with the bride's family. Since your father has married off two sons, he is at sea when the role is reversed and his daughter is to be married! Anyway, everything went off well.

Anand and Arjun and their wives liked Mahesh as well. As for Jaya, she liked him too, naturally, and since she has a master's in physics they seem to be compatible. By god's grace, she can take care of some aspect of work in Mahesh's company later. Mahesh follows Karnatic music and Jaya is happy about this since she does not like film music. God is great indeed.

Appa and I are happy that we are about to fulfil our duty to Jaya. As the poet Thiruvalluvar said, 'No harm will befall in all seven births, one who begets blameless children,' and I am confident that all four of you will live up to your upbringing and give us a good name. Our blessings are always with Jaya and Mahesh. The success of their marriage is now in their hands and in the hands of Lord Venkateshwara.

I had taken a vow two years ago to climb Tirumala on foot whenever Jaya finds a suitable groom. She has found one and as soon as the wedding is over, I plan to make this pilgrimage. Your Appa will procrastinate but will eventually join. After Jaya's wedding, it will be your turn. And then Appa and I will have truly completed our duty to all our children and can look forward to a quiet retirement and close our eyes in peace.

Don't forget to pray to Lord Anjaneya every Saturday since Venkatramaiyer has specifically asked you to say it in view of the series of minor mishaps you had before your departure to America. Think seriously about your future. Good Brahmin girls don't grow on trees and we will have to keep an eye out constantly, which we already are. After your MBA, you will have to find a good job and settle down.

Why don't you reply to me in Tamil? Then I will know whether you still remember your Tamil!

With all our blessings always,

Amma

6

Ravi came back from his internship in Washington with a little more experience and a little more cash, to claim his unkempt room and even more unkempt roommates in Cornell. Back to the Chappy. Back to Malott Hall. Ravi loved Cornell but not Ithaca. *It's nice to be back in Cornell but terrible to come back to dreary Ithaca again,* he wrote to his sister Jaya. She couldn't figure out what he meant but didn't bother to ask. She didn't understand half the things he wrote, anyway. Ravi had never quite believed in love. Hollywood movies had convinced him that what passed for love was lust. But when he fell in love with Deborah, Ravi recognized the symptoms instantly.

When Ravi and Deborah met again in Ithaca, something had changed. Deborah approached their meeting not with the lightness with which they had met on previous occasions, but with quiet excitement. This time they were more interested in each other's company than in exploring famous pubs.

They kissed, gently at first, and then with passion. They spent the weekend exchanging their thoughts, their desires, their nakedness. They sank blissfully into each other's bodies, and for a moment they forgot that they belonged to two different worlds.

As the days wore on, their relationship was transformed. Ithaca had transformed too. Winter was setting in. There was a gentle coat of snow covering the city. The sidewalks and roads had been cleared but the woods, trees and the sloping hills of Cornell wore a sheen of white. The sky was a permanent shade of grey. It was under this bleak ambience that passion filled the souls of two young people.

Ravi told her about the Beebe Lake near his hostel. 'It is believed that if a couple walks hand in hand twice around the lake, they will never be separated. Well, that's what I think.'

'If that's what you think, then let's do it. After all, everything boils down to what you believe.'

'You're getting ahead of yourself. We haven't even walked one round.'

When Ravi visited De Washington, D.C. he stayed with Bala and Senthil. ad moved to Boston with his Marathi H-1B wife.

'Boss, I'm in love,' Bala said gravely when he saw Ravi.

'Love?'

'Yes, in love,' Bala said darkly as if he had committed a crime.

'Bala, that's great! But why do you look like shit?'

'There's a catch,' said Bala. 'This woman has extracted a promise that if I want to marry her, I will abstain from women for three months before I even broach the topic with her again. Only one month is over so far. It's killing me, man.'

'Bala, if you really love her, you have to do this.'

'I know. But right now, I can't fuck her or anyone else, and it's killing me,' Bala said mournfully.

'Just hold on and you'll never regret it. You need to settle down now.'

'And she is perfect, Ravi. Indra is Tamil, and an American citizen. She's great in bed and has a large heart. Even after I confessed that I sleep around, she decided to stick with me. If I pass this test she will take me in.'

'I'm in love too,' Ravi said.

'That makes the two of us.'

'Gopal got lucky. He escaped by marrying out of convenience. He has no fucking idea what love is doing to us.'

'Yes, but after marrying a Marathi girl—that too older than him—he know all about breaking the news to the family,' cautioned Bala. 'Ask him.'

'Whatever happens, make sure you have your parents on your side,' Gopal advised when Ravi spoke to him. 'Don't take the easy option and marry against their wishes. It's tempting to ignore your parents but it isn't worth it.'

It was a visit long overdue but finally Ravi was on his way to meet Deborah's parents in Norfolk.

Deborah's parents fussed over him. He felt odd, a bit like a museum piece being sized up by curators. Her mother was keen to tell Ravi how India had been good to Jews over the centuries. Ravi didn't know there were Jews in India. I hope I can visit India one day and see the Cochin Synagogue, she said. I didn't know we had synagogues, he thought. It's more than 450 years old, she said. He suddenly remembered that he had a friend called Moses in school, when he was in class four. Moses left after a year when his father was transferred to Kozhikode. But Kozhikode wasn't Cochin. Deborah's parents were Ashkenazis. I speak Yiddish but my husband doesn't, her mother said. Thank god for small mercies, Ravi said silently.

Her mother had cooked what she called an Israeli meal. It wasn't very good. If this is the sort of meal Israelis eat every day, no wonder they become bad-tempered and shoot a few Palestinians now and then, Ravi thought to himself. But he was too polite to say so and ate everything on his plate.

'Is this what you eat during Sabbath?' he asked Deborah.

'Today isn't Sabbath,' she said.

'Oh, of course!'

He decided not to ask any more foolish Jewish questions, and concentrated on the father for the rest of the meal. Deborah's father knew next to nothing about India. In fact, after some polite probing, Ravi discovered that he hardly ever left Norfolk. But he loved baseball and the two of them managed to have a rollicking conversation, much to the amusement of the two women.

'He comes all the way from India and all you can ask him is whether he supports Red Sox or the Yankees?' Deb's mother laughed.

'I asked him about Cardinals, Braves, Mariners and the Mets too. But both of us are agreed on the Yankees,' her father proclaimed triumphantly.

After lunch, Deborah took Ravi up to her bedroom. It was a neat room with pale blue curtains and blue-grey upholstery. Framed drawings in charcoal hung on the walls.

'I sketched them,' she said proudly.

They sat side by side on the bed and sipped coffee—warm American coffee made less warm by topping it with cold milk. Deborah looked radiant that day. Her hair looked more blonde than ever, her eyes twinkled animatedly, her lips curved into a smile.

Jaya's marriage was just the opening Ravi needed. He had to raise it now. Or never.

Ravi took off for a week in November. It was good to be back in Chennai. He had not seen Appa and Amma for over a year. The wedding preparations were on and there was a whirl of activity in the house. All their relatives and friends had been invited and Ravi's presence lent the air an extra gaiety—that's what he thought, anyway. The family was together again and they didn't forget to pamper him with murrukkus and badam halwa.

The house looked more beautiful than ever. Two huge banana plants, cut from the stem, were tied to either side of the main gate. A thoranam of mango leaves was strung on a wire and hung above the main door. The plants in the garden were decorated with a long string of colourful bulbs that were lit in the evening. The gates remained open all day. The watchman Varadarajulu stood there, ushering in stream of vehicles. Beggars were given five rupees each, some buttermilk to drink and sent on their way. Flowers were being arranged. Coconuts were being inspected by the servants. The saris had been chosen, the suit for the groom had been stitched. The mandapam had been booked—the most prestigious one in Chennai—and the pandal advance paid. The nadaswaram was fixed and the menu discussed and finalised. The food had been ordered. Accommodation and transport had been organized for relatives and friends.

It was a daughter's wedding—that too, an only daughter—and Appa wasn't about to let it go by quietly. Anand and Arjun and their wives had personally invited some of their close relatives and friends. Armed with a silver plate, a silver chimizh containing vermillion and akshadai—unbroken rice mixed with turmeric, vermillion and a drop of oil—they

went from house to house. The akshadai was placed on the invitation and given to the seniormost male member of the family, while the vermillion was given to the women. Some of the older guests were gifted with silver cups.

Ravi got caught up in the wedding frenzy and had no time to look up his friends. He volunteered to accompany one of his brothers and was promptly assigned to Arjun. Appa even coached them on what to say and how to invite a guest. Whatever you say, say it with humility, he instructed.

Humility came naturally to Tamils. To be called 'a very humble man' was a badge of honour. To be humble and self-effacing was even better. Humility denoted good upbringing. When an important person came to a wedding, he insisted on sitting in the last row. 'No, no, why are you calling me to the front? I'm comfortable here. Please attend to the VIPs first. Don't bother about me,' he would say, till he was forcibly dragged to the front row and made to sit down in the chair earmarked for VIPs. When he was asked to come onto the stage and bless the couple by throwing rose petals and rice on them, he demurred. 'Please ask the elders to do it. My blessing are always with the couple.' Before giving a lavish present he always said, 'Please accept this humble gift as a small token of our affection.' Some were stubborn. They insisted on sitting in the last row and wouldn't budge. The other guests invariably stopped to offer their respects and the crowd started congregating around him, blocking the way of others who were looking for chairs further up.

Once the gaiety and activity wound down after the wedding, Ravi broached the subject of Deborah.

Amma was aghast.

'Ravi, what's all this you are talking about? It can't happen

in our house, you know that. Your father will not even entertain such a thought. Marry a foreigner? Ravi, take such fanciful thoughts out of your mind. You have hardly been there a year-and-a-half and what I feared all along has happened. They are different from us, Ravi. In a fit of emotion, one can get carried away. But these things with foreigners never last. Marriage is not a joke, Ravi. Foreigners are into live-in relationships, divorce, multiple partners. For us, marriage is a sacred institution. You should become a little more mature and come home safely. That's all we want.'

'Amma, she's a wonderful girl. She's intelligent and sweet and she understands me, she knows what she is getting into. She's even willing to come and live in Chennai... Just forget for a moment that she is American. You won't find a better person in Chennai, I promise you.'

'She might be the best girl in the world, Ravi. But these sorts of alliances are not for us. We are not Americans. We are Indians. There can't be any compatibility on this score. Now you think the problem is just language. Tomorrow it may be boyfriends. Then religion. Day after, she might kick out your Amma and Appa. Forget about it. There are lots of wonderful girls here. Just the other day...'

'Amma, I'm not as immature as you think. I know it won't be easy, there will be lots of adjustments. But it's not as bad as you make it out to be.'

'Ravi, for your own good, just forget about her. In any case, even if I agree, your Appa will never forgive you if you do such a thing.'

'I thought you would speak to Appa on my behalf.'

'You and I will both be buried alive.'

'But I have to ask him, in any case.'

'Not now. Jaya's marriage has just got over. If I mention this to him, he will have a heart attack.'

'If he has a heart, that is.'

'Shut up! That's no way to talk about—'

'Sorry, sorry, sorry. I shouldn't have said that. What I meant was that whatever he says, I am quite prepared to take it. But I have to ask. I can't return to the US without asking.'

'This is not the time to ask him such a thing.'

'No time is a good time with Appa.'

'I want you to think about it when you are calmer. You are leaving for America in two days. We will talk again before you leave.'

But they did not speak about it again before he left for the US.

7

First came Amma's letters beseeching him to give up the idea. They were alternately pleading and stern. There was even a parable:

Sri Ramakrishna Paramahansa has spoken of a tired man who had walked a great distance and was resting under a tree. Unknown to him, the tree he was resting under was celestial. He wished for a bed and, lo and behold, a soft bed appeared. He was astonished. I wish for a beautiful girl who can massage my tired limbs, he thought. In a second, a pretty girl came before him. I wish I could satisfy my hunger, he said. A tray of food appeared. Just as he was enjoying the food, the girl and the bed, a sudden thought occurred to him. What if a tiger were to pounce on me now? A tiger pounced on him and killed him. The moral is that you have everything going for you—good upbringing, intelligence, strong character and the best of education. Don't make a death-wish and destroy all that you have gained. It's not worth it. Think for yourself.

Ravi thought for himself and found that he still loved Deborah.

Then the family threw their best pitcher at Ravi. Anand was sent to America. He brought his wife Kanti. Ravi drove down to New York City to meet them.

Ravi's eldest brother had always been a bit of an enigma to Ravi. Anand was nine years older than Ravi, too young to be a substitute father, yet too old to be treated as a brother. So Anand stood—like Raja Bali did in Trishanku—not quite brother and not quite father. Ravi couldn't be too casual or too formal; he couldn't be entirely respectful or totally irreverent. It was a tough balancing act.

They met in New York and drove down to Washington, D.C. on the I-95 where all vehicles on all lanes drove at the same speed, slowing down every other car that wanted to go faster. Ravi took Anand and Kanti to Blues Alley—the finest and oldest jazz joint in D.C.—where sax, bass, trumpet, drums and piano would drown out all conversation.

'Ravi, give up this foolish idea,' Anand said. 'Our father is a broken man. Amma is equally devastated. Don't hurt them any more—they have brought you up all these years with so much love. Look at Arjun and me. We married the girls chosen by them and are none the worse for it.' Kanti looked at Ravi and smiled.

'I'm not trying to hurt them,' Ravi began to protest.

'Ravi,' his brother interrupted. 'Like you, I wanted to come to study in America. I never got the chance. It was too expensive, Appa said, and I accepted his decision. But you had the chance. You got a scholarship and Appa let you use it. No one in this family has had the opportunities you have. You will do a great disservice if you turn your back on us.'

'What disservice?' Ravi retorted. 'Turn my back on whom? And for what? If my friend Senthil, who comes from a village near Punrotti and saves all he can to send money to his parents so that they don't starve, turns his back on them, that's disservice. But our family is not in that situation. I came here to study. I haven't deprived you of anything. How does pursuing my studies and asking Appa for permission to marry Deborah become a disservice to you?'

'Ravi, shut up. There is a line you can't cross. We can't accept an American into our home. If you do that, you are on your own. There is no place in our house for the two of you. There is no point arguing about it.'

'Then why did you come all this way? You could have given me an ultimatum sitting in Chennai.'

'No, Ravi. I want you to understand. That girl will never belong with us. It will tear our family apart.'

Ravi's heart sank. He had wanted to tell Anand that he was mistaken. He wanted to say how much he wanted Deborah to come and live with them in Chennai. He wanted to convince Anand that she would fit comfortably into their lives. He wanted Anand to take back this message to Appa and Amma. But he didn't say another word. He couldn't see the point.

Anjaneya, please give Ravi good sense and guide him, Appa prayed.

The Hanuman temple was right on Royapettah High Road and that was where Appa headed when he heard about Ravi and Deborah the first time. It had come as a shock. Appa had expected great things from Ravi. He thought Ravi was the best of the lot. How could Ravi do this to him?

The abhishekam of the Hanuman deity was done and soon the idol stood dressed in vennai kaappu—clothed in pure white butter with a garland of vadai around his neck. The black granite deity emerged white as snow. The devotees were in a frenzy. They knew their wishes would come true. Anjaneya would grant them whatever they wished for. Appa stood too, with prayers on his lips and bhakti in his heart.

When she heard from Anand, Amma decided she needed astrological help. She went to see the astrologer with Ravi's horoscope.

Venkatramaiyer lived in an old house on Maada street near the Kapaaleeshwarar temple. When you stepped into the Maada streets encircling the temple, you felt like you had entered the past. Many of the houses were over a century old and still retained their distinct features. These four Maada streets had over the years witnessed spectacular festivals and celebrations with colourfully decorated gigantic temple cars pulled by the faithful. Every March, thousands congregated to witness the procession of the Nayanmar idols at the Arubathimoovar festival.

Venkatramaiyer lived in a narrow house that was like a car squished between two giant trucks, with long, narrow rooms like railway compartments, two cycles parked below a steep flight of stairs, tube lights, old musty books piled in no particular order on the shelves and a big twenty-seven-inch TV dominating the drawing room—the only sign of luxury in the midst of an otherwise spartan set of bucket cane chairs and a wooden table.

Venkatramaiyer sat in one of the chairs sporting a spotless white veshti with a long white khadi towel wrapped around his chest and one shoulder. His poonal peeked out from underneath the towel.

As soon as Amma entered, Venkatramaiyer's daughter-in-law brought two cups of hot coffee, placed them on the table and disappeared into the house.

Venkatramaiyer had studied Amma's horoscope several times and he had usually been right. He had fixed up the marriages of Anand and Arjun, he had compared the horoscopes of Jaya and Mahesh and found them suitable for marriage. He hadn't seen Ravi's before and now looked at it carefully.

'Amma, the attraction between the two is very strong. I don't see how they can be separated. I'm afraid you may have to get used to the idea of an American daughter-in-law.'

The family had known Venkatramaiyer for nearly three decades and had never had to consult anyone else. Amma had no reason to fault his predictions this time.

'There may also be an estrangement among the members of the family,' the astrologer continued. 'You have it in your power to be the bridge, Amma. There is a shani patch in your husband's horoscope. It will lift after a year, but that is what is making reconciliation impossible.'

Amma left the house, feeling dejected. She held onto one last straw. She had the power to bridge the gap. She would do it.

She walked to the Kapaaleeshwarar temple, a few hundred yards away.

It was a Friday.

She washed her feet and entered the temple. She took the two fresh coconuts that she had carefully selected and threw them hard on the floor of the specially built stone pit enclosed on all four sides by rickety wooden fences. The coconuts cracked open and revealed their white insides. She nodded with satisfaction and walked in till she was in front of goddess Karpakambal.

While his parents sought divine intervention, Ravi had plans of his own. It had been a long time since he had entered a temple. But Ravi was desperate. He needed someone to talk to. And he was hopelessly in love. To ignore it was cowardice.

To jump into it was foolishness. Ravi suddenly remembered *Thirukkural*.

My good heart, give up either love or shame—
Both these two I cannot bear together.

It was Amma who had instilled *Thirukkural* in her children. He could almost hear her reciting it. Ravi smiled. He had imbibed *Thirukkural* well, to be able to remember an obscure verse like this.

He drove to Pittsburg to pray to Lord Venkateswara. He reached late at night and checked into a cheap motel. At first light, he drove to Penn Hills.

The sight of the gleaming temple rising up against grey clouds lifted his spirits at once. The temple was almost a replica of the temple in Tirupati. White and imposing, the spires rose to the sky. South Indian temples had a certain majesty and this one was no exception. It was one of the first temples to be built in the US, and it was evident that a lot of love and devotion had gone into it. It was smaller than the Siva-Vishnu Temple in D.C. but more beautifully conceived; the resplendent chaturbujam Lord Venkateswara stood on the padma pitam blessing his numerous devotees. Ravi stood in front of him, ran his palms over the fire of the deepaaradhanai and placed them over his eyes.

After the darshan, he sat in the hall with the other devotees. The place was full. Ravi sat next to an old man with an ochre towel wrapped around his sweater. He closed his eyes and prayed. He knew prayers even if he had had no occasion to put them to good use earlier. He recited the *Vishnu Sahasranaamam* without pause and felt extremely proud of himself. He had not forgotten it as he had feared. When he opened his eyes, the old man was still there. The crowd had thinned.

The old man smiled at Ravi. 'Are you from here?'

'No, I live in Cornell.'

'Oh, god bless you. You must be a great devotee to drive all the way on an auspicious day like this.'

Ravi had not known that it was an auspicious day. 'Err... yes, I have come to seek Venkateswara's blessings.'

'He is our saviour,' the old man agreed. 'He will solve all your problems.'

Ravi closed his eyes, partly to concentrate and partly to get away from answering any more questions. He was tired and his body ached from jetlag.

'I heard you recite the *Vishnu Sahasranaamam*,' the man continued. 'You must be coming from a very religious family.'

'Yes.'

'Do your parents live in America?'

'No, they live in Madras.'

'Oh! So you are here to study?'

'Yes.'

'You are not married, are you?'

Ravi opened his eyes with a start. He realized where the conversation was going.

'No, I'm not married. I have to go, saar.'

'Before you go, please give me your telephone number, son.'

'I'm changing my cell-phone next week. So this number is of no use. Namaskaram.'

'Remember one thing,' the old man called out to Ravi as he ran for his life. 'Your heart is your guide. Lord Venkateswara speaks through your heart. Listen to it carefully. Never waver from your devotion to him and he will solve all your problems.'

Ravi folded his hands in prayer and did a namaskaram in front of the garbhagraha, prostrating fully before the idol.

When he finally left the temple, he didn't feel any different. But he knew his questions would be answered.

And for the first time, Deborah went to the synagogue in Georgetown, near her university—the Kesher Israel synagogue. She attended the Hashkama service on Shabbat morning, and sat through the main service as well. And that evening she made sure that meat didn't mix with dairy. It was kosher.

'Aren't you going to pray for us or something?' Ravi had asked her.

'Okay, I'll something,' Deborah promised.

'Praying is better.'

'I thought I would first see how your prayers work out. I just prayed last week for good grades. Anyway, you are praying for both of us.'

'Okay, from now on I'll pray just for myself. You do your stuff, I'll do mine.'

'Fine, I will pray. But my mom, she's praying too—against what we want. And if she is as devout as she claims, we have no hope of getting married.'

'We don't seem to have a hope in hell in any case.'

8

The roads in Chennai curved inwards and outwards and rarely went straight, like a cane bent by weight, or the reverse swing of a fast bowler with an old ball. Ravi's and Deborah's new house stood in the middle of one such meandering road. It was shielded by a long driveway and tall trees. The air was filled with a chorus of chirping birds. The compound wall outside, plastered as it was with large movie posters and election bills, struck the only discordant note. Since all compound walls of Chennai met with the same fate, the wall was ugly and disfigured but not out-of-place.

The locality was posh; it was one of those areas where expatriates lived and was suitably far away from Vedaranyam Street. The rent wasn't low but drawing two American salaries in Chennai helped.

The house had been selected after some deliberation. The driveway curved around the front of the house, encircling a small lawn. A row of crotons of various hues lined the driveway. Maintaining the garden would be a headache with the city struggling without rain or water. But they had wanted greenery and were prepared to take the risk. At the moment, the lawns were green if discoloured in patches. A gulmohur tree stood next to the house, just outside the library window. Its crown was huge and kept the sun away in the afternoon. Money plant creepers entwined themselves around the pillars of the portico. The paint was peeling off the outside walls, but this was true of every house in Chennai. The dust and the heat were enough to wilt anything and anyone.

Deborah had another reason for choosing the house. With its curving road, pebbled driveway and tall trees, it reminded her of her parents' house. When she came out of the house, she could well have been in Norfolk—until the blaring of an Ambassador's horn snapped her out of her reverie.

'What are you up to now?' Deborah asked Kamala athai when she found her sweating over an array of vegetables in the kitchen.

'Seven-vegetable kozhambu,' Kamala athai replied and laughed. 'Yezhukari kozhambu in Tamil. Try getting your tongue around that one!'

Deborah tried gamely but failed.

'If you are serious about Ravi, you have to learn to say that one! Yezhukari kozhambu! But the good news is that you don't have to cook it. Frankly, no Chennai girl in your age group knows how to cook it either!'

On the gleaming black cuddapah stone slab of Kamala athai's kitchen lay heaps of cluster beans, snake gourd, colocasia, raw plantain, sweet potato, brinjal, white pumpkin, French beans and red pumpkin—all cut evenly into small pieces. A Sumeet mixie was placed next to them.

'Ravi likes yezhukari kozhambu. And since he says his tongue has died, I thought I would revive it with his favourite dish. You will see nine vegetables spread out here.' She swept her right arm across the black cuddapah like a magician about to perform his first trick. 'It's called seven-vegetable kozhambu but there can be any number of vegetables as long as they are in an odd number, say seven or nine or even eleven.'

Athai started boiling the vegetables. The heat in the kitchen also began to rise. When the vegetables were half boiled, she added tamarind water, salt and a pinch of turmeric. 'Wait till the smell of tamarind is gone,' she told Deborah, and took some red gram, dal, ground coconut and chillies and fried them. She dropped them into the mixie and its high-pitched whine filled the kitchen. 'Add this to the boiling mixture and top it up with coriander leaves, mustard and fenugreek. That's all there is to it! If you do it well, the entire neighbourhood is supposed to soak in the fragrance of yezhukari kozhambu!'

'Well, that sounds easy. If Ravi develops a craving for this whatever-curry-whatever, I'll send him here!'

That afternoon Deborah was herded by Kamala athai into the thickest part of the city, to get a sense of the 'real' Chennai.

The driver took them to Luz. The traffic was heavy as usual. Pedestrians, cycles, autorickshaws, cars and PTC buses fought for space. Closer to Luz Corner were street hawkers who occupied more than half the street. The car inched its way around Luz Corner between shoppers and groups of people scurrying to visit the temple. It was time to stop the car, get out and walk.

The air smelled of fireworks and fresh clothes and sweat. Deborah usually steered clear of crowds. Crowds made her extremely self-conscious. She felt like everyone's eyes were on her. She tried to look through them but without much success.

'If you want to live here, you have to get used to this,' Kamala athai warned her.

Kamala athai hobbled down the jam-packed street on her crutches. People bumped into her and continued on their way without so much as an apology. At first Deborah tried to make way for Kamala athai by walking in front of her but soon she gave up. She needn't have worried. Kamala athai was enjoying herself and held her own in all the jostling. She liked these boisterous and lively crowds and she liked shopping even more.

Deborah had never seen so many people crammed into such a small space. They walked past the pavement stalls, past rows of clothes shops and into a showroom that sold clothes. Kamala athai walked in confidently and in a few minutes she had persuaded Deborah to pick up three salwar-kameezes. One was a deep burgundy with intricate embroidery. 'It'll look really lovely against your white skin,' she told Deborah, who smiled. She liked the way Kamala athai spoke about white skin, dark skin, fair skin and mango-coloured skin with a complete lack of self-consciousness or ill-will. Finally, they stopped at Ambika Appalam to pick up appalams. Laden with packets, they bumped into another million people before they extricated themselves from the masses and located the car. Deborah was well on her way to becoming a Chennaivaasi.

Getting used to Chennai meant getting used to Tamil talk, that incessant questioning and urge to establish a person's ancestry and identity.

'Where do you hail from?' she was asked.

'Sorry? Hail?' The only hailing she had done was of cabs.

'Where is your home town?'

'Home town?'

'Yes, where do you come from?'

'Virginia.'

'So your family is originally from Virginia.'

'No, they were first in New York and later came down to Virginia and settled down.'

'So you are originally from New York?'

'Not really. My mother comes from Poland, and my dad from Boston and before that from Germany.'

There was confusion. So what was her home town? Deborah didn't have a home town.

'So you are an immigrant.'

'My parents were, not me. I'm as American as you can get.'

'Yes, yes. You're American,' it was agreed. 'But not American American.'

'The only American Americans are the American Indians,' she explained.

There was a confused pause.

'Oh, you mean Red Indians!'

Deborah squirmed.

After her identity—or lack of it—was established, the conversation shifted to their relatives and friends who had migrated to the US. Deborah had to listen to what each one was doing, how well their children were doing in school and how hard the parents worked. Each one was nothing short of a CEO or, at worst, indisposable in the company where they worked. Cities like Montana, New Jersey, LA, San Jose, Palm Beach, Houston, Phoenix and Baltimore were named as though they adjoined Chennai. They reeled out their list of relatives proudly and were surprised that Deborah hadn't heard of any of them.

'You must be knowing Shanmuganathan, popularly called Sam Nathan. He heads the investment unit of Citibank.'

No, she didn't.

They forgave Deborah for her ignorance, thinking that Deborah was your typical, uninformed American girl.

Getting used to Chennai meant getting used to the smell of urine. It wafted out from the most unexpected places. When Deborah went to the Music Academy, it came from behind the electricity transformer on the broken pavement. Further down, the smell struck unsuspecting pedestrians at the intersection of Avvai Shanmugam Salai and T.T.K Road. The Tamils felt no hesitation in lifting their veshtis and relieving themselves against a wall on the road as long their backs were to the traffic.

But Deborah's greatest challenge was learning Tamil. It was a challenge she accepted with determination. She swore she would learn the language. And in a span of about a year, she did.

Learning Tamil was akin to a rite of passage in Tamil Nadu. Tamil wasn't a language to be trifled with. Memories of the anti-Hindi agitation were kept alive in Tamil Nadu with a periodic dosage of Tamil chauvinism. Tamils still talked about how anti-Hindi agitation broke out all over Tamil Nadu in 1965 and the great Tamil leader Annadurai was arrested. A 'Hindi demon' was garlanded with chappals, and one day twenty-four people were killed under police firing. That sealed the fate of Hindi in Tamil Nadu.

Deborah's intention was noble. She wanted to feel at home in Chennai, in Ravi's world. She got hold of Ravi's Tamil teacher from his old school and hammered away at studying Tamil with dedication. Slowly, she started understanding

Tamil quite well—except the Tamil of the local politicians which the Tamils themselves found hard to understand and even harder to believe. She liked the language, her only grouse being that people spoke so fast.

'Tamil is killing me,' she complained to Ravi on a particularly tough day.

'It killed me a long time ago, Debbie. My mom was adamant we take Tamil as our second language and killed whatever chances I had of becoming prime minister.'

'Why prime minister?'

'You have to know Hindi if you want to hold any meaningful position of office in New Delhi. In fact, in a place called Karaikudi, Mahatma Gandhi had once declared that the famous Tamil leader Rajagopalachari would be his natural successor. But Rajaji didn't speak Hindi, and soon Nehru—with his command over Hindi and certainly over English—took over. That's the power of Hindi.'

'Shouldn't I learn Hindi then? There's nothing to prevent a foreigner from becoming prime minister!'

'No. But I would rather you become the president of the United States than the prime minister of India. '

Getting used to Chennai also meant her colleagues in office had to get used to Deborah. When Deborah and Ravi first came to Chennai, their colleagues made life anything but easy for Deborah. Mike, Anwar, Anita, Govind and Narayanan weren't overtly hostile. But it was obvious that they resented Deborah's intrusion into their cozy group. They considered themselves whizzkids and when they saw the smart young blonde from America, they treated her with contempt and went about systematically excluding her from every important decision. Deborah couldn't imagine Tamils could be so arrogant. In a way, she felt relieved when she saw that the US was not the only country to discriminate against foreigners in the workplace.

Ravi found it a lot easier to get accepted. That was only natural. For one, he was next only to Mike in the hierarchy. Second, it was easy being a Tamilian in Chennai. Even if one was a Brahmin.

At first Ravi tried to protect Deborah from the hostile environment but then he realized she had to build her own equation with the others. He could be a catalyst but nothing more. Rejected by Ravi's parents and viewed as an oddity by the locals, Deborah tried to overcome her loneliness by working harder and longer. There was enough to do, fortunately, and she pounced on her work eagerly and tried to shut out the world outside. Things did change. One by one, her colleagues came round. Grudgingly at first, but when they got to know her better, willingly.

Deborah stepped onto the portico one day to find two men at the gate. They were waiting patiently, and hadn't even rung the bell. She quickly walked up to them.

'I want to have a word with you, madam,' the older of the two said respectfully, in English.

'With me? Or with—'

'Yes, with you, madam. It's about my son here—Govind.'

Deborah looked at the lanky youngster wearing a dark blue long-sleeved shirt and even darker blue jeans, and saw a blank pair of eyes staring back at her.

'What is it?'

'My son has got admission into an American university. I have arranged for his finances. We need your help to get him a visa. It is extremely difficult to get one. The American Consulate here is—'

'Visa? I have no idea how to get one…'

'We wanted your help to talk to someone in the American Consulate…'

'I don't know anyone in the US Consulate here.'

'If you want, you can help, madam. They will definitely listen to you.'

'They don't even know me. Why should they listen to me?'

'Madam, please, it will be a big opportunity for my son,' the man said, folding his palms together. 'You will be doing my family a big favour. You will be like a goddess for our—'

'Sir, I have no idea. I don't know anyone…'

'You are from America. They will listen to whatever you say.'

Getting used to Chennai meant getting used to cries of help from US-visa seekers.

Beyond her attempts at learning Tamil, finding acceptance for her Jewishness, her accent and her blonde hair, her toughest test was to explain her relationship with Ravi to friends and foes alike. In fact, when it came to this, Ravi had an equally difficult time. The Tamilians were used to film stars, tennis players, golf champs and New Yorkers living together. They had read about it in the papers, seen it in movies. But to have their own homegrown boy living with a white girl came as a shock.

Living together without getting married was not unusual in the United States. Some even had children before marriage and proudly flaunted their children like a badge of honour. For every code of civilized conduct, there were several that broke it. For every set of conservative values, there were several sets which ran diametrically opposite. Everything had an antithesis. That was the strength of the US. It was also its bane. The Americans scrupulously observed the rules of the road, stopped at red lights, gave way to pedestrians, waited patiently for their turn in a long queue, sorted out their garbage into neat lots of paper, bottles and refuse and kept it out on the allotted day of the week, filled the parking metre with dimes and quarters if it threatened to expire, and ran up the American flag every fourth of July. But when it came to the norms of human relationships or the pursuit of inner peace, most Americans didn't consider these relevant to their search for happiness.

Living together wasn't Deborah's or Ravi's first choice. They had wanted to get married first and with Appa's consent. But that didn't happen. So they battled hostility, curiosity, awkwardness, rudeness and friendly advice before they were left alone.

Tolerated as an oddity but not quite accepted.

9

It started auspiciously enough. Deborah had been coached well by Ravi and Kamala athai. When Amma entered Kamala athai's house, Deborah walked up to her, went down on her knees and did an elaborate namaskaram.

Amma stood frozen, before her right hand reached out to touch Deborah's head in blessing. Deborah straightened up. 'I wanted to do this when I met you for the first time,' she said.

Amma's eyes grew moist. It was the last thing she had expected Deborah to do and she was struggling for words. 'Deborah, I have been waiting to meet you in person,' she said, pulling Deborah up on her feet. Ravi had expected Amma to react the way she did. Amma had taught the children that you can't show anger at a person who falls at your feet. That was a lesson Ravi never forgot. 'Fall at my parents' feet and they will agree to our marriage,' he had said and Deborah had agreed to try it out.

Amma was struck by Deborah's beauty. She looked almost like a Punjabi girl, she thought, but fairer. And such lovely blonde hair. No wonder Ravi was moonstruck. If only she were an Iyer girl...

Amma's first task was to dissuade Deborah from marrying Ravi. She thought she could achieve through persuasion what Appa couldn't through ostracization. 'Deborah, my child, you will find it difficult to adjust to our family,' she explained gently. 'Ravi has been brought up in an orthodox way. You might be attracted to each other now, but once you get married and have children, and your individual beliefs and traditions start asserting themselves, you will find nothing but despair. Think about that before you do something rash.'

When reasoning failed to make any impact, Amma resorted to pleading with Deborah. 'Ravi is impulsive. He does things rashly and regrets them later. Sometimes, in the full flowering of youth, one tends to get carried away by physical attraction. Soon the physical attraction will die and you will find that he is very different from you. Please leave him now so you save him and yourself from future heartbreak. Please leave us. This is not the family or the place for you. Don't do something now which you will regret later.' Deborah was getting stressed out. Just when she finally had an access to Ravi's family, the door was closing on her.

Appa was furious that his son had chosen to live openly with a foreign woman in the heart of Chennai. It was as bad as living with a whore. People would talk about it. Ravi had done this to spite him, Appa was convinced. He had brought disgrace to the family and Appa was determined that he would pay for it. Ravi's act went against everything Appa stood for.

Where had he gone wrong, Appa wondered. Hadn't he brought up his children in the best manner possible, taught them all they needed to know? Love meant nothing to Appa. Respect for tradition, strong morals, faith in god and obedience to parents—these were the values he stood for. He had been strict, but only because he wanted them to be virtuous, incorruptible. Certainly Ravi had always been a bit of a rebel, even turning into a non-vegetarian. But how could things have gone so wrong?

When Appa heard about Deborah and Ravi for the first time, his first reaction wasn't anger or shock. It was pain. Pain in the deepest recesses of his being. A pain that no one—not even Amma—had seen before. Ravi's act had brought back an ancient memory. He thought he had come to terms with it, but it came flooding back now.

1955.

Eight years after India's independence, what was still unacceptable to the north had already been accepted by the south: partition. After all, the Tamils had not seen the bloodbath that preceded it. Partition hadn't affected them the way it did the Punjabis or Bengalis. The Tamils thought India was better off giving Pakistan to the Muslims. The fact that most of the Muslims in Madras chose to remain in their city and not leave for an alien country only vindicated the Tamilian stand that partition was a north Indian phenomenon.

The Tamils were pragmatists. They didn't expend their energies unnecessarily. They had their own problems with the north to deal with: removing the imposition of Hindi, better share in revenues, greater representation in the government. And local problems too: problems of caste and the domination of Brahmins in the bureaucracy, the demand to carve out a separate state of Andhra from the Madras Presidency with Madras as its capital.

In this confused phase of a nascent Indian democracy, Appa found a job with a British company in Madras. His father had arranged for him to join the company. Not that Appa needed any recommendation. His fine mind and diligence impressed his bosses and they soon decided to send him to London for a four-month training stint.

Appa was very excited about travelling to London. He had never been on a ship before. It sailed from neighbouring Ceylon. But first he had to take a train from Madras to Dhanushkodi with his father, who insisted on accompanying him. They left for Egmore station and reached so early that there weren't any porters around to carry their luggage. The station had a leisurely air about it, like the Royapuram railway station in Madras, but it was far more impressive. They sat on top of their bedding until the train pulled in. The train was called the Boat Mail; it would take them directly to the harbour from where the ferry to Thalaimannar operated. Powered by a steam engine, the Boat Mail cut through the fast-receding evening and blew dust and smoke right into their compartment. Appa spread his bedding and covered himself with a bedsheet to avoid the soot. His father barely noticed the dust and smoke—he was busy giving his son a list of dos and don'ts, with more don'ts than dos. Don't lean too far over the railings of the ship. Don't smoke. Don't drink. Don't eat meat. Behave with humility. And beware of foreign women. You will be enticed by them, Appa was warned.

There were several pilgrims in their compartment, but since it was night, they didn't have to talk to their fellow passengers. When the Boat Mail pulled into Dhanushkodi railway station the next morning, it occurred to Appa that his father was as interested in seeing him off as in visiting the temple at Rameswaram, where the linga of Ramanatha was the presiding deity. It was a rare opportunity, his father told him excitedly. Rameswaram was a new experience for Appa. Father and son walked through long corridors and past intricately carved pillars for a darshan of the deity, stopping at each of the twenty-two wells to take the ritual bath. The water in each well was supposed to taste different from the others. His father had thoughtfully brought along extra veshtis so they could undertake the drenching without ruining their clothes. While doing their prathakshinam around the temple in their wet clothes, they recited all the shlokas they knew. With the blessings of Ramanatha, Appa didn't have to fear the success of his trip to London.

The next day Appa boarded the ferry to Thalaimannar. His father bid him goodbye from the shores. He wasn't coming any further. Appa choked back tears when he saw the receding figure but he didn't have much time to wallow in self-pity because the water was choppy and the ride bumpy. His stomach churned and he thanked his stars that he had eaten only idlis for breakfast. The torture lasted two hours until the ferry anchored at Thalaimannar. Then he had to take an overnight train to Colombo. As he waited for the train at the forlorn platform of the station, he felt a sense of apprehension dissipate the excitement he had been feeling all this while. He was in a different country. He was alone. When he finally reached Colombo, he was exhausted.

Appa was one of the first passengers to reach Elizabeth Quay the next evening. *SS Orantes* was waiting at the docks. It was a large ship and only grew bigger as Appa approached it. His company had arranged a second-class ticket for him through Thomas Cook for the handsome sum of 850 rupees. His father had converted some money into pounds sterling at thirteen rupees to a pound. He touched his wallet every now and then to make sure it was still there. He was shown to his cabin. There were four beds, two on each side. Two tables under the circular window looked onto the dark waters. Appa placed his favourite book and a picture of Ganesha next to his bed. The journey had started well, he thought.

The ship streamed out of Elizabeth Quay into the Indian Ocean towards Marseille. The waters enveloped them on all four sides and even the comforting light of the Ceylon shore had vanished. Darkness descended quickly and all Appa could hear was the dull swishing of the water as the ship made progress.

The next morning, Appa was greeted in bed with tea and biscuits. He decided to stay in bed a while longer. Breakfast had been divided into two rounds—the first between eight and nine, the second between nine and ten. He missed both and sat in his cabin, munching gratefully at the idlis packed by his Ceylonese hosts. This perked him up and he got ready to explore the ship. Most of the other passengers were already on the deck, taking in the fresh air. It was clear and sunny. There were cards, deck tennis, table tennis, billiards, darts and even a gym. A few of the passengers ventured into the gym but most were content just to laze about on the deck. Not wanting to exert himself, Appa avoided the gym and played everything else, including a few rounds of billiards.

It was lunchtime when he finally dragged himself away from the billiards table. When he saw the generous lunch spread, the second doubt crept into his mind. How was he going to survive the journey on this food? For what lay before him were non-vegetarian delights. There was hardly anything for a vegetarian. All that he could salvage was bread, salad, fruits and ice-cream. Even the ice-cream had egg, he suspected, and avoided it. He wasn't sure whom he should take the problem to. The captain? No, he searched out the cook—a man with a splendid white cap—and explained his dilemma. The cook couldn't quite fathom why the young man couldn't eat meat or fish and all he could muster up the next day was some boiled vegetables.

Bread and boiled vegetables. The journey was slowly turning into a nightmare. It was bearable the first day. By the time the passengers got together for a dinner party on the deck the next day, Appa's enthusiasm had diminished. He saw couples dancing into the night and felt envious and hungry. The spring in his step had disappeared. At the end of the third day, Appa was famished. He stopped playing billiards and preferred to sit in his cabin and read, all the while thinking of food. The elderly gentleman who was his cabin mate also stayed in the cabin for an entire day since he couldn't cope with the rocking of the ship. The Arabian Sea was rough. The few idlis packed in Colombo had long disappeared. He tried to grab as much fruit as he could during meal times but it was never enough. On one occasion, when Appa was trying to take three apples away, a gentleman with a bowtie caught him by the hand and said, 'One fruit each, leave the rest alone.' Embarrassed, Appa dropped all the apples and ran away.

By the fifth day, his cabin mates were worried about his condition. The elderly gentleman was the most concerned and kept checking Appa's pulse every six hours. Finally, in desperation, the gentleman made his way to the chef. He swore him to secrecy, forced him to take out the beef pieces from the broth, had boiled vegetables put in and served to Appa. 'One word of this to that man and he will commit suicide. It's best we keep this between us,' he said and the chef solemnly agreed.

Vegetables in beef broth tasted delicious. Appa ate with relish, little realizing that his principles and religious beliefs were being compromised to appease his hunger. For the rest of the journey, this carefully concealed charade was played out.

Fortunately, after five days, the ship reached Aden and the passengers were allowed to go on shore. The Aden harbour was swarming with people. Appa bought a large box of Arabian dates, enough to last him the rest of the journey. Much to his surprise, some of the shopkeepers spoke to him in Hindi. Since Hindi was as alien to him as Chinese, Appa requested them to speak to him in English. When they understood each other in English, Appa's first question was about vegetarian food. There was good Arab food available and they served him falafel and bread with ta'miyya and foul. Appa ate like there was no tomorrow. After this, he felt much better and promptly bought himself a cream-coloured silk shirt.

Soon they had left the turbulent waters of the Arabian Sea and ventured into the calmer Red Sea. It was a tranquil twelve-hour journey through the Suez Canal and all the passengers stood on the deck admiring the manmade canal cutting across the desert. The two banks were alarmingly close. Ismailiya came on the left and the Sinai stood forlorn on the right. When Port Said finally came into view, Appa's relieved cabin mate bid him goodbye. 'Take care of your health, my boy,' he said affectionately. 'Remember, when you go abroad, you have to stop being a vegetarian. Otherwise you won't survive too long.'

'A bowl of vegetable soup will keep me alive till the end of time,' Appa replied.

The man laughed loudly.

10

Appa visited America for the first time in '82, the year *Gandhi* won the Academy Awards and *E.T.* ran to full houses. 'Ebony and Ivory' was on everyone's lips, *Dynasty* on everyone's TV. More than 25 million Americans smoked marijuana and President Reagan had declared war on drugs. Thank god none of my children have to study here, Appa thought, relieved. When the largest cash robbery in American history occurred in New York, where 9,800,000 dollars was stolen from an armoured car, Appa thanked his stars that he had always lived in a safe city—Madras.

But Appa had returned impressed with the Americans. He had met his suppliers and struck deals. They were tough bargainers but forthright people: direct, frank and surefooted—just like him.

By the time he visited the US in '84, Michael Jackson's *Thriller* had broken all music industry records, the Los Angeles Olympic Games had made the US a world sporting power and Edwin Moses a household name, Madonna sang like a virgin and President Reagan was on the verge of being re-elected. But what left a lasting impression on Appa was *Amadeus*. He wished someone would make a movie on Thyagaraja in the same way. Thyagaraja is infinitely superior but there's no one to make a movie on his life, he complained to all those who cared to ask him about his visit to the US. Just imagine how wonderful it would be if, like Mozart's first performance on stage, the arangetram of Thyagaraja were to be portrayed on screen. Think of the impact it would have on millions when Thyagaraja starts singing 'Dorakuna Ituvanti Seva'—'Is it possible to get a darshan of Lord Hari?'

When Appa visited the US again he had a new concern. If my sons come here, they will end up getting married to an American, he worried. But Appa had not been unimpressed with the US. He realized its strength and potential. He admired its people and the intellectual atmosphere of its universities.

So when Ravi asked Appa for permission to study abroad, Appa couldn't bring himself to refuse him. Cornell was a prestigious university. Ravi's admission was a result of his excellent academic record. To deny Ravi would have been to deny his son what Appa had prepared him for. He couldn't even use college fees as an excuse since Cornell had given Ravi the best financial package they could offer.

So Appa agreed.

But when Ravi wanted to stay on in the United States after his graduation, that was an entirely different matter. His worst fears were coming true.

1955.

By the time *SS Orantes* reached Port Said, Appa had regained his health with a daily diet of vegetables in beef or chicken broth, salads, boiled vegetables and fruits. The dates purchased from Aden had long since vanished. It was time to replenish stocks. Appa got off at Port Said to write a hurried postcard to his parents, assuring them that all was well. A tall Egyptian wearing a flowing grey galabiyya came over to Appa.

'Are you Hindi?' he asked gruffly.

'No, I'm Tamil,' Appa replied.

'I thought you are Hindi.'

'No, I'm Tamil.'

The Egyptian paused thoughtfully.

'Where is Tamil?'

'I'm from India and Tamils are from—'

'Of course, that's what I thought! You are Hindi.'

'Not really, I'm Tamil.'

The Egyptian laughed. 'No, no, I mean Indian. An Indian is called Hindi in Arabic,' he explained.

'Oh!' was all Appa could say.

'Nehru is a good man,' the Egyptian said. 'I like him.'

'Nasser is also a good man,' Appa said in return.

'Egypt–Hindi brother–brother,' he said, locking his fingers together.

'Yes, we are brothers,' Appa agreed and the Egyptian came forward to hug Appa in a show of unwarranted bonhomie. Then he kissed him on both cheeks.

Appa muttered something about the ship sailing soon and extricated himself politely from the warmth of the embrace and the wetness of his lips.

'Bye-bye, brother,' the Egyptian called out cheerfully.

Appa waved meekly and fled.

As he was running, he had the presence of mind to buy some falafel to eat in the safe confines of his cabin. He wanted to buy one of the famous Egyptian cotton shirts but he didn't want to get stuck with another friendly Egyptian. He also saw some lovely bananas on the way. Appa was fond of bananas. In fact, most Tamils were. Madras boasted of a variety of them, from the tiny malavaazhai—small sweet bananas from the hills—to the more common yellow poovambazham or the long green pachavazhai.

The Egyptian bananas piled up before him were much bigger than any he had seen in Madras. They looked a bit raw. He asked for half-a-dozen and the scraggy Egyptian held out a bunch of nearly unripe ones. These are fit only to make curry and not to eat as fruit, Appa thought and selected another bunch. The fruits in Madras ripened fast, became sweet and just as quickly became overripe. Overripe bananas were dipped in milk and made into pachadi. The ripe ones were soft. They tasted delicious.

It was a gentle journey across the Mediterranean. As they neared Marseille, Appa's excitement grew. He was going to see Europe. It was a dream come true.

The train ride from Marseille to Paris was like travelling through the Garden of Eden. Lush, green and heavenly. When the train stopped, he got off to stretch his legs and buy some fruit. One banana cost the equivalent of one rupee. Appa quickly put it back since the price of two bananas in Madras was one anna and for a rupee he could get thirty-two bananas. If I start converting everything into rupees, I will end up eating nothing, he told himself. But he couldn't help it. To spend a whole rupee on a banana? Ridiculous.

From Paris to Calais and Calais to Dover. Then a train ride to London Paddington. It had been a three-week journey to the heart of the western world.

Appa arrived in London in July. Since he hadn't been sure whether he would be received on arrival, his father had thoughtfully booked him into the Indian Students' Hostel in Earl's Court at one pound sterling per night with breakfast thrown in. Fortunately Appa didn't have to wait long on the platform before the representative from the company sought him out and took him to his residence.

Hardworking and brilliant, he was soon absorbing all that he could learn. They were eight of them: four British, two Irish, one American and one Indian—himself. The non-British shared a guesthouse just outside the company premises and took every opportunity to spend time together. Even war-weary London had much to offer in terms of entertainment. Theatres, parks, pubs—Appa stuck to soda and water—cricket, palaces, there was so much to see. With religious rigour, the four non-Britishers took off every weekend to do some sightseeing. Oxford, Cambridge, yachting, the countryside. By the end of the second month, they had started going out in pairs, depending on each one's interest. Soon it was down to Appa and the American girl, Jennifer.

Jennifer and Appa shared a passion for literature and tried to connect everything to books. She was different from the other English girls, informal and easygoing. Appa had found the other girls in their group reserved—whether they were turned off by his skin colour or whether it was their natural reticence, he couldn't tell. But Jennifer was friendly. She called him Tom because she couldn't pronounce his name. Appa didn't mind; he liked being Tom to her. She was a good-looking girl with an undistinguished American nose. But what fascinated him the most was the way she spoke about writers and poets, with the confidence of an English don. Appa's fascination slowly turned to infatuation. It's just her white skin, he tried to convince himself, but he knew it wasn't. The more indifferent she was to him, the more he sought her company. He waited for Jennifer every day after work and they spent the evening together strolling through parks or window-shopping on Oxford Street. Later, they walked by the river till they reached the docks and the warehouses.

She talked about Boston and he about Madras. She took him to see a movie at Cinerama—on a full-blown 70-mm screen. And when the streetlamps came on, they took a bus to Hyde Park and lay on the wet grass, counting the stars.

Jennifer was a girl at peace with herself. She was clearly attracted to him but she didn't seem to need him the same way he craved for her attention. He sometimes felt like the orphan Pip in front of Estella.

He felt foolish. He had been taught to be immune to a woman's charms. His father had warned him against foreign women and exhorted him not to give in to his baser instincts. Appa had done precisely that.

Just when he thought she was going to ignore him completely, she turned up in his room one day. Tom, I love you too, she said. He stood speechless. He had never told her about his feelings. He stood awkwardly, his heart pounding. She threw her arms around him and kissed him.

They were in love.

11

Chennai was a religious city. Not for nothing was it considered the last conservative bastion of Hinduism. This was not very surprising because Chennai was a city where different faiths had coexisted for centuries and carved out niches for themselves. Almost every street had its own shrine—whether a shrine on the pavement or a pillayar where the outline of an elephant's trunk could be seen on the bark of a tree or a colourful cement gopuram enclosing the deity. Over time, the shrines grew bigger, until both the temples and their gods became formidable, attracting bigger crowds every day. Some streets were still adorned with churches from the time of the British, Portuguese and even the Armenians. There were a few mosques too, in prime locations, imposing and grand, and even a lone Buddhist shrine. It could safely be said that in spite of the inroads made by many political parties which claimed to have 'lack of faith in god' as a crucial electoral plank, the believers outnumbered the disbelievers. And even the disbelievers secretly worshipped the same gods behind the closed doors of their homes. In a city that believed in god, it was important not to be left out of god's munificence.

There was also a Jewish cemetery in Chennai—a reminder of yet another faith which had flourished in the city not so long ago. The Jewish presence in Madras began at the time Madraspatnam, as it was known then, was founded. They were mainly Portuguese Jews. Along with the Armenians, they formed the thriving trader and merchant class of the area. With affluence came privileges. They were given permission to live in the White Town. In 1687 there were six Jewish diamond merchants living there. The next year, when the Corporation of Madras was founded, three of them were appointed as Aldermen.

The Jews had arrived.

If you went north of Muthialpet, you would come to a dirty road, as dirty as any other road in Chennai. The importance of the roads in Chennai was usually directly proportional to the amount of dirt in them. This road was indeed special, since it had seen better days and had a lot more dirt. A veneer of affluence could be seen behind the dirt and grime. This was Pavalakarar Theru or the Coral Merchants' Street. The Jews of Madras set up shop here in the late-seventeenth century to trade diamonds from the Golconda mines in return for corals and other stones from their counterparts in London and other European cities. A synagogue came up nearby and there was a cemetery on Mint Street.

Deborah thought shifting out of Kamala athai's house would dissuade Amma from visiting them too frequently, but Amma wasn't one to give up so easily. She often landed up in their new house, especially when Ravi wasn't there, and worked on Deborah.

'Deborah, I ask you as a mother, don't come between Ravi and his family. Since the day he saw you, we have been living a life of stress and worry. Appa is a broken man. I don't want to die with sadness in my heart.'

'Nor do I, Amma. But I can't leave Ravi just like that...'

'You are like my daughter. Why should I ask you to leave? I am not asking you on a whim. You may be in love with Ravi but the sacrifice you make by leaving him will be for the greater good of the family—'

'Ravi loves me too, you know. Don't his feelings for me matter at all?'

'Of course they do. But you are young. Such feelings disappear over time. What matters in the end is the understanding that comes when you belong to the same culture.

'Amma, you should talk to Ravi first.'

'My dear child, I have no doubt that the attraction is mutual. But I want you to see reason even if he doesn't. There will be pain but from this pain will come a better life for both of you.'

'Frankly, I can't see what better life can come of separation.'

'What pleasure do you get by seeing us suffer?'

Deborah was close to tears. 'Amma, please stop. I can't take this any more!'

'Take what? After taking our son from us, what else have you left to take?'

'You're harassing me!'

'Harassing? You don't know what the word means. You have no idea of the torture you have put us through. Appa is a mere shell of his old self...'

'Stop it, Amma,' Deborah sobbed.

While Appa was busy excising Ravi from his life and Amma busy trying to dissuade Deborah from marrying Ravi, Ravi himself was quite amazed at Deborah's transformation. While he had grown more and more American in the US, she was growing more and more Tamil in India. In fact, it was Ravi who had been most reluctant to return to India. There were just a handful of Americans in Chennai and hardly any Jews. But that didn't seem to bother Deborah. She had come to India with the enthusiasm of a tourist and the tenacity of a mountaineer.

But Amma had started bothering her, and it had become quite intolerable. Deborah was nevertheless determined to stay on. Each time she was frustrated, she would bury her face into a pillow and cry. She didn't want Ravi to see how unhappy she was. She kept up the pretence of enjoying herself.

Ravi saw her tear-stained pillow and admired her determination. He hadn't expected her to last more than six months. He waited for her to ask him if they could shift back to the US. But that day never came. Deborah went through phases of excessive attention from colleagues when she wanted anonymity, hostility from relatives when she craved support, indifference from acquaintances when she longed for their friendship, and casual treatment from those she wanted to be taken seriously by. But she was still going strong, Amma or no Amma.

Deborah visited the Jewish cemetery to regain her composure. It was the only relic of Jewish presence in Chennai. She wasn't quite sure if it would help her but she was willing to try. Remember, her mother had always told her. Remembrance was what kept our race alive through the holocaust. Remember our past. Don't let it slip away. It will anchor your life and give you peace, wherever you are, whatever you do. Deborah had promised her mother that she would remember. Maybe a visit to the cemetery would anchor her existence in Chennai.

A corner of the big Christian cemetery on Lloyd's Road had been carved out for the Jews. *Solomon Franco, 1763,* the first tombstone said. *Issac Sard, 1709,* said the next. *Esther Cohen, 1964,* said another.

So the Jews remembered. They remembered their presence in Madras, their contribution to the city. As Deborah looked at the tombstones, she thought of her mother, proud of her Jewish heritage. But not blind to the follies of man, Deborah realized. For her parents had seen both sides. She remembered what her mother had told her.

The first time we visited Jerusalem and your dad and I looked up at the Golden Dome of Al Aqsa mosque above the Western Wall and saw the stones rain down, I felt nothing but hatred for the way we Jews were targeted in our own temple.

The next day, your dad and I decided to go to Kotel a second time, so that we could go back to America with the love we had felt the previous day—not with hate and disgust. Just as we were entering the periphery of the old city, someone called out to me. I turned around and saw a young Palestinian woman. She wore a black abaya over her body and her head was covered but I could see her face. Normally I would have hurried away, especially after the nasty experience the previous day. But she stood with such quiet dignity, her eyes so gentle. With her stood six more ladies, all wearing black and about the same age, except one.

'Can we speak to you for a minute?' she asked us in halting English.

We stood still, not saying yes or no, just staring at them.

'You are from America?'

We nodded.

She started to speak hesitantly. 'We are Palestinians. Our husbands have been snatched away from us by the senseless violence between the Jews and us. Fatima here,' she continued, pointing to the younger woman, 'lost her husband and both her sons last month in the shelling by Israeli tanks in Abu Dis. And Umm Omar here lost her daughter—she was a girl of fifteen—to a bullet from a Jew living in a settlement near Al Ram. And Umm Ahmed has just lost her husband and son—all of nine the boy was—to Israeli bullets; stray bullets, we were told. We are mothers and wives. We don't hate Jews. All we want is to raise our families in happiness and peace. We have not found either and we are not sure we ever will. There are hundreds like us all over Palestine. But all we want is for those amongst us who still have their families and happiness intact to feel that the future is worth living for.

'We know you are from America. We want you to take this message to your people. Americans should come here and talk to us and see for themselves. Talk to the Israelis and tell them to stop. What we need is peace and with peace will come friendship. Give us a chance. Otherwise this senseless killing will continue. And you and I and all of us will be helpless spectators.'

She stopped. The others nodded. They probably didn't understand a word of English, but their eyes glistened. The lady had spoken in broken, accented English and I had some trouble following. But very few could have spoken with greater feeling. I knew then that we all spoke the same language—the language of a mother, the language of one who has lost happiness in return for nothing.

I was at a loss for words. I wasn't sure why they chose us. We probably looked like any other Jewish American couple. I said something to the effect that I understood their anguish and promised that Americans had the same sentiments as they did. 'Whenever you see the happy face of your child, just remember that you are the most fortunate in this world,' she said before she left.

That single conversation removed in one moment the hatred I had been feeling. The more we thought about it, the more we were convinced that there was a divine hand in our meeting these women. Maybe it was god's way of answering our doubts. Your dad and I rushed to the wall. And as we saw the golden dome looming behind it, we felt the wall turn golden as well. We had found peace.

Deborah sat on the stone bench, her cheeks wet. The shadows of the evening surrounded her. Yes, mom, I love a stranger to my religion, she thought. Then she went back to transforming herself into a Chennaivaasi.

When Amma got after her, there was no one Deborah could turn to. She hesitated to go to Kamala athai. It wasn't a good idea to involve the family without Ravi's knowledge. He would prefer she went to him first. But she didn't want Ravi to know, because there was no knowing how he would react and the last thing she wanted was to be the cause of further conflict in Ravi's family. Only Chinnamma the maid, and Padma the cook, saw their memsahib suffer quietly. But who were they to interfere in what was going on?

Soon Deborah had reached breaking point. She wanted to leave Chennai, leave Appa and his rules, leave everything in India. Even Ravi. She just couldn't take it any more. So she went back to America.

Ravi, I need time to think. I need time to get used to this. I promise you, I'll be back.

Ravi had seen this coming. He said he would go with her. He hadn't found peace in Chennai either.

No, you stay here. I just need time. *And some space. For myself.* I'll come back.

But would she? She wasn't sure. Maybe she had got carried away. Maybe she was immature. Maybe Amma had a point. Maybe she was not fit for this kind of life after all. But then, what of her love for Ravi? And his for her? If she left, wouldn't he lose everything? Or would his family finally accept him again?

Deborah drove down the road slowly, enjoying the swaying of the trees on either side. It was in the midst of this greenery that Deborah had grown up. As children, she and Sophie would bounce up and down inside the old Chevrolet, while their father cursed whenever he hit a bump on the long, uneven road. The house stood alone among fields of uncut wild grass. Their closest neighbours lived a mile away. By the time Deborah graduated high school, the road had been paved and a lively neighbourhood had come up. In fact, their house was one of the smaller ones. The others had bought larger tracts of land and built spacious villas with huge Corinthian pillars. The white pillars gleamed in-between the trees like a tiger baring its teeth through tall grass.

Deborah's parents' house was a graceful, comfortable space. The tall trees shut out the outside world and the house seemed untouched by time, an anachronism in the middle of a two-lane road that brought with it fast cars and faster people.

Deborah was home.

12

It was Varadarajulu, the watchman of Vedaranyam Street.

'Varada! You, here? What happened?' Ravi's heart stopped for a moment.

'No, no, chinnadorai, don't worry, nothing has happened. Nothing at all…'

'Are you sure? Why are you here? Anything wrong?'

'No, chinnadorai, nothing has happened. Don't worry.'

Ravi relaxed a little. 'Then what brings you here, Varada?'

Varadarajulu hesitated. He looked down, his eyes refusing to meet Ravi's.

'Nothing… I was just passing by, so I thought—'

'There must be more to it than just passing by, Varada. What is bothering you?' Ravi asked anxiously.

'Well, chinnadorai, if you will not misunderstand me, I have something to say. In fact, I should have come to you some time ago but I was not sure…'

'What is it? Do you need any help?'

'No, chinnadorai, thanks to your father, I am well looked after and my children are being looked after too.'

Then, if not money, what did Varadarajulu want? Ravi wondered.

There was a brief pause and Varadarajulu stood there awkwardly, trying to find the right words.

'Chinnadorai, actually it's not my business… please don't misunderstand me…'

'I won't, Varada, you know me well…'

'Come home, chinnadorai,' he said in a rush. 'You have spent too long outside. I don't know what has happened between you all and I have never asked your father or brothers about it. But it doesn't look nice, chinnadorai. You cannot stay alone. You must forgive them and come home. After all, you are the youngest. That's why I have come, chinnadorai. The house is not the same without you, chinnadorai, not the same…'

Ravi looked at the watchman. His face was still cast down, his lips were pursed and his bushy moustache covered his cheeks. Varadarajulu had come all the way to call him home? Ravi turned away abruptly so that the watchman wouldn't see his eyes turn moist.

'Varada, my friend, it is they who don't want me home.'

'What is this formality between family members? Forgive them and come home…'

'Varada, believe me, it was not my decision. I never wanted to stay away. Why should I? But they didn't allow me to live there. They…' Ravi stopped. The words refused to come out. 'Varada…' He shook his head and went inside the house.

Varadarajulu stood outside, unmoving. When Ravi returned after several minutes, he was still there.

'Varada, I cannot return to Vedaranyam Street if they do not allow my friend from America to come with me.' Ravi's voice was steady again. 'It is not my choice, Varada. It is theirs.'

Deborah stayed in Norfolk for several days. Then she spent a few days with Sophie in Buffalo and then went to D.C. to stay with Diana. She met up with her old friends and spent a crazy night out till she was fully sloshed. She felt hot lips over her own. Hands on her breasts. Lips touching her nipples. Kissing. Then slipping lower and lower till she could hear someone moan. It was herself.

She woke up late the next day with a severe headache. Diana was sitting next to her.

'I saved you from John, Debbie,' she said.

'You shouldn't have.'

'I fucked him instead.'

That night they had another wild party.

'Let's celebrate Passover,' Deborah said.

'You pass over every day in any case.'

'Shut up. I mean the real one.'

'That was months ago, Debbie,' said an exasperated Diana.

'Then let's do Shavuot.'

'Well, at least you're getting closer.'

Deborah got drunk again. Diana ended up saving her from Benjy this time.

'You shouldn't have,' Deborah protested again.

'You were too far gone to enjoy it. You did the moaning and I did the screwing.'

Deborah took out Ravi's photo from her drawer. She saw two smiling faces peering into the lens—Deborah and Ravi, taken during his convocation ceremony at Cornell.

It had been a perfect day. Cornell was bathed in spring sunshine. There was still a nip in the air, but the sky was bright and blue.

Long before the scheduled time, crowds had started filling the football field. Parents walked about with cameras, camcorders and water bottles, trying to spot their children in the mass of black gowns and black hats wading through the football field to the beat of a live orchestra.

Deborah sat in the front row and kept an eye out for Ravi. He came into the field with the MBA contingent and waved at her.

It had been a perfect day.

The good news was not just the graduation. The company in Washington where he had interned wanted him back, this time for a permanent job. After lunch, Ravi and Deborah ran off to celebrate in the only way they knew—with some intense lovemaking. In the evening, another round of celebration followed with his roommates and classmates and a lot of shouting and drinking. Some of the parents who had come down for the function gave up trying to control their children and joined in the fun. The restaurants ran full. The hotels were booked up. The streets were crowded with proud parents trying to get their children to pose for photographs. The vineyards surrounding the Finger Lakes region made brisk sales. Wines were tasted, bottles bought. Beer was flowing. It was a good time for everyone in Ithaca—at least for those two days.

Those were the two faces that grinned back at Deborah in the photo.

Diana could see that Deborah was troubled and she liked saving her from lustful men and celebrating Jewish festivals on successive nights. But Deborah was getting drunk too often, lurching from one party to another, moaning about headaches through the day only to spend the evening in a drunken orgy. It was almost as though she wanted to disappear into another world.

'What's biting you?' Diana asked her finally.

'I'm just having a good time.'

'No, something isn't right.'

'Hey, I'm just living it up!'

'What's the problem, Debbie?'

'I want to get screwed!'

'Shut up! What happened between you and Ravi?'

Deborah was silent.

'Nothing. Just nothing.'

Diana looked at her, exasperated. 'Nothing! Is that all you have to say? Nothing! Fuck you. Fuck Ravi.' Diana got up.

'Okay, I feel empty inside. Lost. There's a hole inside me. I don't know what to do.'

Diana sat down. 'Then fill it.'

'I can't. I thought I was through with Ravi. And Amma and Appa. His mom and dad. After all, I belong here. But I want him now.'

'Call him.'

'I can't. What will I say? If I hear his voice I'll want him... I'll cry.'

'Then cry, you idiot. Cry.'

'I think I still love him.'

'Then love him, silly.'

'I still want him.'

'Then go to Chennai. You don't belong here.'

13

From where Deborah was sitting, she could see the aircrafts land. It was late afternoon and the warm rays of the sun hit each aircraft like a laser beam. A puff of dust when the wheels touched the runway, and seconds later the aircraft disappeared behind the boarding gates.

There weren't too many people on the flight from D.C. to New York. Deborah placed her handbag on the floor and wrapped her legs around it. That was what Ravi had taught her to do. The first time she and Ravi left for India, Ravi had kept the two handbags on the floor and wrapped his legs protectively around them. It was an old habit, Ravi had explained, founded on a fear of losing one's handbag or briefcase. It was from his father that he had picked up the habit. Of course, inside train compartments, Appa usually went a step ahead and insisted on tying his suitcase with a chain lock to the iron rod holding up the lower berth. All their suitcases sat stoic and chained like toothless rottweilers.

'Good afternoon, ladies and gentlemen. Delta announces...' came the boarding call.

The time had come to make her journey again. And this time there was no going back.

But now it was Deborah's turn to be surprised. Amma had changed.

Once Amma realized that if she persisted she would lose Ravi too, her attitude to Deborah became different. Amma couldn't afford to lose Ravi a second time. If they were destined to be together, Deborah had to be accepted into the family.

'What's with Amma? Is she okay?'

'Just about,' said Ravi.

'Did you say something to her?'

'A little.'

'I hope you weren't harsh on her.'

'A little.'

'Was that really necessary?'

'A little.'

Amma made a sincere attempt to like Deborah. It wasn't too difficult. It was just that she had prevented herself from liking her earlier. But Ravi had left her with no illusions about where he stood if Deborah were to leave him. Don't think I'll ever forgive you, Amma, he said and that was that.

So Amma decided to devote her energy to introducing Deborah to the traditions and mores of the Tamil Brahmins. Religion. Karnatic music. Music Academy. 'I prefer to sit in the balcony. Those who truly love and understand Karnatic music sit in the balcony. Ground floor is of course more expensive but most of those who sit there have come to be seen rather than to truly enjoy the experience,' Amma said with a sniff.

She taught Deborah how to appreciate Karnatic music. 'One shouldn't open the mouth like a croaking frog,' she said on one occasion. 'Listen to this singer; she sounds

like shells rolling around inside a metal vessel,' she said on
another. When a singer was not able to reach too high or too
low a pitch, Amma likened her voice to a greasy mustard-oil-
coated pole where one could neither go too high nor slip
too low. And so Deborah's music education went.

Cooking. Some special dishes—vegetarian, of course—
and those that Ravi particularly liked. Like paruppusuli
and more kozhambu. She wrote out the recipes in a special
notebook.

And Deborah's first silk sari. From Nalli, where the best
saris came from.

Like all good mothers, Amma lobbied with Appa for their
entry into Vedaranyam Street.

'Sometimes I don't know whether he is your son or you're
his son,' she admonished her husband. 'Both of you are
behaving like children.'

'I can't have a white woman as my daughter-in-law,' Appa
said.

'I don't know why you are being so stubborn.'

'I am not stubborn. Ravi has decided to go his own way
and that's that.'

But Amma was undeterred and poured all her efforts into
making Deborah a Chennaivaasi.

'I want you to have a typical Brahmin wedding,' Amma
told Deborah. 'I want to see you in a koorai pudavai. You will
be the envy of every Brahmin girl.'

'What's that?'

'Koorai pudavai is a traditional sari worn when the thaali
is tied by the groom around the neck of the bride to signify
the giving away of the bride to the groom. The way it is worn
symbolizes Ardhanareeshwarar—the god who is half woman

and half man, signifying the unity of Shiva and Shakti. The koorai sari has to be nine yards and it is either brick-red or yellow without a single black thread in the weave. The bride wears it in such a way that the left side depicts the female element and the right side the male element. The sari pleats weave inward on the left side while on the right side the pleats fall straight to indicate the veshti pattern worn by men. The left arm is bare, revealing the bride's jewellery, while her right arm is covered by the folds of the sari, like the angavastram covering a man's arm. The extra portion of the sari hanging down behind is folded, brought to the front and tucked into the pleats. So we really struggle with draping the bride in a koorai pudavai. The right pleats, the right folds and the right balance.'

Deborah's head was whirling with traditions and customs. Wasn't there an easier way to get initiated into TamBram life?

Amma saw the transformation of Deborah in front of her eyes. She admired her determination, her tenacity and her love for Ravi.

She knew she had to bring Appa round to accepting Deborah. Only she could do it. It needed effort and, more importantly, time.

And that was one thing fate decreed otherwise.

Amma died.

14

It had been sudden and unexpected, as death often is to the living. She had been hale and hearty, her body kept active by years of brisk housework and, subsequently, by keeping pace with the grandchildren. She was up before everyone and slept after everyone. Right through the day, she kept manifesting herself in every part of the house, advising the cook on how much salt to add or warning the servants not to water the plants excessively or cajoling her grandchildren to recite the *Vishnu Sahasranamam* or keeping tabs on whether the lunch tiffin-carrier had been sent to Anand on time. In the afternoon, when the house was quiet, she would be stretched out on the living-room sofa, reading Tamil magazines or books. In the evening, she made sure the lights were switched on and a hot tumbler of coffee was ready as soon as Appa's car turned into the driveway, that the money for the next day's milk packets were handed over to Varadarajulu and that the daughters-in-law got enough free time to spend with their husbands—this she ensured by asking her grandchildren to come to her with their homework. Managing a joint family was a full-time job, and one she did with enthusiasm and relish.

But one night Amma went to sleep and didn't wake up.

It was a silent but massive heart attack. Appa didn't hear a sound or even feel a stir. When he woke up the next morning, he was surprised to find her still asleep and reached out to wake her up. He knew instantly that she was no more.

Appa was devastated. He had always prayed that she would outlive him. I can't learn to live all over again without her.

Just the previous morning Amma had said she was going to the temple and left early. On her last night she had made sure that the plastic bag and money were kept in the verandah for Varadarajulu to get the milk packets in the morning.

When Ravi rushed to Vedaranyam Street that morning, Appa embraced him and held him tight. They sobbed together without exchanging a word. A large slab of ice in the middle of the living room formed the bed. On it lay Amma lifeless, her face peaceful. That evening, as he watched his mother's remains being consumed by the leaping flames, Ravi thought that perhaps in death she had achieved what she couldn't while she was alive—bringing father and son together. The next day, they went to collect the ashes. All that remained of his mother could be collected in a metallic urn.

In the end, that was what was left of Amma. That and the wonderful memories of her existence.

For the next thirteen days, Ravi remained at Vedaranyam Street to participate in the rites. Anand was dispatched to immerse the ashes in the Ganga at Benares. Ravi wanted to accompany him but was requested to stay back. As the youngest son, he didn't have much to do but he stayed, because Appa had asked him to.

It had been almost two years since Ravi had last slept in his old room. It felt strange to be sleeping in his bed again.

He could see the old cellotape marks on his wardrobe from posters of Monica Seles and Catherine Zeta-Jones. Very little had changed. The wet patch on the far corner of the ceiling, above which the water tank lay, the long chipped mirror on the wardrobe door, the papyrus painting gifted by his uncle after a trip to Egypt, the dark teak wood writing table with its bulky uncomfortable chair and the antique clock that managed to run accurately long after the Roman numerals on its dial fell off. There was even a wooden chair in the corner—the chair in which Amma sat whenever he had Tamil homework and needed her help.

He cried. Ravi had dreamt of returning to live in Sundari with Deborah, in the midst of his parents and his brothers and their wives, the whole family together, with Amma presiding over them. And now Amma was gone, never to return to Vedaranyam Street.

Appa seemed happy to see Ravi back in Sundari. But something held him back. He made a few enquiries about Ravi and his job. Ravi answered them patiently. Not a word about Deborah.

'Amma died without her last wish being fulfilled,' Anand told Ravi after he came back from Benares.

'What was that?'

'She wanted you to return home.'

'But I have returned home.'

'Here. To live in Sundari.'

Ravi did not rise to the bait. This was a no-win conversation.

'She prayed to all the gods she could think of. You could have… maybe just for her sake you could have…'

'I never knew this would happen.'

'None of us anticipated this. But you could still have come back…'

'It wasn't up to me. You people also had a role in what happened. It was your decision as much as mine.'

As the days went by, there was no sign that Appa had changed his mind about Deborah. Or given Ravi's predicament a second thought.

Ravi felt cheated.

When the thirteenth day came and all the relatives started leaving after the afternoon feast, Ravi went to Appa's room to say goodbye.

'Why are you leaving?'

'What do you expect me to do?'

'Stay here. There is enough room here for everyone.'

'Even for Deborah?' he asked quietly.

'No. No, Ravi. It is not easy for me to accept this…'

'Then there is no place in this house for me either.'

Appa did not respond.

'Appa, when I leave this house today, I will not enter it again until you have changed your mind about Deborah. When you change your mind, you will come to my house to say so. Otherwise you can forget you ever had a third son,' he said, his voice quavering in anger.

'Ravi, this is hardly the time…'

'When will that time ever come?' Ravi said furiously. 'Enough is enough. If ever you want me, you will come home.'

Appa made no effort to stop him from storming out. He didn't say a word, not even a silent goodbye. Appa had not wanted Ravi to leave. But he let him leave Sundari that day. Amma's death had not softened his pride.

Part 2

15

A gecko chirps.

Ravi looks around but he can't find the bloody creature. When he decided to to take the day off, the last thing he wanted was a chirping house lizard. Not to mention mosquitoes. Before he settles down on the extravagant extra-soft king-sized mattress brought back from the US, he lights up the mosquito coil right in the middle of the room, shuts the bedroom door, switches the air conditioner on full blast, and wraps himself in a thin razai. In spite of his best efforts, a few mosquitoes manage to find their way into the room. But such are the hazards of living in Chennai.

Ravi has not slept for two days. Working for a US subsidiary in Chennai is a bit of a strain. But now he settles down to his afternoon siesta. The very thought of his Chennai colleagues slaving away in the office or outside in the sun, sweating and fuming in the heat—100 degrees Fahrenheit and rising—soothes him. Chennai is at its sweaty best.

He closes his eyes and dozes off.

Ravi had not counted on the house lizard.

It chirps loudly.

'Damn it!' He turns around, puts the pillow over his head and tries to shut out the world.

It chirps again. He can hear it from under the pillow. He looks around but can't figure out where the chirping is coming from. Under the bed? Behind the wardrobe? Or the curtains? But there is no sign of it anywhere.

He looks blankly at the ceiling. The chirping has momentarily stopped but sleep eludes him now. He thought sheer exhaustion would put him to sleep, but that isn't working. Maybe he can read a book and lull himself to sleep, he thinks.

There it is again, the chirping. The gecko is hiding behind the wardrobe. The wardrobe is made of solid wood—he had picked it up from a second-hand furniture shop. The house is full of antique furniture: the writing table in the library downstairs, the re-upholstered sofa set, a few side tables and the ornate crockery cabinet. The bar is made of mahogany, new but treated to look old.

The gecko chirps again. Ravi used to take a great delight in ridding the house of geckos. It is an old habit that he picked up in his childhood, from his father. Appa disliked house lizards but not enough to kill them, merely to evict them from the house. A perfect blend of aggression and non-violence. Appa didn't believe in indiscriminate killing. Even when his children went after the ants making a beeline for the food on the dining table, Appa stopped them. 'Just dust them off; don't kill them. They are not red ants. They are just pillayar ants—completely harmless.'

When he saw a gecko on the ceiling, Appa would take a long-handled ottadai broom—used to get rid of cobwebs— and chase it round and round the room till it dropped down in exhaustion. If it was already on the floor, it usually tried to climb up but soon dropped down again and lay immobile.

Lizards get exhausted very easily. That was the first lesson Ravi had learnt. When exhausted, they lose their grip on the wall and fall to the floor. Appa would sweep the lizard into a plastic container, take it outside the house and throw it into the overflowing municipal dustbin or in the dry open drain a few metres away. Due to Appa's magnanimous gesture, the lizard lived to chirp for another day and the house was also rid of it. Ravi doesn't quite recollect how effective this remedy was, because the house at Vedaranyam Street always seemed to have more than the normal share of geckos.

Ravi looks at the wardrobe and decides that he is feeling too comfortable to get up and chase his tormentor around the room. He closes his eyes. It has been more than a year since Amma passed away and more than two years since he arrived in Chennai from the US. But he has not returned to his house since Amma died nor has he seen Appa or any of his brothers. He glimpsed Arjun once at a wedding but they pretended not to see each other.

The gecko chirps again. Ravi keeps his eyes closed. Suddenly a new thought enters his head. The chirping of lizards portends something or the other. What did it mean now? It is not as if Ravi is superstitious. But these rules had been ingrained into him all his life. When he joined college, his father refused to let him join on a Tuesday. 'No one should do anything important on Tuesdays, said Appa, and that was that. He joined the next day—a safe Wednesday. It was a good day—'Muhoortha naal,' Appa observed with satisfaction. Since Ravi joined a day late, all the good seats were already taken. Even certain flight schedules were declared inauspicious—it was either the wrong time or the wrong direction. 'You can't travel north today,' Appa declared one day and that was it. He had to postpone his departure. 'Don't open the bank account till noon, it's Rahukalam,' said his mother on another occasion. When he went to the bank after twelve, the counter had closed. The next day was a Tuesday, not desirable either. Ravi had to wait two days before he could open an account. When he stood first in class—and it was not a routine occurrence—Amma promptly performed drishti to neutralize the evil eye. The evil effects were dissolved in vermillion mixed with water and soot. And so life went on, overcoming obstacles both real and imagined with strict rules. When Ravi moved to the US, one by one these superstitions fell by the wayside. It was inevitable. He even joined his new job on a Tuesday—and that was indeed a big break from tradition. He just made sure it wasn't Rahukalam, as a minor concession to his upbringing.

It's funny how house lizards remind Ravi of his family. Ravi remembers how Narayanan mama had rung up one night—it was nearly one in the morning. Appa had picked up the phone. A gecko had fallen on Narayanan's head. Narayanan had opened the door and the gecko had dropped on top of his head.

'Athimber, can you tell me what to do?' Narayanan asked Appa.

'Is it dead or still alive?' Appa asked sleepily.

'No, it ran away.'

Amma had woken up in the meantime, fearing the worst. Late night calls usually meant something was wrong.

'Who is dead?' she asked.

'Your brother is on the line…'

'What happened to him?' Amma said anxiously.

'Nothing. A lizard has fallen on top of his head. He wants to know what he should do.'

'That's it? This is why that idiot is calling? That too in the middle of the night?'

'He also sounds slightly drunk…'

'Drunk? How many times… Give me the phone. I'll talk to him,' she said, getting up.

'No, no, this is not the time to say anything. It won't make any sense to him. Just put him out of his lizard misery for now.'

'Then tell him to have a hot bath at once. That should cure both his drunken state and the curse of the lizard.'

Appa dutifully told him.

'What does it mean? Falling on the head must mean something,' Narayanan said.

'It doesn't mean anything much,' Appa said impatiently. 'If it ran away after falling on your head, you need not worry. You just need a head bath.'

Ravi hears another round of chirping from behind the wardrobe. South-east, Ravi notes. He must check this out.

With a sigh, Ravi gets up and goes down to his library and locates the book, the fat omnibus book of Tamil customs. It had been presented to him by Amma just before he left for Cornell.

The chapter on house lizards is towards the end. The first few pages are devoted to lizards falling on humans. Ravi realizes that instead of chirping, if it had fallen on his forehead, he would have been crowned king; if it had fallen on his eyes, he would have been imprisoned; if it fell on the right hand it spelled good health; if on the left hand, he would have had a night-long orgy. Unfortunately, the lizard had merely chirped. He scans the pages till he comes to the part about lizard chirping. The entry reads:

Tuesday. If the chirping is from the south-east, it portends gain of relatives.

Portends gain of relatives. Ravi leans back in his chair and reads those words again. It can mean only one thing: Kamala athai is coming home. She is the only relative with whom he can claim proximity.

There is a barely audible knock on the main door.

Who would come at this time of day, and in the middle of the week too, when he is supposed to be in office, Ravi wonders. He gets up and goes to open the door.

It is his father.

Appa.

16

The figure in the doorway stands still, looking at Ravi with unblinking eyes. Whether it is with apprehension or expectation, Ravi can't quite fathom. Appa is wearing his usual white cotton veshti, long-sleeved shirt and rubber slippers. There is a streak of white vibhuthi across his forehead with a vermillion dot at the centre.

The shock of seeing Appa robs Ravi of his speech. He wants to say something but can only stare. His words stick in his throat like an overripe lemon.

'Aren't you going to invite me in?' Appa breaks the ice.

'Please come in, Appa,' Ravi says, recovering just in time. When he calls his father 'Appa', the word comes out hesitant and strange.

Appa takes off his slippers outside the door.

'You don't have to take them off.'

'It's okay. I can't wear chappals inside the house.'

Appa walks into the drawing room and looks around. It is spacious and well-kept but not ostentatious. Queen Anne furniture from the United States, with a three-seater sofa, a love seat and high-backed chairs, occupies one side of the drawing room. The upholstery is rich burgundy with thin gold stripes. The centre table is elegant oak. On the other side of the drawing room is a small alcove, which has just enough place for an intimate arrangement of three chairs—not Queen Anne but old Moore Market cane—for a cozy chat between friends. But a cozy chat is not uppermost in Appa's mind right now. Where should he begin?

'Please sit down,' Ravi says, motioning to the sofa.

Appa hears the words come out stiff and formal. He sits down on one of the chairs. 'These days I'm not able to sit on chairs with too much cushion,' he offers in explanation.

Ravi switches on the overhead fan. At least there will be some noise to dispel the awkwardness. Strange. Instead of anger, he feels awkward.

Appa looks around the room. Ravi sits on the opposite chair.

'Have you come alone?' Ravi asks after a while.

'Yes, da,' Appa nods. 'I have come alone.'

For a moment Ravi detects sadness in Appa's voice but he brushes it away as his imagination. He has not heard his father's voice for a year. Maybe that is the reason it sounds different. It sounds familiar, of course, but like an echo from the past, like hearing someone's voice through a speakerphone—distant yet familiar.

When Ravi was thrown out of Sundari, it hurt him. He couldn't begin to understand how to react. With anger? Bitterness? Pain? It was a strange feeling. One day in, the next day out. It was as if he didn't belong to them any more. Not even his brothers had stayed in touch. Only Amma had continued to talk to him. But she was dead.

And now Appa had turned up.

'How are you, Ravi?' Appa asks. His voice sounds tired.

'I'm fine,' Ravi answers stiffly. 'You are keeping well?'

'So far I have managed to keep my body and soul together.'

When Appa says 'keeping the body and soul together', it could mean anything from doing extraordinarily well to living a life of penury.

'Would you like something to eat?' Ravi asks.

'Nothing, I have finished my lunch,' Appa answers.

'Coffee?'

'No, don't bother.'

'We have a Brahmin cook. She can make you coffee or tea.'

'Coffee,' Appa says finally. 'I'll take a little bit of coffee. Just half a cup will do.'

Half a cup means a full tumbler when it comes to Appa. He likes the pretence of asking for half a cup and getting a full one in return.

Ravi leaves the room swiftly. It is almost as if he is looking for an excuse to run away from Appa. Meanwhile, Appa gets up from the chair and examines one of the paintings. It is a Jamini Roy. Amma used to love Ravi Varma's works. She had two of his paintings at her ancestral residence and doted over them. But after she got married, her brother took away one of them and broke her heart. Much as she had wanted the painting back, she could never pry it out of her brother, especially after Ravi Varma's work started fetching enormous sums in the art world. Appa still remembers that episode. He secretly wants to get it back one day—for Amma's sake.

Appa goes around the sofa and comes face to face with a photo of Deborah and Ravi. They are looking at the camera with their arms around each other. It is a lovely picture, taken in the evening with the warm glow of the sun lighting up their faces. They look so happy together. Amma had tried telling him about Deborah but he had brushed her off. And when he sees Deborah in this picture…

Appa's face clouds over.

A gush of old memories overcomes him.

1955.

They were in love all right. For a fortnight they forgot all about sightseeing and just saw each other as much as they could. They held hands. Kissed. Hugged. Lazed in the den. His infatuation grew. He had never been this close to a girl, not even a Brahmin one. When he was in Presidency College, the most he had done was speak to a girl for a few minutes before she moved away shyly. How easily Jennifer had slipped into his life.

When they went to the Covent Garden market one evening, he picked up a bunch of red roses for her. The evening felt romantic, despite the cold, steady drizzle. They stopped at a café for tea and cake. She leaned against his shoulder and sipped hot tea. He didn't want the moment to end. No wet evening would ever seem bleak again. One night, in a moment of weakness, he made love to her.

She hadn't provoked him. But he had given in to his baser instincts, as his father would say. The next morning he woke up to a different world. A world of guilt and remorse. He couldn't believe what he had done. He prayed to all the gods he could think of, to all the pictures of Ganesha, Shiva and Hanuman that he had kept above his desk. Sex before marriage was taboo. He had never believed that he was capable of doing something like this. He loved Jennifer but felt that he had crossed a line.

The next day, he extracted a promise from Jennifer. It was more an admission of his weakness than hers. The next time they made love, they should be engaged, even married. Why he sought her promise when he was equally responsible for that moment of passion was something Jennifer couldn't understand. But Appa knew he had to marry Jennifer before taking their relationship any further, and for this he required his father's permission.

It wasn't going to be easy. Fathers of Chennaivaasis were fathers. Full stop. They weren't friends. They were fathers who took their role seriously. They brought up their sons in the best way possible—the best way as they defined it. 'You may not realize it now, but when you grow up, you will be grateful to me,' was the usual refrain. Sons saw their father as a figure to be obeyed. Not as a friend to chat with or a confidante to discuss private affairs with. The daughters were luckier. Their mothers were far more accessible. When the sons needed to talk to their father they usually depended on their mother to intervene on their behalf. So it was with Appa's father, the quintessential Chennai father. Appa had to look elsewhere for help.

So he turned to his stepmother. He wrote her a long letter, explaining the circumstances of how he had come to fall in love with Jennifer. He begged her to intercede on his behalf and make Appa agree. As he waited for her reply, his feelings for Jennifer only grew.

As each day passed, Appa's hopes faded. He prayed to his gods to put sense into his father's head and make him see things his way. When he received the reply a month later, Appa's world was shattered. He had been ordered by his father to return to India immediately. If not, his father threatened to come and take him back forcibly.

That summer in London came and went. The cricket grounds were vacated and the days grew shorter. Jennifer could never understand why his father's consent was so important if Tom truly loved her. Appa felt that it wasn't right to shrug off years of parenthood for one swift brush with love. Winter was setting in when the time came for Appa and Jennifer to say goodbye. He knew he was leaving behind a part of himself and Jennifer knew she would never know another Tom.

17

Deborah has not reached the office. She sits inside her Tata Indica. She turns off the ignition, crosses her arms and waits. There is a procession crossing the main road, the people shouting slogans as they inch along, armed with colourful banners. Deborah doesn't bother to hear what they are shouting. This is not the first time she has been stopped on her way to and from work. She is used to being held up at the same spot several times a month—for processions, for the motorcade of the governor or the motorcade of the chief minister or the motorcade of no one in particular. The police are out to make sure the mob doesn't get out of hand. Deborah looks at the agitators. They are animated all right but they don't look violent.

The men in the silver Maruti next to her Indica stare at her. She is used to those leering eyes by now. It bothered her when she first came to Chennai two years ago. At every corner, on every footpath, people stopped and stared. She felt their eyes burn into her white skin. Soon she stopped going for walks. Now she has realized their stares are just inquisitive and they mean no harm. White skin and blonde hair are not easy to adjust to. The men in the Maruti don't even bother to avert their gaze when she glares at them.

By the time Ravi returns, Appa has gone across to the alcove and sat down on one of the cane chairs. Ravi sits down next to his father. A swarm of mosquitoes attacks them mercilessly. Appa looks at Ravi as he gets up to switch on the fan. This Ravi, he is a carbon copy of his mother, Appa thinks.

'You look more and more like your mother,' Appa can't help saying.

Padma walks in just them and father and son sit quietly as she places two cups of steaming coffee before them.

'Can I have my coffee in a tumbler?' Appa asks hesitantly.

'Of course, ayyah,' she says. 'How many spoons of sugar will you need?'

'Two,' he answers. At least the old man has no problem with his sugar, Ravi makes a mental note.

Inside the car, it is stifling. She turns on the ignition to run the AC. The road is packed with cars. Pedestrians fight for space on the pavement since they can't spill onto the road, jampacked as it is by cars and lorries. People sweat and curse. The procession continues without break. The police do nothing. Several crows sit on the trees and watch the fun.

Some street urchins have gathered around her car. Three or four faces flatten themselves against her window and peer into the car. One of them asks for money as soon as she makes eye contact. Beggars used to trouble her earlier. Even in D.C., she always dropped a quarter into the hat of beggar or trumpeter on the sidewalk. But poverty in India has numbed her senses. It is something she cannot reconcile with. She now looks at them with unseeing eyes, like other Chennaivaasis do.

The first thing she has learned in Chennai is that her time is not her own. She has to share it with others, many of whom come in uninvited. Ravi doesn't find it strange since he is himself a product of Chennai. She pointed it out once or twice and Ravi brushed it aside. 'I know they should have asked, but now that they have come, let's not make a big deal of it,' he said. It bothered her. She longed for some uninterrupted free time and the more she longed for it, the less she got it. Initially, she put it down to people's curiosity. As the days went by, she realized it wasn't curiosity but that friendship and hospitality were taken for granted. 'They would do the same if we went over to their place,' Ravi said reassuringly. 'This behaviour is the direct outcome of the break up of the joint family system. The ethos of being together exists even if families have become nuclear. This is simply a way of reassuring oneself of another's affection.'

'Dai Ravi, I have a request,' Appa says finally.

'A request?'

Appa clears his throat. 'I know my sudden arrival here has come as a shock to you. But I have a request. You are, of course, at liberty to say no.'

'What is it?'

Appa clears his throat again.

'Of course, you are at full liberty to say no,' he repeats.

'What is it?'

'I was wondering if I can stay with you for some time.'

'Stay with me? Here?' Ravi says without trying to disguise the incredulity in his voice.

'Yes.'

'But why? You have a mansion in—'

'Yes, I know. But of late it has started resembling a bhoot bungalow.'

'Bhoot bungalow! Why?'

'It's a long story, Ravi, and it is getting more unpleasant by the day. You know what your mother was like. She was the stabilizing influence in the family. After she died, the centre that held that house together collapsed. And one by one, things started going wrong, terribly wrong. I couldn't stay there a day longer. Your brothers, well…'

'What happened?'

'Many things. I don't know where to begin. I don't want to burden you with all the stories right now. I'll tell you in good time. All I can say now is that after the way your brothers have treated me, I have nowhere to go. That's why I've come here. To ask you if you can take me in. It's purely temporary, I promise.'

'Has something happened?'

'You will know in due course. I have nothing to hide. I thought of renting a flat and moving out of Vedaranyam Street. But your mother spoilt me so much when she was alive that there is no way I could survive more than a few days alone in a new house. I thought of going to a hotel, but for how long? I had no option but to come to you. All I want is to stay here for a few days, that's all.'

'Well… it's a bit of a surprise…'

'I know, I know. I couldn't talk to you before… but it all happened so quickly…'

'I'm not sure if this is the best place for you to stay.'

'I understand. Things happened so fast…'

Ravi has no idea what these 'things' are, but isn't interested in them yet.

For a moment he had hope. Even though it was impossible, he thought for a brief second that Appa had come to ask his forgiveness. But that obviously isn't what brings him there. Ravi feels deflated. Appa has killed his hopes, yet again.

This man sitting in front of him has come to him for his own selfish reasons. It is not that Ravi continues to nurse the burning rage he had felt when he was thrown out of Sundari. Not after all these years. There was a time when the mere mention of Appa's name made him fume. Appa had treated him badly. Even his brothers had ignored Ravi and Deborah. Only his sister Jaya had kept up the relationship. But she was in Bangalore with her husband. In fact, Appa was no more in his life than his uncle in Ambasamudram who sent him a New Years' card every year.

'I know it is a little late for me to apologize for the way I have treated you and Deborah...' Appa begins.

'Apologize? Don't start! You don't even know what it means.'

'I know you will have to ask Deborah as well,' Appa second-guesses Ravi, his voice betraying a slight hesitation.

'Yes,' Ravi says, his voice hardening. He feels no sympathy for the man who robbed him of his family. 'I don't know why you have come to me when you can go elsewhere,' he says harshly. He is about to continue when Padma enters.

A strong aroma of filter coffee fills the room. Appa picks up a tumbler by the brim, holds it several inches away and pours a stream of hot coffee into his mouth. The coffee stays in his mouth for a few seconds before disappearing. A quiet sense of satisfaction overcomes his being. It is a feeling only Tamil coffee-drinkers are privilege to. Hot steaming filter coffee gliding through the gullet, tickling the tastebuds. It is not a sensation easily matched. Appa looks at his son. When Ravi was barely twelve, he tried to imitate his father and ended up scalding his tongue. But the determined young boy practised for months until he could pour hot liquid into the hollow below the tongue in such a way that it didn't scald the mouth or the tongue but trickled smoothly over the tongue and down the throat, warming the body and sending a powerful aroma of coffee into the nostrils.

Ravi gingerly picks up his tumbler. He has not tried it for some time. He tilts his head, raises the tumbler a few inches above his mouth and carefully pours coffee into it. He can feel the hot liquid searing the back and sides of his tongue, but nestled in the hollow below the tongue, it instantly cools just that little bit to slide down his throat. He hasn't forgotten how to drink coffee. He feels reincarnated. The reincarnated filter coffee drinker.

Emboldened by the coffee, Ravi challenges Appa: 'Why don't you stay with Jaya?'

'I can't stay in a daughter's house after her marriage. I could only think of you.'

'You didn't think of me all these years,' Ravi says quietly. 'How long are you planning to stay here?'

'I don't know, Ravi. I have some work to do, which requires my presence here in Chennai. I will not stay too long, Ravi, I promise you.'

'I don't know how long is too long.'

'Just give me a chance.'

'For what?'

'To stay with you… and for many other things, Ravi. But for now, just to stay with you.'

'You should ask him to stay,' Deborah says finally.

Her answer takes Ravi by surprise. 'I thought you would say no and make the decision for me,' he says, pouting, even though she cannot see him from the other end of the line.

She laughs. 'You can't say no when your father wants to stay with you.'

'Yes, I can.'

'You can't. Besides, if he is appearing out of the blue like this, something must have happened. He needs you now. You can't turn him away.'

'Why do you keep saying you, you, you all the time? It's us. This is your home as much as mine.'

'I know, Ravi, but it's really you he is returning to. He's your dad.'

'Debbie, he's hardly acted like one. And after what he did to us… particularly to you… why should I let him stay?'

'Ravi, you can't say no. If you treat him the same way he treated you, what's the difference between the two of you?'

When she puts it that way, the decision is obvious. They are stuck with Appa.

When Ravi goes back downstairs, Appa is in the library.

'Appa, I talked to Debbie… you can stay with us if you want to. But please remember that Deborah also lives here. I don't want any complications because of you.'

Appa nods. 'Ravi, I understand.'

'I'm not sure you do. You never did understand anything. Anyway, there's no point talking about it now. Just finish your work—whatever it is—and leave.'

Ravi stops. He hasn't spoken so bitterly in years.

Appa doesn't reply.

'When do you plan to move in?' Ravi asks.

Appa looks up anxiously. 'Right now. I have all my things in the car.'

'In the car?'

'Yes. is that okay?'

'What's the hurry?'

'Ravi, I will tell you all in good time,' Appa sighs. He suddenly looks very old.

Ravi stands up abruptly. 'Do my brothers know you have come here?'

'No, I haven't told them. I wasn't sure if you—'

'Our guest bedroom is upstairs. Can you—'

'Don't worry. I still walk three miles every morning.'

That's three miles more than I do, Ravi thinks.

Four suitcases are unloaded from the car and Appa feels a little relieved. Ravi has accepted him, at least for now.

Before Deborah comes home, Appa paces up and down the drawing room. Then he goes out and paces up and down the verandah. Then up and down the driveway. And finally up and down the lawn.

How does one greet the girl who his son has been living with for the last two years? Does he treat her like his daughter-in-law? Or his son's girlfriend? Or somewhere in-between? Appa has never handled such a situation before and is clueless. For two years, he has ignored her and Ravi, pretended they don't exist.

A cool breeze from the sea sets in, bringing some relief from the sweltering heat. The trees sway gently as the city cools down. Appa continues to pace up and down the lawn till Padma brings out a dabara and a tumbler of coffee. He doesn't want to drink his coffee in the garden. He goes inside and settles down on the Queen Anne.

'Does she normally come this late?' he asks Ravi, looking at his watch. It is six.

'Six is not late,' Ravi declares and goes into the library.

Appa drinks his coffee alone.

Deborah arrives ten minutes later. She has been a bundle of nerves all afternoon. 'What do I call him?' she had asked Ravi on the phone. 'Uncle, Appa, what? Maybe I should call him uncle. He might take offence at me calling him Appa.'

'Call him Appa, Debbie. And frankly, I don't give a shit whether he takes offence or not. You could call him an ass, for all I care.'

'Shut up. Behave yourself.'

A few minutes later she was on the line again. 'I'm wearing trousers, is that okay?'

'Deb, just come. Things will sort themselves out. He should learn to accept you as you are.'

'Hi, Appa! How are you?' Deb says now, trying to sound cheerful as she enters with a leather satchel and a huge white plastic bag. Then she does something that Ravi taught her and she had used with good effect on Amma: a namaskaram.

Like Amma, Appa is stunned. His hand instinctively reaches out to touch her head in blessing. He is visibly moved. 'Deborah, I don't know what to say…'

'Appa, what matters is that you are here. I hope you are comfortable, or has your son not taken care of you?'

Appa recovers a little.

'He has taken very good care of me,' he says unconvincingly.

'I picked up some stuff for you,' says Deborah, rustling through the plastic bag. 'I know you are a strict vegetarian and Ravi and I have slightly different eating habits. So…' Out come two new stainless steel casseroles.

'No, no,' he protests. 'I didn't want to give you any trouble.'

'It's no trouble, really. I picked it up on my way home.'

'You shouldn't have. Wait a minute…'

Appa goes briskly up the stairs and returns with two gleaming casseroles. 'I bought these so that you could make food separately for me,' he smiles. 'I wasn't sure whether I should make such demands on you!'

They now have four new stainless steel casseroles.

'By the way,' she says, lowering her voice to a whisper. 'Padma the cook is not a Brahmin. I hope this won't be a problem.'

'Don't worry. It doesn't bother me at all. I know we are living in a different era. I'm not that old-fashioned,' Appa says.

For the first time all day, Appa breathes easy.

18

Chinnamma, the maidservant, had come in the afternoon that Appa appeared and went up to Padma quietly and asked, 'Who is that man?'

'That's Ravi saar's Appa,' Padma replied.

'Whose Appa?'

'Ravi saar's.'

'Ravi saar has a father?'

'All men have fathers,' Padma answered.

'What about women? They don't have fathers or what?' Chinnamma said irately.

'Women have only mothers-in-law,' Padma retorted, at which they both smirked. 'Anyway, this means one more set of clothes for you to wash every day. God knows how long he is going to stay.'

'Also, one more mouth for you to cook for.'

'And no chicken and fish for god knows how long,' Padma sighed.

On that pessimistic note, they went about attending to their respective work.

The bus ride is as comfortable as it can be in a Pallavan Transport Corporation bus. The rush hour has not begun and Chinnamma easily finds a seat in the ladies' section. The bus is old and dust sprays in through the broken window like fine drops of rain. The passengers look weary and are drenched in sweat. One of them has brought a basket full of fish into the bus and it sits right in the middle, blocking the way. The fish is still fresh and the stench somewhat bearable. The passengers step around the basket carefully. They are used to this kind of thing. A Christian priest with a French beard is engaged in an animated conversation with his neighbour. Some college students are chatting, their conversation scattered with curses. Is this what they teach in school? Chinnamma wonders. But she is tired. She closes her eyes and lets the grinding noise of the engine and the hot wind outside lull her to sleep.

Chinnamma has had a difficult life. When she was a young girl she ran away from Burma with her mother, father and two sisters and crossed the treacherous jungles and mountains into India. For days they struggled against animals and nature. It rained and the jungles were thick. Bleeding and famished, they were getting weaker by the day. The nights were terrible and the forests full of dangerous animals. Her youngest sister was dragged away by wolves. Her mother survived the journey only to die of malaria a few days after their arrival in Calcutta. Chinnamma, her father and surviving sister came to Madras and settled down to a grim existence.

Chinnamma was forced to start work at a young age. They had no choice. Her father was a cycle-shop assistant and barely earned enough to feed them. She joined the household of a Chettiar family to help the woman of the house with her chores. She did all the washing, cleaning and sweeping, but not the cooking. She wasn't allowed into the kitchen because she was untouchable. Chinnamma stayed in their house all week and went home on Sunday to spend time with her father and sister.

The Chettiar lady was kind but strict. She cursed easily. With her nasal voice, these curses took on a more pungent tone than intended. Fortunately, very few of them were aimed at Chinnamma. They were reserved for the milkman who came late, the postman who passed their house by when she was expecting a letter, or the shopkeeper who charged a little extra for the brinjals. Chinnamma listened to the choicest curses and committed them to memory. Since she only had to cook for her two sons, the Chettiar lady had not bothered to hire a cook and spent most of the day in the kitchen. In the afternoon, she lay on the wooden bench in the courtyard in the middle of the house and let Chinnamma massage her legs.

'I'm not young any more. I keep asking my sons to get married, but all they are interested in is distributing our family wealth to some cause or the other. They say they are fighting for India's independence. They keep saying that independence is imminent. God knows what this independence is all about. My husband, when he was alive, made good money under the British. He lived an honest god-fearing life and did business with the English businessmen... Yes, press that part ...ammaada... it feels good.'

Chinnamma pushed down on that part with her frail hands.

'Ahh... that's where the pain is...'

Chinnamma pressed harder.

'Your hands are thin and young. Or I would have asked you to press even harder. Nothing like a pair of sturdy hands on an aching body... The other day, I let that slut Kaveri massage my legs and the thevidiya nearly crippled me for life... Frankly, I don't see anything wrong with these

Englishmen. They let us Chettiars flourish. After all, we are
the business caste and making money is our duty. When I
tell my sons this, they just laugh. After listening to Mahatma
Gandhi, they think everyone else is a fool. They are both
hell-bent on squandering their father's wealth. God knows
where all this will end. I keep praying every day, asking Him
to put some sense into my sons' heads,' she concluded
philosophically.

Chinnamma listened silently. That was what was expected
of her.

In the evenings, the Chettiar lady's other elderly friends
on the street dropped by and they gossiped about what
was happening in the city. Their loud voices carried to the
verandah where Chinnamma sat folding clothes and listening
in silence. They talked about the gathering independence
movement with complete detachment, as if it was happening
elsewhere.

The Chettiar lady had a habit of calling Chinnamma
'Sudraponnu'. Chinnamma hadn't given it a second thought
till she heard the woman's sons cautioning their mother
softly one day.

'Don't call her that!' the elder son said. 'Sudras are being
outlawed by the new set of laws.'

'Yes, that's what I have been saying. Sudras have been
outlawed by other castes as well, since the time of Manu.'

'No, amma. Untouchability has been outlawed. It's going
to be illegal to practise untouchability. Gandhiji, in each
one of his messages, talks about it. He calls them Harijans—
children of god. He says India will truly be free only when
the caste system is abolished.'

'Then who will do the cleaning and sweeping? Are you

planning to ask the Brahmins to do it or what?' She laughed aloud, enjoying her little joke. Caste hierarchy was a zero-sum game. If one had to be pushed up, another had to come down.

'Amma, you don't understand. You should not differentiate on the basis of caste.'

'Then what happens to us Chettiars? Do we also become Harijans or what?'

'We don't become Harijans, amma,' her son said, exasperated. 'There should not be any distinction on caste lines between a Chettiar or a Brahmin or a Harijan.'

'But there is a distinction!' she said in surprise.

'Okay, amma,' he sighed. 'Just promise me you won't call her by that name, that's all.'

'Then what shall I call her?'

'Ask her her name and call her that.'

The Chettiar lady was appalled at the thought of calling an untouchable by name. The fact that she had allowed her to roam about in her house was freedom enough, she thought. But in deference to her sons' wishes, she started calling her Chinnaponnu—the little girl. Chinnaponnu later became Chinnamma.

By the time Chinnamma reached marriageable age, she was good at household work. She got married and had a son. But her husband died young, barely five years into their marriage. Chinnamma had to keep working all her life to make ends meet.

She has to change buses on the way and it is late afternoon when Chinnamma finally reaches the cheri. The slums haven't changed much since she first came to live there. When Chinnamma came to Madras, she moved seamlessly into the vast slum network of the city. Over decades, generations of labourers built thousands of hutments and made Madras a slum-friendly city. She remembers when she, her husband and their son lived in a thatched hut, surrounded by dirt and squalor. Even when Madras was parched, the ground near their hut was damp with stagnant water seeping out from broken drains. The stench of putrefying matter was unbearable at first, but with time they got used to it. The mosquitoes found it an ideal breeding ground and soon thick black blankets of mosquitoes covered the slum area. The inhabitants struggled to keep their body and soul together. Malaria was common. The Municipal Corporation had no interest in disinfecting the water. In any case, the slum was outside the pale of legality and non-existent in their records. The slum- dwellers were left to their devices. Soon politics and slums learnt to coexist. Slums thrived because they were vote banks. Even when permanent three-room flats were built to shift the slum-dwellers from the squalor, they were soon rented out and the inhabitants moved back to the slums. They now had rents from those flats as additional income.

And so life went—neither permanent nor temporary, neither legal nor illegal, neither human nor animal, neither dead nor living.

While her husband slept outside on the charpoy, Chinnamma slept inside with her son, throwing the long thalappu of her sari over him to ward off mosquitoes. They had one full meal a day and for the second meal, they took it one day at a time. If the people she worked for gave her leftovers, she gave it to her son first, then her husband, and finally herself. If there were no leftovers, they drank konjee with pickle. Even after the death of her husband, poverty didn't deter her from thinking ahead. They had just one son and she was determined to give him a good education. He went to a public school—a euphemism for poor education. The teachers there were more famous for their absence than for their teaching skills. But Chinnamma was firm. She made sure her son studied whatever he could from whoever he could. Even though he failed a couple of years, he finally managed to get admission into a local college. Chinnamma was overjoyed and the entire colony rejoiced at the news. After he got married and became a senior foreman in a factory at Palani, she went back to living alone, barring monthly visits from her son and daughter-in-law.

Her present solitude does not bother her. She has several friends in the slum but they are not very important to her. She is a loner. She has become numb from losing everyone in her family, one by one, right from the time she ran away as a child from Burma into the hills and jungles of India.

It was Deborah who convinced Chinamma to move into a locality closer to their house. You can't commute one-and-a-half hours a day, she insisted and made her shift into a small two-roomed outhouse nearby. They paid the rent, which made it easier. Deborah had been appalled at how the slum-dwellers lived, though Ravi was unmoved, having seen it all his life. In fact, the only thing Deborah could never reconcile with in India—even after two years in Chennai—was the crushing impact of poverty. Every time she passed a slum, it touched a chord within her. It's inhuman, she said with a monotonous regularity which Ravi attributed to the naïve American in her.

To be treated as a human being who deserved respect was a new experience for Chinnamma. Deborah was young enough to be her daughter, or even a granddaughter. Ravi and Deborah did not seem to care that she was a non-Brahmin. They paid her well and made sure extra food was cooked every day so she could take it home with her. You have suffered enough, Deborah told her one day. I don't want you to suffer more.

The place looks the same. The stagnant brackish water is just where it used to be. The smells of decaying plants and drying urine waft towards her. The slum looks bigger than before. There are more thatched huts. A single spark and the entire colony will be reduced to ashes, she thinks again. She has always dreaded something like this. It happens all the time in Chennai and the inhabitants live in constant fear of seeing their dreams engulfed by flames.

There is noise and bustle. She hears a mother shouting to her children to come back inside. She passes by the drunkard Chellappan's hut but finds the door closed. Nobody answers her knock. Out drinking again, she says to herself and continues to walk through the slush. A few boys are playing cricket on the roadside. The nicely paved road on the outskirts of the slum is like heaven for the children. The ball bounces well and there is enough space to hit fours and sixes. Each time a vehicle passes by, they run for safety to the side of the road before resuming their game.

She goes straight to the house of Thambi Maarimuthu. He is the local don. His reputation is wide. His friends are many. Thambi Maarimuthu still keeps his house in the slum since that is where he started more than a decade ago. Now he owns several houses in the city but continues to stay amongst the slum inhabitants. In keeping with his status, it is the only proper building in that patch—a concrete oasis in the midst of a thatched desert.

Thambi Maarimuthu is at home.

19

Ravi wakes up with a start. For a second he thinks he is back in Vedaranyam Street. Appa is playing a tape.

'Kousalya suprajaa raama, poorva sandhya pravartate.'

'You, incarnated as Rama, son of Kousalya, the crack of dawn is fast spreading in all directions.'

Not a day began at Sundari without the blare of the *Suprabhatham* belching out of his father's prized possession— the 'National' tape recorder. Every day, seven days a week. The alarm clock of Vedaranyam Street.

'Uthishta narasardoola karthavyam deivamahnikam ...'

'Wake up, embodiment of valour,

To utter hymns and perform divine duties.'

Memories come flooding back, too fast for Ravi.

'Uthishto uthishta Govinda...'

'Wake up, O Govinda! Wake up!'

In Tirumala, Lord Venkateshwara is woken up at four in the morning every day with the *Suprabhatham*, Appa had explained to Ravi and his brothers. The loudspeakers strung all around Tirupathi carry the music across the hill station, over peaks and valleys, waking up the pilgrims. This is how the Lord is woken up. And so should we be woken up too.

The vibrations in praise of Lord Venkateshwara fill the ether and unleash positive energy, Appa went on to elaborate to four sleepy children.

'Wake up, husband of Lakshmi,

To protect the three worlds.'

All four would grudgingly brush their teeth and go down to the dining room for their Bournvita. Appa was religious and tried to bring up his children the same way. They sat through lessons in Sanskrit. A shastrigal came every weekend to teach them prayers—*Vishnu Sahasranaamam, Rudram, Chamakam*. They learnt them all by heart. They were even taught the basics of Karnatic music. Jaya sang the best of all. Those like Ravi who couldn't sing were taught to differentiate between one raga and another. If you don't know Karnatic music, you can never appreciate our religion and culture, Appa said with an air of finality.

It wasn't easy being a child at Vedaranyam Street.

As the mellifluous voice of the *Suprabhatham* filled the ether, Amma made four tumblers of Bournvita and two tumblers of piping hot coffee—one for Appa and the other for herself. It was a daily ritual. The first edition of strong filter coffee always went to Appa.

'What is it, Ravi?' Deborah asks.

For a moment, he has forgotten her. 'It's the alarm clock, don't worry. Appa has started all over again! He has put on this musical wake-up call, the *Suprabhatham*. My brothers and I were forced to wake up to this every single morning, even on a fucking Sunday.'

'You know, I think you quite like it.'

'I have had no choice but to like it,' he laughs. 'I even thought for the longest time that it was compulsory to wake up to this or the day would be a disaster!'

'It definitely sounds nice. In fact, the voice is terrific. Is it M.S. Subbulakshmi?'

'No, but close. Don't tell me you actually like it?'

'Yeah, it's soothing... monotonous and musical at the same time. I like it.'

'I wish he wouldn't play it so loud, though. He has never learnt to listen to anything softly. Every damn thing he plays is loud. Appa actually believes it fills the ether and unleashes positive energy. The only concession today is that he has put on the *Suprabhatham* at seven in the morning—which is very late by his standards. Otherwise, he thinks he is still at Vedaranyam Street.'

'Who knows why he left that place. Let him feel at home here. That's the least we owe him.'

'We owe him nothing, Debbie,' Ravi cuts her short. 'Don't be under any illusions.'

Ravi gets up and closes the door, shuts out the *Suprabhatham* and walks across to the window, to draw the curtains, letting in a strong ray of light.

Appa was as fastidious about his food as anyone else. It was, therefore, natural that when he left Vedaranyam Street for Ravi's house, he bought bright new stainless steel casseroles for his own cooking. He wanted his food to be cooked separately in these gleaming casseroles. Not mixed with chicken gravy or mutton stock. Vegetarianism was as sacred as virginity.

Cooking was the exclusive preserve of women in any Chennai household. Not that they chose this form of drudgery willingly. Given a choice, they would happily exchange their ladles and stainless steel casseroles for some rest and leisure. But the men refused to go anywhere near the kitchen. They couldn't even make a cup of coffee. At best, they stood outside the kitchen and discussed all the other chores that had to be done. Appa was no different.

The men of Chennai were fastidious about their eating. The food had to be fresh. Not even a day old. The aroma of hot rasam and sambhar had to permeate the bedrooms and other corners of the house. Appalams had to be round like the full moon, freshly fried, crisp and crunchy. To keep them crisp in the humidity of Chennai was no mean feat. Like the Chennai flowers wilting under the blazing sun, the crisp chips collapsed in the humidity. Limp chips were no chips. The men refused to eat them. The women folk ended up eating the limp chips mixed with cold rasam.

Now, as Appa watches Deborah and Ravi gulp down idli and chutney for breakfast he realizes how much Chennai kitchens have changed. Appa is not a breakfast person. All his life, he has had lunch at nine-thirty every morning—a full meal of rasam, sambhar and curry and thayir sadam with the hottest pickles, preferably avakka. Now he sits with them and sips from a tumbler of hot coffee.

Ravi swallows another idli.

'Ravi, don't gulp down your food. Eat slowly,' Appa warns and immediately looks embarrassed. 'I'm sorry. For a minute I thought we were at Vedaranyam Street!'

Ravi can't help smiling but doesn't say anything.

'If you gulp down your food, it doesn't stick to the body. The nutrients do not get absorbed into the system,' Appa feels the need to explain to Deborah. Ravi has heard this a million times as a child.

Dinner at Vedaranyam Street was a big affair. The children sat cross-legged on the floor in the kitchen, in a semicircle around Amma. Amma kept a large stainless steel vessel in front of her, containing sambhar-rice. Another big vessel shaped like a funnel stood next to her holding crisp appalams. The small container below the funnel-shaped vessel collected the oil in which the appalams were fried. Another, less obtrusive vessel had beans curry or bitter gourd curry. The children always groaned when they saw bitter gourd but Appa was adamant. It stimulated the part of the brain that dealt with mathematics and that was that. They ate bitter gourd and did well in math.

Amma was the presiding deity. One by one they held out their hands. Amma took a large spoon, scooped up some sambhar-rice and placed it on the outstretched palm. A small spoon of curry and a bit of appalam was placed on top of the heap. They stuffed their mouths with this mixture. One by one, starting from Ravi—the youngest—then Jaya, Arjun and finally Anand, the food was administered. Then the next round. And the next. Until the vessel was empty. Then a vessel of curd-rice was placed in front of Amma by the cook and the empty sambhar-rice vessel removed. The rounds started again. This time each scoop of curd-rice was crowned with a piece of narthangai pickle, salty but not spicy. The children loved it.

When guests came over, all the children were treated to the same ritual. Only the semicircle around Amma became wider and the size of the vessel larger. Once the children had been fed, the men ate at the dining table. After they finished, the women sat down to eat, usually on the floor.

As Appa watches Ravi gulp down his idli, he is fascinated. In some ways, his children have not changed at all. And in other fundamental ways, they have.

The phone rings.

'Ravi, this is Anand. How are you, da?'

'Anand?' Ravi says in surprise. It has been years. 'How are you, anna?'

'I'm fine, da.' Anand's voice has become heavier with time. There is a sense of urgency in his tone. 'I was wondering if you had heard from Appa, by any chance.'

'Yes, he is here.'

'He is there!'

'Yes.'

'Can I speak to him?'

Ravi turns to Appa, who is sitting in the sofa watching him. Appa waves his hand and says softly, 'No, I don't want to speak to him.'

'Why not?' Ravi asks, lowering his voice and covering the mouthpiece with his hand.

'He just wants to talk me into coming back,' Appa says.

'Sorry, anna, I… I don't think Appa is in the best frame of mind to talk to you now. I will call you later whenever he is free… I'm sorry.'

There is a pause at the other end.

'Ravi, this is not a game. I want to speak to him.'

'I know, but what can I do?'

Another brief pause.

'Ravi, let me tell you something. Appa came to your house without even informing us that he was leaving. He just vanished. We were worried like hell.'

'Yes, I knew only later that he hadn't informed you.'

'We were worried sick. Ravi, enough of all this drama. Tell Appa he should come back now. If he has a problem, he should sort it out with us. God knows we have tried to make him happy…'

Ravi listens quietly.

'He has been acting strange ever since Amma passed away,' Anand continues. 'He is getting increasingly cranky. Sometimes a tiny thing becomes a major crisis. I have tried everything to make him happy. But—'

'Anna, I understand. Why don't you call a little later? Maybe Appa will speak to you then.'

'Ravi, I don't understand this sudden bonhomie between you and Appa. First, he walks out on us. Then, of all places, he goes and plonks himself in your house—a place he hasn't seen in his life and a son he hasn't seen in three years. Now he refuses to speak to me. What the hell is going on?'

'Anna, all I know is that he is staying with us for the present. He is the one who made this decision. If there is something between you both, then it is best sorted out directly.'

'Ravi, that's exactly what I want to do—sort it out between us directly. You must persuade him to return. There's no point in you getting into this.'

'I agree and I'm not even trying to get into it. But the decision to return is entirely his own. I can't persuade him without knowing what the hell this is all about.'

'Ravi, don't be idiotic!' Anand says, irritated. 'This is his home and he has to return and it's your responsibility to see that he does. He can't keep staying at your house.'

Something inside Ravi snaps.

'I don't give a damn where he stays. In fact, I don't give a damn about you or Appa. After two years of not even bothering to find out whether I'm alive or dead, neither of you have any business telling me what to do and where my responsibilities lie.'

'You better be careful about what you say,' says Anand furiously. 'I don't need a sermon from you.'

'Nor I from you.'

'Fine, if you both want to gang up against me, so be it.'

'If you insist on seeing conspiracy where there is none, that's your headache, not mine.'

'If you say so.'

'Yes, I say so.'

Ravi hangs up.

20

'Thangachchi,' Thambi Maarimuthu calls Chinnamma affectionately. She is twenty-five years older than him but the name 'thangachchi'—younger sister—has stuck. The cheri ladies called her that when she moved in as a youngster. After several decades, whenever she went there, they still called her thangachchi. Chinnamma called him Thambi—younger brother. 'I told you you needn't return the money till next year... not till next year. Why have you come now?'

'I can only return the money when I have it and not when you want me to,' she retorts in mock anger.

'You are turning logic... logic on its head,' he laughs. 'That's what all those who can't pay me say. But not those like you who return the money before time!'

'Thambi, I am fortunate to live in a nice household. They are nice people. They pay me well and look after me well.'

'Brahmins?' he asks.

'Yes, the man is but not the lady...'

'Brahmins, Brahmins... can't you people get away from this Brahmin worship?'

'You don't understand, Thambi. They might be Brahmins but they are not like the others. These are decent people.

They looked after me very well. In any case, the amma of the house is American.'

'American?'

'Yes, American.'

'Good looking?'

'A thousand times more than all the girls you go to bed with every day,' Chinnamma says and he doubles up with laughter. 'Don't laugh. Everything in life is not a Brahmin–non-Brahmin affair, Thambi. There is life beyond paapaan for many of us. For you too, some day. I owe that family for—'

'For throwing a few crumbs your way?'

'… for treating me like a human being. For treating me as one of them.'

'You talk as if… as if they take you out to a restaurant every evening.'

'Short of that, they have done a lot for me,' Chinnamma says.

'The problem with us is that we get carried away… carried away when the paapaans throw a few crumbs our way,' says Thambi Maarimuthu, shaking his head from side to side. 'That's what has kept us where we are—doomed to be second-class citizens… second-class in our own Dravidian land. When someone with guts… guts like EVR took them on, then we saw their true colours. Challenge them, EVR used to exhort us. We challenged them… challenged and won whatever we have got till now. It is not charity done to us by these Brahmins. We can't be condemned to a life of servitude. To destroy Brahminism has to be the goal of every self-respecting Tamilian. We need our rights, not their charity.'

'Thambi, now you are talking like a politician. You can never build a new society by destroying someone. Speak loudly if you can replace them with your own people who are as good as them. But if you are after votes, then these speeches should be made in public places, not in front of a poor person like me.'

'You are not poor at all, thangachchi. You are one of the richest persons I know—at heart. I cannot forget how your husband and you saved me... saved me from becoming a street child when I came to this cheri as an orphan. That one year I spent in the cheri, going in and out of your house, made me understand what parents were.'

Chinnamma and her husband had taken him into their house. Maarimuthu—he wasn't Thambi then—and her son had kept each other company. Maarimuthu refused to go to school with her son, but he was off every morning ragpicking. She insisted that whatever he did, he should come back and sleep at night in their house. The streets were no place for a youngster. By sleeping at Chinnamma's home, he avoided any run-in with the police who pounced on his gang of ragpickers to exhort money, and evaded the older rowdies who tried to rope in the youngsters for worse things. Most importantly, Maarimuthu felt the warmth of living in a family.

'That's why I cannot say no to you for anything,' he continues. 'The fact that I have made money and got some notoriety as well is nothing in front of a person like you. You have worked so hard...'

'Enough, Thambi. You make me sound like a great person. Anyway, here's the money. I will come to you if I need anything else. For now, be happy that I have enough to give back your loan and lead a decent life.'

'Bestowed on you by Brahmins,' he says.

Thambi Maarimuthu was an important link in the underworld chain. His operations had started modestly,

when he got together a band of men to protect the people
of his cheri from being harassed by the law. For this, the
cheri took care of him and his men. His services came in
handy and he soon realized there was money in it. In a few
years, he started to provide protection for a fee. Alongside,
he set up a moneylending business for fishermen and other
such communities. They borrowed in the morning and
returned the money in the evening with interest. As his
coffers grew, so did his businesses. Now he was more into
financing operations—both legal and illegal—rather than
roughing people up. But he had to keep up the strongman
image and took up such contracts for a price. He didn't
enjoy doing them but they maintained his reputation as a
person not to be trifled with. His political links had grown.
The Tamil political parties sought him out to get votes. And
when Thambi Maarimuthu requested the cheris under his
protection to vote for one of his choice, they listened.

As he speaks, there is bitterness in his voice. He is a
Brahmin-hater and isn't afraid to show it.

It was no longer easy to be a Brahmin in Chennai. Slowly but
surely they were being stripped of everything, even their self-
respect. Used to being revered, admired and obeyed through
centuries, they were now reviled, mocked, even ignored.
It wasn't easy to adjust to this sudden change of status.
Appa remembers how, at the height of the anti-Brahmin
movement, the gleaming white walls of Chennai were
scrawled with virulent slogans: *If Shiva and Vishnu produced
Ayyappan, how can god exist? Drive them out of Chennai!* Anyone
with a Brahmin-sounding name had to pay exorbitant sums
to get admission into a college, even if he or she stood first
in the entrance exam. Brahmins started giving their children

neutral names like Ashok Kumar or Vishwajit. Brahmin deities were garlanded with chappals in the morning, though some of the miscreants quietly went at night to the same gods to seek forgiveness since some Brahmin deities were also worshipped by non-Brahmins.

It wasn't as though Brahmins grudged the non-Brahmins wealth and power. At the same time, they refused to do anything to correct thousands of years of social subjugation of the non-Brahmins. The non-Brahmins who looked for a new social structure found that the Brahmins were not about to surrender. In the end, it required the efforts of Tamil leaders like E.V. Ramaswamy Naicker and Annadurai and organizations like the Self-Respect League. And fortunately for the Tamils, the struggle for social independence of the non-Brahmins went side by side with the political independence movement. When the Mandal Commission Report caused much consternation and bloodshed in the north in the late eighties, the Tamils were bystanders who had already achieved a high degree of social integration and looked at the north with resignation.

A new Tamil Nadu was born.

At the same time, a new kind of discrimination started—this time against the Brahmins. Whether in jobs, or admission to colleges, or in assigning marks for exams, or for selection to public sector companies, or in transfer of civil servants, Brahmins were given the short shrift. They were made to pay huge bribes, institutionally discriminated against and sidelined.

'You TamBrams would do well to learn from us,' Deborah says thoughtfully, as Ravi and she walk down Boat Club Road at sunset, dodging cars and cycles.

'You?'

'Us, Jews. I've now seen enough of you guys to know that you actually need a role model for survival.'

'How?'

'Jews were a minority too, but we endured neglect and persecution and turned our adversity into our advantage. We refused to disappear. You guys seem to be giving up without a fight in Tamil Nadu and are keen to move out at the drop of a hat. No wonder I see rows and rows of oldies reading *The Hindu* and drinking filter coffee every morning while waiting to hear from their sons and daughters in the US.'

'We TamBrams do well wherever we go. That's the confidence we have in ourselves. I don't have to physically be here in Tamil Nadu to thrive.'

'That doesn't mean you look for an exit strategy and run away. We too did well wherever we went. But we didn't give up and leave. We stayed and made sure we got our due in the country where we were born. Even now, there are more Jews outside Israel than inside it.'

'Don't worry, like the Jews, there will come a time when there'll be more TamBrams outside Tamil Nadu than inside it!' Ravi laughs.

21

The first to visit after Appa's arrival is Kamala athai. When Appa appeared like Duncan's ghost that morning, Deborah called Kamala athai to give her the news. Kamala athai was shocked at first, then amused, and finally excited at this new development. Unable to contain her curiosity, she comes over as fast as her legs and crutches can carry her. She hobbles into the living room, puts down her crutches on either side of the sofa, and sits down.

Appa greets her warmly if sheepishly.

'So you have finally found your way into your son's house?' she asks.

'Yes, Kamala,' he says with a sigh. 'Life has come full circle. I was born alone and now I am alone once again. As the *Kural* says, even those loved are luckless, unless loved by those they love. I seem to be luckless.'

'Stop this self-pity!' she admonishes. 'You have a wonderful son and an even lovelier daughter-in-law-in-waiting. Instead of thanking god, you are moaning…'

'No, no, that's not what I meant. All I meant was that my own thinking has evolved and come full circle. The moment I realized I was isolated within my own family, I was struck by how foolish the whole thing was. If only I had come to my senses a bit earlier—'

'First, you moan, then you regret. Now, stop this. You have taken a bold step even if it's come late in the day. I am proud of you, anna. You have swallowed your ego and come in search of reconciliation. Now tell me, what's next?'

'What do you mean?'

'Well, are you asking them to get married or not? I have been telling them to do so all the time, but they keep saying the time hasn't come. So do something about it before you leave this place.'

Appa is suitably chastised and he nods his head. In any case, he can never say no to his youngest sister. If there is anyone who can speak to Appa in that fashion, it is Kamala athai.

At this time of year, the weather can get sultry. But it rained last night and the morning is surprisingly pleasant. Ravi opens the window and looks down at the garden. Appa is standing there. For a second, Ravi had forgotten about him.

Seeing Appa, Ravi feels as though a part of his life has suddenly rewound. Walking around the lawn in his yellow silk veshti with his angavastram slung across his shoulders, Appa holds a cane basket in his hand, going purposefully about denuding the flowers. His figure is skinny and his face drawn.

Deb stirs behind him. 'There goes Appa,' Ravi says, turning around. 'He has cleaned up all the flowers from our jasmine creeper.'

'Why?' she asks, yawning.

'For his puja. I wonder what he is up to. Our puja room is all of one Torah and one bronze idol of Ganesha.'

'Have my roses been cleaned up too?' she asks anxiously.

'Don't worry, he has left those alone. I presume he knows they're yours. He's not going to take liberties with your stuff!'

'I don't mind a few roses, especially if it's for the gods…'

'And there goes our hibiscus…'

Appa goes about his daily routine, as if he is back at Vedaranyam Street.

Since the time he was born, Ravi has seen Appa in the garden at Vedaranyam Street every single morning, picking flowers. Jasmine, roses, hibiscus, champangi and pavazhamalli were woven into garlands with strings made of banana fibre. The banana fibres themselves had to be cut and made to certain specifications. Before his puja, Appa made sure the garlands were liberally sprinkled with rose water and attar. On entering the puja room, one was ambushed by the instant rush of fragrance. The gods stood resplendent in their flowery glory surrounded by lamps of different sizes—shaped like ohm, suryan, chandran. Appa had a lamp for every type of worship from Eka arathi to Pancha arathi, Kumbha arathi to Nakshatra arathi, Deepa arathi to Navagraha arathi. To ring in the arathi, he collected a range of bells, from the loud gong to the simple nandi bell.

Appa walks around the garden, enjoying the early morning dew rubbing against the soles of his feet. The garden isn't as big as his own garden at Vedaranyam Street, but the flowerbeds make up for it. Carefully laid out under Deborah's supervision, red hibiscus hugs the compound wall, while rose bushes and jasmine creepers line the inside walls.

Appa is engrossed in his puja for a long time. By the time he finishes, he has added his own three framed photos to the existing bronze Ganesha idol and the Ark of the Torah—photos of Gayathri, Hanuman and Ram. Appa smiles when he sees the Ark, the Torah covered in fabric, the yad, silver crowns on the handles and the silver breastplate, and the mat aligned in the direction of Jerusalem. So Deborah wasn't an atheist as he had initially feared.

After lunch, he walks into the drawing room and finds Deborah reading the newspaper.

'Sorry, I have kept you away from your work. Please don't worry about me. I make myself comfortable anywhere.' Appa remembers Ravi's admonition the previous day and adds, 'It's not my intention to dislocate your lives…'

'Don't worry, Appa. I can work from home. Was your food all right?' She changes the topic.

'Couldn't be better,' he answers truthfully. 'After a long time, I ate in peace. You are the one who didn't eat properly. You should have had whatever you normally eat every day. I am not fastidious about what you people eat. Don't feel constrained—'

'Don't worry, Appa. I am quite used to this food,' she says. 'Just because I'm from the US doesn't mean I need to eat meat all the time!'

'No, no, that's not what I meant…'

'That's exactly what you meant,' she laughs.

'I just don't want you to change your lifestyle because of me. The last thing I want is to be a burden to your lives.'

'You're not a burden. You have said that three times already, don't say it again.'

'Fine. But if at any point of time you don't want me here…'

'I'll tell you straightaway if that will make you happy!'

'In fact, on Saturdays, I'm very happy with just a bowl of fruit for dinner. That's the day for Hanuman. A bowl of fruits will cleanse the system too. Amma used to follow this religiously twice a week. I try to do it once a week, that too only if I remember.'

'Well, you needn't starve for our sakes…'

'No, a bowl of fruits on Saturday suits me fine.'

'Okay, Appa, take that as done. You are only making my job easier by starving.'

Appa looks at her closely. Amma had told him she was good-looking. When he sees Deborah now, he agrees. Ravi has made a good choice. But how Appa wishes she had been an Iyer girl.

'You are a beautiful girl, Deborah. Ravi is indeed lucky,' says Appa suddenly, catching Deborah by surprise.

'Thank you, Appa,' is all she can say.

'You know, we Tamils are partial to fair colour. In this case, you're not just fair but genuinely good-looking. When I was adamant about not seeing you both, Amma said I should meet you once, at least for your looks. That was her way of enticing me!'

Deborah blushes furiously.

'And now that I have finally see you, Amma is no more.' Appa turns away and looks out of the window. A sudden surge of emotion chokes him. If only Amma were alive.

News of Appa's arrival spreads fast. Soon Appa's friends start frequenting Ravi's house. At first they are hesitant. What will Ravi say? they wonder. But they come anyway. Besides, they are dying to see his pretty girlfriend. She is a novelty and they all want to see her so they can tell their wives how she looks, how she behaves, how she lives with Ravi and how she treats Appa. They have never seen something like this in Chennai. On all these counts, they aren't disappointed. She is beautiful, has blonde hair, behaves respectfully and gives them all authentic 'dikakshun' coffee. They even understand her accent.

And for the colour-conscious Brahmins of Chennai, fair skin is everything. She has passed the test.

'Dai, you are lucky Ravi has selected someone like Deborah to live with. She is beautiful and her skin is like ivory! Ask him to marry her quickly. They have wasted enough time waiting for you to say yes. You can finally stop being pig-headed about this.'

For once, Appa agrees.

The fact that she is a white woman is not mentioned by Appa's friends. It's not their problem because Deborah isn't getting married to one of their sons. They are generous with their words and advice but if it had been one of their own sons, ivory skin and beauty wouldn't have mattered and the fact that she was white would have brought out the worst in them. They would have reacted exactly as Appa had.

They find Ravi very hospitable, which comes as a surprise to them, prejudiced as they are after Appa's raving and ranting. Ravi too makes sure not to let his antagonism towards his father show in front of Appa's guests, even though he deeply resents their intrusion into his home.

Some, who are not quite Appa's friends but distant acquaintances, also come to visit. Appa is not surprised. He know they come for vambu or gossip. They come to carry tales about Appa. They wonder what he is going to do about the house. They casually ask how Ravi is and what Deborah is doing. Whether they have children or not. Oh, they are still not married, are they? Appa is no fool. He sends them on their way after a cup of coffee.

Appa manages to spend more time with his sister. For the first time since his retirement, he finds time to sit with Kamala and discuss just about everything under the sun. Politics. Chennai roads. Water scarcity. Their parents. The changing times. The cinema. Usually it was Kamala who sought Appa out for advice and talked to him about her problems. Now, for the first time, Appa opens his heart out to her. It is a strange reversal of roles.

'Kamala, you were right. I'm happy to be here with Ravi and Deborah. But I still can't get over how all three of my sons turned out the way they did. When I look at them, I wonder what I did wrong. I gave them a good Brahminical upbringing. Since childhood they have been taught to distinguish right from wrong. I even engaged a Sanskrit teacher to teach them the shlokas. They used to sit like parrots in front of the porch—even our father used to sit on that old reclining cane chair and listen to them chant—wearing their silk veshtis and repeating dutifully after the teacher. After their poonal, every one of them continued to say their *Gayathri* and do their *sandhyavandhanam* every day. After all that…'

'You never gave them space to be themselves. You expected them to do whatever you wanted them to do.'

'But what else was I supposed to do?' Appa asks helplessly. 'At that age, they are hardly in a position to know what is good for them. It is for us parents to give them what we can. It's up to them to use it later in life.'

'Maybe, but times have changed, anna. Nowadays no child accepts anything unquestioningly. They want to ask questions, debate and find out why before accepting anything. You never allowed them to question you. Whenever they asked something, you shouted at them and there ended the conversation.'

'But they still performed well in whatever they took up.'

'Out of fear. When that fear went away—especially after they entered college—they felt free to do as they pleased. What they did was a sign of defiance rather than a flaw in their character.'

'Even their school marks were so good…'

'Oh, anna, it was never enough for you.'

'That was just my way of pushing them to do better.'

'It looked as if you were picking on them all the time. Even when Anand got 98 in maths, you asked him where the remaining 2 per cent went. I'm sure the children resented it.'

'Maybe I overdid it now and then. But I was strict for a reason. I didn't want them to make do with what they had achieved. That was the age to push them, get them to compete, to take pride in academic achievement. And each one did very well in school. That's only because I taught them not to be satisfied with anything less than the best.'

'You put a lot of pressure on them.'

'Yes, but they can handle it at that age. Even Anand got admission in a well-known US college…'

'And you didn't send him. Later you agreed to Ravi going and Anand was so upset that you never gave him that opportunity.'

'Yes, that's what Ravi told me during one of his outbursts. That Anand was jealous of him. But Kamala, studying in the US is expensive. Ravi got a scholarship. Anand can't hold that against me.'

'I'm sure he isn't holding it against you. But you never listened to those three boys, you never let them be boys. You never encouraged them to talk to you. You just gave them orders.'

'You talk as if I enslaved them or something…'

'No, you certainly didn't, anna,' Kamala says quickly. 'You gave them everything a father could. But how you give is as important as what you give.'

'And what about Ravi? His decision has nothing to do with my strict upbringing. I never imagined he would—'

'Before you proceed any further, let me just say that I am proud of him…'

'Of course, so am I, but—'

'No buts. He has all the qualities you would want in a son. What irks you is not his character but that he didn't listen to you. So what? You gave him all you could so that he could think independently. You can't sit in judgement on him now.'

'So do you want me to sit quiet when Arjun goes to bed with those actresses?'

'No, not at all. But why did you stop them from seeing Tamil movies in the first place when they were in school and college? You forced them to see movies on the sly. You stopped Jaya from going over to her friends' houses if they had a brother. Their world, their friends, their lives were controlled by you. There's bound to be a reaction. I'm not supporting them, anna. But this is not entirely their fault. That you must accept. You had some role to play.'

'At least none of them took to drinking,' he says lamely. 'There is still hope.'

'That's why I'm proud that you have taken this step and are trying to patch up your relations with Ravi. I can see that he is already changing.'

'I'm not so sure. He wants me to clear out of the house as soon as possible.'

'He has his pride. Just be patient.'

22

L ike many old-timers in Chennai, Appa prefers the beachfront for some peace and quiet away from the mayhem of the city. Marina beach.

The waves in the Bay of Bengal were not as benign as Appa would have liked. They crashed onto the beach in repressed fury. But the people loved the Marina and came out in full force to celebrate it. And just as well they might. It was popularly referred to, at least by the Chennaivaasis, as the second-longest beach in the world, spanning tens of miles. It was built in the late 1800s by Governor Mountstuart Elphinstone Grant Duff, a remarkable contribution from a man who was otherwise an ineffectual governor of Madras. His vision was to make this a lung for thousands. It was to become a lung for millions. Soon Beach Road became the most celebrated road in Madras. The row of buildings built in the Indo-Saracenic style made the skyline look grand. To the north was the red brick façade of the Presidency College complex, which produced two Nobel Prize winners—Sir C.V. Raman and S. Chandrasekhar. Appa never forgot to remind his sons of this fact, since he was himself from Presidency.

But the Marina had changed over the years. Successive Tamil Nadu governments had made the skyline as ugly as possible by adding incongruous buildings, restaurants and even a swimming pool to the beach. Hawkers, balloon-sellers, toy stalls, food carts and ice-cream carts invaded the sands and the beach was littered with their debris. The well-known Tamil writer Bharanidaran even took the pen-name Marina. The sands concealed the broken hearts of spurned lovers and the waters hid the remains of broken ships, torn apart by cyclones. Over the years, the beach and its endless white sands gave the people of Chennai the assurance that all was well, in a way that no other part of the city could.

Appa loves the Marina. The ceaseless gurgle of the waves, the wind rustling through his hair, his veshti blowing in the wind, his feet sinking into the soft sand, the backs of all the dark statues—Avvaiyar, Thiruvalluvar, Bharati, Veeramamunivar, Kannagi and others—dotting the landscape, and the warmth of the sundal, murukku and molaguvadai sold by the vendors.

A walk on the beach triggers so many memories. It was here that Appa brought Amma the day after their wedding. It was a blazing afternoon and the two had sat quietly under the shade of a large fishing boat, just enjoying each other's company. 'When I was studying in Presidency I dreamt of bringing a girlfriend here, but I never had one. It's only after marriage that I am getting this opportunity,' Appa had told her. Every weekend, Appa brought his four children to the beach. Anand and Arjun were allowed to wade into the waves by themselves. Ravi and Jaya had to hold Appa's hand before they were allowed to wet their feet. When Appa became a grandfather, he brought Anand's son and daughter here all the time. And so life went on, from one generation to the next; the Marina remained the same. The waves, the sea breeze, the sinking sand and the boundless skyline. Whenever he returns to the beach, it gives Appa a sense of continuity despite the chaos around. Even though there are ten times more people on the beach than there were a decade earlier, Appa still goes to the beach for peace and quiet.

As he walks on the beach and his feet sink gratefully into the sand, Appa feels unwanted. The driver has taken the day off and he had to fight a battle to find an auto-rickshaw to bring him here. He has never felt unwanted before; there was always someone to look after him. Amma was always there. He had not realized how dependent he was until his wife died, and first his sons and then his daughters-in-law started ignoring him. He feels sorry for the poor wives, they had to listen to their husbands, after all. They had even stopped their children from talking to him. It had become unbearable. Appa had been left with no choice. For the first time in his life, he was at the mercy of those who didn't want him.

Appa continues to stare at the rushing waves and a wave of emptiness sweeps over him. He dreads having to stay in Ravi's house any longer. He prays that things get sorted out quickly. Just when he was looking forward to retirement, a quiet life at Sundari, watching his grandchildren grow, god took away his life partner. And now he is taking away everyone else too. When exactly did things start to go wrong?

It would have been a full-moon night, but for the thick clouds covering the sky, drenching Chennai with pre-monsoon showers. It only took a few minutes of rain for the entire city to be flooded. If the rain had continued for a few hours, Chennai would have become the Venice of the East. The Chennai drainage system had collapsed long ago. After decades of clogging, not even rats lived inside the drains for fear of suffocation.

Arjun had not returned from office; he had called to say he would be working late. Anand and his family were in Kodaikanal on a holiday. Only Appa lay awake.

The house was quiet. It had seen better days, noisier days, days when one barely knew how many people were living in the house. Food was cooked in vast quantities and consumed as in a wedding. When the lights went out in one part of the house, they came on in another.

Change, of course, was inevitable. One by one, they left. First, Kamala's husband got a transfer and they moved to Delhi. Anand and Arjun graduated, got jobs and got married. The house gained two daughters-in-law even as it lost a daughter when Jaya got married and moved to Bangalore. Ravi went off to the US. The ammanji mannis left. The retinue of servants became smaller. Navaratri kolus became smaller in size. And then Amma's death. A sudden quiet shrouded the house. Now, Sundari was a shell of its old self. Anjali, Arjun and their son had a large bedroom on the first floor. Anand and his wife Kanti stayed on the ground floor, their son and daughter shared the vacant room upstairs and they had converted the adjacent room into a study. The bags of grains and dal in the storerooms, the aluminium bins, the jars of pickle and uruli had long disappeared. The guest rooms were empty. Appa continued to occupy the first room on the left. After the death of his wife, he shifted his library into his bedroom and one more room became empty.

It was still raining.

Appa stayed awake as was his habit. He couldn't sleep till the rest of the house was at rest. The rain brought mosquitoes. Even the fan above was not strong enough to drive them away. He pulled a sheet over him. It was nearly midnight

when he heard the main gate creak open. He got up, opened
the front door and switched on the porch and verandah
lights. Arjun's Zen drove in. Close behind was a jeep.

Both vehicles pulled up at the portico. Arjun got out.
From the other side of the car, a lady got out. A couple of
policemen emerged from the jeep.

One of them marched up the steps to the verandah.

'Saar, you must be...'

'I'm Arjun's father.'

'Namaskaram, I'm Inspector Basheer,' he introduced
himself. 'This is my colleague Vetrivel.'

'Namaskaram.'

Arjun stood silently in the verandah looking in the other
direction. The woman stood next to him.

'Saar, I found your son and this lady in a compromising
position inside your son's car in Saidapet. It was raining
heavily and the car was parked by the side of the road. When I
approached them, they claimed they were married. I decided
to accompany them here and see for myself.'

Appa turned to the lady.

'Well, dear, why don't you go in?' he said to her gently.
'And you too, Arjun. It must be late for both of you.'

The woman walked past Appa into the house. Arjun
followed without a word.

'Inspector sir, she is my daughter-in-law and Arjun is my
son. It's disgusting what they did in public. I apologize on
their behalf. I don't know how to thank you for bringing
them here safe and sound. I ask you to kindly forget what
happened today. This will not happen again, I assure you.'

The inspector nodded.

'Saar, you are sure this is the way you wish to handle the
matter?'

'Yes, and I deeply apologize for the inconvenience they have caused you.'

'No, no inconvenience. But…'

'They shouldn't have behaved like this. These days youngsters think they can do what they want and get away with it.'

'Yes, they should have been more discreet.'

'I agree. If you will please wait a moment…'

Appa went into the house. When he came out a few minutes later he had several hundred-rupee notes in his hand. 'Please accept this from me for all the trouble they have given both of you,' he said, pressing the money into the inspector's palm.

'No, saar. Why, why all this?' Inspector Basheer protested even as his palm enclosed the notes.

'Don't refuse, Inspector sir. This is only a small token for the great help you have done us today.'

'Please tell your son not to indulge in anything like this again. It doesn't behoove someone of your stature to have a son who behaves like this.'

'I will warn him to be careful in the future. I hope you will be discreet about this matter…'

'Of course, saar, you can count on us. We don't want the good name of your family to be besmirched.'

'Thank you. That's reassuring.'

'Saar, I'll take your leave.' The inspector saluted smartly and got into the jeep. The rain had decreased to a steady drizzle.

Appa switched off the verandah lights and closed the door behind him. Arjun and the woman were standing in the drawing room. Appa took in her heavy makeup, glittering bangles and sequinned sari.

'What's your name, amma?' Appa asked.

'Revati,' she whispered.

'Revati, you look like a nice girl. Please don't come to these parts again. I will ask Arjun to drop you after a few minutes, after the police jeep goes out of sight. Arjun has a wife and a child. Please do not come near him or near this house again.'

Revati looked at her feet and nodded.

Appa took Arjun aside.

'Appa, I'm sorry, Appa… I was suddenly—' he started.

'Your apologies can wait. First pay her whatever you owe her, then drop her to the nearest taxi stand. And thank your stars that nobody is awake at this time or our name will be in the dust.'

But the next morning, all of Vedaranyam Street knew what had happened the previous night.

Appa wanted to seek the help of Anand. He was the elder son and might be able to talk to his brother. But that dream vanished only too quickly. Anand himself fell from grace and it happened so suddenly…

Anand had taken a loan from Karim Basha, real-estate don from Triplicane, and lost it all in a cinema misadventure.

Cinema, cinema, cinema. Chennai was full of it. Politics, social life, culture and values were defined by cinema in Tamil Nadu. Literature, music and dances underwent changes. Even religion did: film stars were akin to gods. Kollywood, they called it proudly.

Anand lost ten lakhs. For backing a flop.

'Actually, it's more than ten lakhs,' he confessed to Appa. 'So Karim Basha took collateral. I notionally pledged my share in this house as collateral.'

'Idiot, what the hell have you done? You have started partitioning the house even before my death! Even before you have asked for partition? That's not even legal collateral. He can't touch you in court.'

'Maybe it's not strictly legal. But that's not really the issue. The issue is that these guys are not going to give me any more rope and I don't think confrontation will get us much more than a few broken bones. The only practical way out is to pay up, collateral or no collateral.'

'Karim Basha! Of all things, you had to go and take money from a Muslim financier. Where does he live?'

'In Triplicane.'

'But Triplicane Muslims are nice people. It is you who screwed up. Don't you have any common sense? Business comes naturally to these Muslims. They are born businessmen. They can do very well without green horns like you borrowing money from them and burning it overnight. Why are you venturing into areas you know nothing about?'

'One has to take a chance in ventures like these.'

'Chance? Haven't I told you time and again not to go after financial windfalls? It has ruined generations. Even the great poet Bharatidasan was ruined because of films. Money has to be earned. The day I retire, no one will come to help you or me if you lose your job, remember that, Anand. No one will touch a failure. And all you and your brother can think of is where to find the next prostitute or how to gamble away your salary.'

When Appa walked out to the waiting car, he looked back at Sundari. The only thing familiar to him was the large, looming house. The people inside had become almost unrecognizable.

23

THIS DOCUMENT OF ARRANGEMENT of properties belonging to the family and its members and the free consent of various members of the family made on (date) day of (month and year) BETWEEN Thiru _____, aged ___, Karta of the Hindu Undivided Family, Thiru _____, aged ___, and Thiru _____, aged ___, and Thiru _____, aged ___, all sons of the Karta and members of the Hindu Undivided Family and Thirumathi _____, aged ___, daughter of the Karta and a member of the Hindu Undivided Family.

WHEREAS the above five persons constitute a joint family governed by Mitakshara school of Hindu Law owning immovable properties more particularly described in S.No. 1 to ___ of Schedule A attached hereto.

AND WHEREAS in view of the internal family quarrels amongst the family members, the members are not able to continue their joint enjoyment of the properties belonging to the family and therefore all the members have voluntarily and of their free will agreed to put an end to such a situation and have also agreed to partition the joint family.

Appa looks up from the partition deed in front of him. The lawyer Vaidyanathan is slouched in the chair across from him, a half banian barely covering his torso, both arms across his chest. A towel is thrown across his shoulder. He is humming an out-of-tune Karnatic song.

Vaidyanathan and Appa go back a long way. They were classmates in school. They had a similar upbringing—those days every Brahmin kid had a more or less similar upbringing—and soon became close friends. Vaidy's father was wealthier and that was obvious from the Desoto that came to drop him every day to school. When they both entered Presidency College, Vaidy started driving the Desoto himself. Appa's father made do with a smaller but gleaming black Flying Standard 8, which Appa subsequently inherited, fortunately while he was still in college. Even marriage didn't end their friendship. So it was natural that when he needed a lawyer, Appa could think of no one but Vaidy.

'Vaidy, do you have to include this line about internal family quarrels?' Appa asks.

'Not if you don't want it,' Vaidyanathan replies and continues humming.

'Dai Vaidy, I don't want this thing to become a public spectacle.'

'That's bound to happen so you may as well be prepared.'

Appa sighs. 'I suppose so. The best thing would be to sort this out by mutual consent. Arjun and Anand shouldn't take this to court. Then it will never see the light of day.'

'They won't take it to court. Why should they? They already have possession of the house so they will simply continue to live there. Why should they partition it? Frankly, you were foolish to move out. It might have been the right thing for you emotionally, but in practical terms you have done everything short of signing away the house to your two sons.'

'Possession without money, Vaidy. As one says, the best thing one can gift detractors is an elephant! They will have this elephant as a gift from me. They have to maintain it and pay for all the expenses.'

'And you will stand in the middle of the road with a begging bowl?' His out-of-tune humming grows louder as the conversation becomes more intense.

'Well, unlike them, I don't have to depend on the house for my survival. But you have a point. It's true that Arjun and Anand would be happy if the case dragged on for years and in the meantime I just folded up and died.' Appa shakes his head.

'Dai, that's what all sons want their fathers to do—just fold up and die.'

'Then their share will become bigger. If I die, they can dupe Ravi and Jaya out of their share—Ravi wouldn't be too interested and Jaya is not the kind to put up a fight. Arjun and Anand will rule the house. Maybe even sell it and get a few crores to settle their debts.'

'Dai, what you say is possible but unlikely. Ravi is not going to sit and watch and Jaya's husband won't let this go even if Jaya does. When it comes to property, even a cat becomes a tiger,' the lawyer laughs. 'But remember, it's not a good policy to hold onto any property till the very end. That's a sure way of making your children pray for your early death rather than your long life! Partition it soon so that they can also enjoy it.'

'… and gamble it away!'

'Kaaamoooo… Let's have one more round of coffee,' the lawyer calls out to his wife.

'This means they will wait for me to go to court. Which means I have to persuade them to accept a partition by mutual consent. They neither have the money to monetarily compensate Ravi, Jaya and me nor do they have the guts to move out of the house and seek compensation. We would be left with a house divided into five parts—the kitchen for Jaya, verandah for me, bathrooms for Ravi...' Appa chuckles at the thought. 'But Vaidy, you know, this house can be partitioned without too much trouble. It has fourteen rooms apart from the kitchen, living room and so on. It's quite huge.'

'What about your other assets?'

'They are all mine, not part of the Hindu Undivided Family. The land at Besant Nagar is in my name. So are the fixed deposits. All bought or saved up from my job.'

'Can you prove that?' Vaidy asks. By this time, the song he is humming has become unrecognizable.

'Yes, I have accounted for every penny. All I got from my father was this house at Vedaranyam Street and some stocks and shares, which I sold a couple of years ago and distributed to my children as startup money. You did the deed that time too. Come to think of it, if they really want money, I can buy them out of their share of the house. They get the money and I keep the house intact.'

'Dai, don't you think that thought has occurred to them? If they do that, they will have hardly any money left to start afresh. The longer they hold onto the property, the greater the chances of a bigger loot.'

'But they wouldn't have dreamt their father would file a case against them!'

'Yes, they wouldn't have dreamt their father would be foolish enough to file a case against them and literally hand the house to them on a platter!'

'At least you will be writing history. This will be the first time that the father files a case against his children to

partition property!' says Vaidyanathan's wife as she enters
with a tray and two tumblers of coffee.

'Just what we need for a hot day. Two hot coffees and a
draft partition deed!' Appa laughs.

'It's all written in my head, Vaidy. When the river dries
up, nobody blames the river. It's because the heavens have
run dry. Similarly, when a son starts misbehaving, there's no
point in blaming the son. I'll be blamed,' he says.

'You are not heaven.'

24

Deborah is stuck in traffic again. There is a PTC bus in front of her, overflowing with sweaty passengers and spewing undigested black carbon monoxide as it tilts precariously to one side. She sighs and closes her eyes.

Deborah had never imagined the kinds of things she would have to deal with in Chennai. Her life had not prepared her for this. When she came to Chennai two years ago, Ravi had protected her from the quirks of the Chennaivaasis, and from the hostility of his parents and brothers. It was not as though she was miserable in Chennai. She liked it: the ambience, the people, even her office colleagues. But it had taken them some time to warm up to her and it had taken her a while to let them in.

The singlemost determining character of her birth—her Jewishness—made no difference here. This surprised her, used as she was to hearing stories of the Holocaust. But it shouldn't have surprised her. Jews were no strangers to India. There was even a Jewish kingdom in Kerala, probably the only one outside Israel.

It is funny how the world has turned upside down in the last three weeks. It is not that Appa is difficult or demanding.

It is just that his very presence makes their world a completely different one.

Still, it is time she had a heart-to-heart with him. No use pretending everything will sort itself out magically just because Appa lives in their house now. Appa must see things for what they are. He has to accept them, so that he, in turn, is accepted by Ravi.

The car behind her honks and Deborah is jerked back to reality. The traffic is moving again. She shifts gears, as she has done several times in her life, and drives towards Thiru Vi Ka Bridge.

Deborah comes back early from office the next day. Appa is in the library, sitting near the window, engrossed in a book.

'Appa, if you are not too busy I'd like to talk to you.'

'No, no, I have all the time in the world. What is it?' Appa closes the book hastily.

'I wanted to speak to you about, well, so many things... Sometimes I wonder where I should start. There's so much to tell you...' She takes a deep breath and continues, 'Appa, Ravi and I have been living together without getting married. I know this is difficult for you to accept. I have seen how people react to this here. That's the way it has been for more than two years. When we first came to Chennai, we came with every intention of getting married but only after seeking your consent. I was sure you would give it. Ravi wasn't so sure but I was. That's why I insisted on taking this job in Chennai, even though Ravi wanted to stay on in the US. But you proved me wrong.'

Appa looks away. He stares at the swaying gulmohur tree outside the window. He is searching for the right thing to say, the right words to convey his feelings.

'Ravi tried to wait you out and even worked on you through Amma. When you still didn't approve, we thought of moving back to the US,' she continues. But there hadn't been any openings in the D.C. office for the two of them and they had no option but to stay on in Chennai for some more time. Before they knew it, one and then two years had gone by. 'But we couldn't go back and we had to stay here. Those are lost years as far as Ravi is concerned. I don't have any family here, so I didn't lose anyone. But Ravi had everything here in Chennai. Everything.'

She pauses. She knows how much Ravi has lost just to be with her – his parents, brothers, sister, all his relatives.

'We still hope to get married, soon, I guess. I don't know. I love Ravi deeply and I know he loves me too. That's what's kept us going here in Chennai… especially after all of you shunned him.'

'Yes, we let you down,' Appa says, his voice barely audible.

'I've always wondered how you guys could be so cruel to Ravi. Didn't you feel for a moment that Ravi belongs to you? I know your values are different, but why didn't his brothers come to see him? I just don't get it, Appa…' Her voice breaks.

'I'm sorry,' Appa whispers. 'You will never know how remorseful I am about the whole thing. How ashamed I am that I didn't even let you step into our house. I have, in the last several months, played and replayed the whole episode like a video in my mind, again and again, and each time I feel devastated. I feel small. I feel helpless. I think god is giving me a second chance by bringing me here to you. When I took the decision that Sundari was no more for me, the only place I could turn to was yours—not my daughter's. That's when I knew this is god's way of bringing us together.'

'It's never too late to start, Appa.'

Deborah is crying softly. Appa sees her tears, but doesn't console her. There isn't much he can say. He closes his eyes and covers his face with his palms. The two sit quietly, helpless at their inability to go back in time or go ahead without closing the chasm between them.

'I'm sorry if I've hurt you, Appa, but that's how we both felt. I don't think about it any more but I know Ravi still does.'

Appa understands. He thinks about it too.

'Amma was against me too and she tried hard to dissuade me from marrying Ravi,' Deb says. 'But once she realized I wasn't about to go anywhere, her attitude changed.'

'You know, when Amma died, my link to you was gone. She understood exactly what I wanted, even when I didn't. When she died, something in me died. I lost the capacity to think and communicate. In some ways, I think Anand and Arjun took advantage of that and the result is this.' He stretches out his arms. 'I have run away from my own home!'

'It can't be as bad as all that!'

'It is, Deborah,' Appa says, shaking his head sadly. 'But I am not going to remain a bystander now. Nor should Ravi. After all, he has every right to claim a part of the house. He is still a member of the Hindu Undivided Family.'

Deborah nods uncertainly.

'The house is worth a lot today. Even if the land is sold, it should be quite a sum. It's not the money I am interested in. It's the house. Our home. It belongs to all of us. Not just to my two sons.'

Deborah nods again, this time in understanding.

'I am determined to get it back… just as I am determined to get Ravi back. And you.'

Deborah knows she must play her part too. From being a total stranger to Appa, she suddenly finds herself thrust in the role of confidante. She has to be the bridge between Ravi and Appa. Like Amma was, she thinks.

25

His two sons have not contacted him yet. Appa had written a detailed letter outlining the options available to them and asking them to come to a mutually agreeable settlement. He had wanted the first letter to sound reasonable. Appa had asked Ravi to read it before he sent it, but Ravi did not want to. He said he didn't care.

Anand calls in the morning around ten o'clock, long after Ravi and Deborah have left for office. Arjun and I would like to meet you in an hour or so, he says. Appa agrees. Finally his sons will see reason. He asks Padma to make three coffees around eleven. My two elder sons are coming and they normally drink coffee, he tells her. If there is any murukku, you could bring that out too, he adds.

Deborah rings up after a few minutes to give instructions to Padma on what to make for the dinner that evening. Some sort of curry and Mysore rasam.

'Ayyah has asked me to keep some murukku and coffee ready soon. His sons rang up and said they are coming to see him.'

'When did they call?' Deborah asks sharply.

'A few minutes ago, amma.'

'When are they coming?'

'Ayyah said at around eleven o'clock.'

Deborah pauses. 'Are you sure?'

'Yes, amma.'

'Okay, Padma. Call me if you need anything.'

When Arjun and Anand walk in to meet Appa, Chinnamma is in the house. She has already dumped the clothes into the washing machine and is sweeping the bedrooms on the first floor when she hears them enter. The voices settle down in the drawing room. They do not sound familiar but are strained and at times abrupt. Like servants in any household, Chinnamma has mastered the art of listening in on conversations from a discreet distance.

The maidservant community is abuzz with the news that Ravi's father has come to stay. In any case, Deborah is always news. Now the maidservants wait every evening for Chinnamma to give them the gossip. Why is Ravi's father staying with them? Is he trying to split the two? Or is he trying to persuade them to marry? And how is Deborah-amma dealing with the new arrival? It can't be easy with the old man around. That too without any non-vegetarian food. Poor white girl!

Chinnamma is not the gossiping sort. Even though she has grown up in the slums of Chennai for the best part of her life, she has no time for gossip. In any case, for Chinnamma, Deborah is special. She can never speak ill of her. Not that there is anything ill to speak about. But the thought does not even cross her mind. This disappoints her maidservant friends who congregate to gossip every evening. Chinnamma usually keeps them entertained with harmless bits of news. So when Chinnamma carefully keeps an ear open to the conversation in the drawing room, she has Deborah's best interests at heart. She doesn't want the men to plot anything behind Deborah's back.

When Chinnamma enters the drawing room to sweep the floor, Anand tells her, 'Amma, don't clean this room today, we have something to discuss.' She promptly withdraws.

Padma comes in next with a tray with three tumblers of coffee.

After a while, Anand and Arjun persuade Appa to withdraw to the guest bedroom upstairs, and Chinnamma and Padma are shut out of the conversation.

Deborah is distracted. Ever since Padma informed her that Anand and Arjun are coming over, she has not been able to concentrate. She thinks of telling Ravi, but decides against it. Appa knows what he is doing, she thinks. Let him involve Ravi if he wants to.

After the heart-to-heart with Appa, something changed between Appa and Deborah. She realized she cared for him, in spite of everything. She realized that beneath his stern exterior, he was vulnerable. He needed her. And perhaps she needed him too.

She looks at her watch. It is eleven. She picks up her handbag, slings it across her shoulder and walks down to her car. In twenty minutes, she is home.

Deborah opens the door and walks in, half expecting to see the three of them huddled over papers and plans. The fan is whirring furiously but there's no one in the drawing room. She goes to the kitchen. Padma jumps up at the sound of her footsteps but relaxes after seeing Deborah.

'Are they here?'

'Yes, amma. They came in about twenty minutes ago and now they have gone to Appa's room.'

As Deborah climbs the stairs, she can hear a loud voice from behind the closed door of the guest room. She isn't sure whose voice it is, but knows it cannot be Appa's. She hesitates outside the door for a moment. Then she goes into her own bedroom. She leaves the door open and switches on the fan.

It is a hot day. And things are obviously getting hotter by the minute. She can hear voices being raised, louder and sharper. She sits on the bed, waiting and wondering. It's between them, she tells herself. I should not interfere. After all, it is Appa who has agreed to meet them. She waits impatiently and glances at her watch every now and then. The voices grow louder by the minute. The fact that she cannot hear Appa's voice troubles her. When there is a pause in the shouting, she assumes Appa is speaking. Most of the conversation is in Tamil and she is not yet adept at following an excited pair of voices in Tamil. When the shouting does not cease even after several minutes, she gets up, crosses the corridor and knocks on the door. Suddenly the voices become silent.

'Who is it?' asks a gruff voice.

'Deborah.'

The door is opened by a tall man; Deborah assumes it is the eldest brother, Anand. She has seen photos of Ravi's brothers and she can see the resemblance. Anand stands across the doorway. Deborah looks behind him into the room and glimpses Appa sitting in the cane chair, his right hand holding his forehead, his face cast downward. Arjun is nowhere in sight.

'What do you want?' Anand asks.

'I was about to ask you the same question,' says Deborah.

'We had to discuss something with our father,' he says shortly.

'It sounded more like an argument than a discussion.'

'Deborah, this is something we can discuss only with Appa.'

'Then discuss it, don't shout.'

'I suggest you stay out of this,' Anand says sharply.

'I'm afraid I can't,' she says calmly.

'Why?'

'Because this is our house. I don't want Appa— or, for that matter, anyone—to be shouted at in our house.'

For a moment, Anand is at a loss for words.

Deborah takes advantage of his momentary confusion to walk into the room. Appa sits without moving. His left hand clutches a sheaf of papers. He doesn't look up. Arjun comes into view. He is shorter and thinner than his elder brother and stands at the edge of the bed, holding another sheaf of papers. Deborah realizes they are legal documents. She instinctively moves closer to Appa. Anand has recovered by now and quickly stands between her and Appa.

'Deborah, I suggest you leave us alone for sometime. He is the one who called us and even if it's your house, he is still our father.'

'Exactly, he's your father. Treat him like one.'

Deborah stops in front of Anand. He glares at her. 'Okay. Now leave us alone.'

'I want to speak to him first.'

'I suggest you don't interfere, Deborah. You are unnecessarily treading on ground you have no business with.'

'Let Appa tell me that.'

'Not now.'

'Right now.'

'Not now. You will have to wait.'

'I will not wait. And if you don't give way, I…'

'What? What will you do?'

'I will call the police.'

Anand looks into her eyes. 'You wouldn't dare.'

'I would. Why wouldn't I dare?'

She brushes past him and goes up to Appa. Anand stands near them, looking a little helpless.

'Appa, what's the matter?' she says gently.

Appa remains silent.

'Appa, say something. What's going on?' She kneels in front of him so that she can see his face. It is creased with dried tears. He opens his eyes and they are red and swollen.

'They want me to sign the document…'

'What document?'

'… sign away the property at Vedaranyam Street over to them. At least my share.'

'And do you want to do that?'

He shakes his head.

'Then tell them.'

'I have… several times… They won't listen…' His voice breaks.

Deborah grabs the papers from Appa's hands.

'Stop it, Deborah,' Arjun says. 'Don't try anything funny. This is not America. And this is none of your business.'

'Yes, it is. As long as it is Ravi's business, it is also my business.'

'No, it isn't,' Arjun replies. 'You are not even married to him. Whores don't have rights, not in Chennai anyway.'

For the first time, words fail her. She is too inflamed to speak.

'You bastard.' It is Appa. He is up in a flash and before Arjun can react, Appa has slapped him.

In one swift movement, Deborah tears the sheaf into half and flings the papers to the floor. 'You'd better get out of this house immediately,' she whispers as she turns to leave. 'Or you'll both be very, very sorry.'

As she charges down the stairs, her hands begin to tremble and she feels giddy. She runs to the library and locks the door behind her. She buries her face into the leather couch and bursts into tears.

Appa runs behind her but the door is locked. He reaches for the phone and calls Ravi.

Chinnamma is already at the door. 'Deborah-amma, open the door,' she pleads.

Deborah is not listening.

'Amma, please open the door.'

26

Deborah had known that living with Ravi would cause nothing short of a scandal in Chennai. She had been prepared for it. But Arjun's remark wounded her deeply. It wasn't just the fact that he had said it, but the venom with which he had spat it out.

She doesn't go to office the next day, feigning a headache. She doesn't have a headache. She just feels numb, drained, lifeless. She tried to sleep in the afternoon, hoping to feel better in the evening. But she feels exactly the same.

She lies awake at night, tossing and turning. Ravi puts his arms around her but nothing helps. When it happens for the second day running, he gives her a sleeping pill. It is almost dawn when she finally falls sleep.

When Ravi finds Deborah sliding down from the bed to the floor a few days later, he doesn't stop to think. He takes out the car, bundles her into the back seat and rushes her to the hospital. Deborah is quickly wheeled into the emergency room while Ravi waits outside. 'God, please help her,' Ravi prays as he leans against the wall, which is brown with the prints of generations of people who have leaned against it.

There is a shuffling of feet and someone gets up next to him. He quickly sits down. The plastic chair is screwed on to a long metal stand holding five other chairs in a row. The backrest is broken and he is careful not to lean back. A receptionist sits behind a large wooden table, engrossed in the local Tamil weekly *Ananda Vikatan*. Now and then, he is interrupted by the telephone which he picks up with great reluctance and after replying in a crisp, almost abrupt voice, he returns to his magazine. Appa calls after a few minutes. No, he hasn't gone in. No, he has no idea how long these things take. Yes, he will call back as soon as the doctor tells him something. Ravi absorbs himself with the buzz in the waiting room to take his mind off Deborah. There is constant movement around, with people coming and going, telephones ringing, the honking of cars, buses, scooters and auto-rickshaws in the distance.

In a few minutes, he walks to the doctor's room again to ask what the latest is. No one seems to know. 'Don't worry,' they reassure him. How can you say don't worry when you don't know what the hell is happening, he curses them mentally and goes back to the waiting room. 'Fuck you, Arjun,' he whispers and looks out of the window.

It is only when they wheel Deborah into the private room that the doctor emerges.

'She is fine,' he says.

Ravi breaks down and weeps like a child.

The chat with Appa had been difficult but necessary. Sitting in the darkness of the library, Ravi was all set to tear him apart. When it ended late into the night, Ravi came away with a very different impression of his father. Not sympathetic, but different. For Appa revealed many things to him including the reason he left Sundari when he did.

'I want you to leave right now,' Ravi had said. 'I don't think it's good for Deborah. Or even me, for that matter. After all, what am I getting out of this? Do you really think I care for my one-fifth share in that house of yours? Do you think I came back for that damn house, leaving behind the offers I got in the US? I came back to be accepted into my family, not to be treated like an outsider...'

'Ravi... I am truly sorry. I wanted to heal this rift. Your Kamala athai was adamant I take the initiative and do something to show that I am truly repentant. That's why I came to your house.'

'No, you came because you were kicked out by your sons. But does that really matter now? Can you give me back my home? Can you welcome me and Deborah into that house again? Can you bring back Amma? You can't... you can't bring back a single damn thing. So what the hell are you trying to give me back? Just go to hell.'

'Ravi, I wish I could. I wish I had another chance. I wish I could go back in time.'

'Can you bring back Amma?' Ravi screamed.

'Ravi, I cannot undo what has happened. But where can I go? I have nowhere to go... no one to go to...'

'You could go back to Vedaranyam Street. You could continue to stay there and still fight your case in court, since the property is what provoked you to leave the house in the first place.'

'Ravi, that wasn't the real reason... I was too ashamed to tell you... You have no idea how they treated me the last few months. Not just Anand and Arjun. Even their wives. I've stopped being a factor in their lives—'

'You tried to stop me being a factor in your life and ended up being a non-entity in everyone's lives instead.'

'You do not know how they treated me. They didn't even allow my grandchildren to talk to me. Walking into Sundari was like walking into a cemetery.'

Appa stopped and looked down. A tear slid down his cheek. Ravi looked away. He hadn't come to make his father cry.

Appa had returned from his daily evening walk when he felt an unfamiliar tightness across his chest. He was out of breath. He lay down on the bed, removed his shirt and switched on the fan. After half an hour, the breathlessness remained and so did the dull pain in the chest. Then the sweating started. He asked Anjali to call Arjun. Arjun said he was going out to attend to something important and left. Anand was contacted in the office and he told Appa: 'Take some Tylenol and rest. It's nothing. Don't get scared about every little thing. These days everything feels like a heart attack to you. You are getting old and it's about time you cut down your silly long walks.' His condition did not improve. With rising panic, Appa asked Anand's wife Kanti to fetch the doctor. She asked Appa to take a sleeping pill and rest, and went upstairs to her children.

'I rang my friend Vaidyanathan, who immediately came home and took me to Malar Hospital. The doctors assured me that it was a strain and nothing more. I had done more than my quota of walking and that had affected my breathing, that's all. For a moment I thought I was having a heart attack. Maybe what Anand said was true. I'm getting scared for everything. But how was I to know? This episode showed me where I stood in front of my sons and their families. I was simply an old man who ate, slept and complained, but gave money whenever they wanted it. It was then that I decided to leave Sundari. I could not stay there a minute longer. That wasn't the Sundari I grew up in. That wasn't the Sundari I wanted to bequeath to my children. But where could I go? I could think of no place to go but yours.'

Ravi listened to the story in anger. Appa probably deserved to be treated shabbily, but to wish his death was not something Ravi could think of, even in his dreams.

'Appa, I still think it's best that you leave,' he said, more kindly now. 'You can't go back to Vedaranyam Street. Maybe Jaya's house is the change you need. If not, we could arrange something…'

'I need some time, Ravi. I don't think I can leave today…'

'No, not today. But sometime soon. It'll prevent us from having further misunderstandings. I don't see a happy ending to your problems or mine as long as we are in this house together. Let us part with the knowledge that we came together as father and son, if only for a short while.'

Ravi got up and left the room. Appa continued to sit in the library, under the glow of the lonely table lamp.

When she wakes up, Ravi can sense it.

'Ravi,' she calls out uncertainly.

'Darling, I'm right here.'

She hears his voice but can't see him. It is dark in the room. The night light in the corner is turned the other way. 'Where am I?' she whispers.

'You're fine, don't worry,' Ravi replies. His palm touches her hand and tightens around her wrist.

'Where am I?'

'In the hospital, but there's nothing to worry about.'

'Shit!'

His face comes close to hers. She can feel his hot breath. 'Don't worry, Debbie. You're just fine.'

'Hospital! Shit!' Her voice cracks.

She can feel his face, his palms touch both her cheeks. 'Debbie, believe me. You're fine. Just close your eyes and sleep.'

'What happened?'

'Don't waste time asking too many questions. What's important is that you're fine. And that you're with me.'

She has no energy to argue with him. She cannot see him but can feel his lips on her forehead. 'I love you, Ravi,' she says and gives in to her tiredness.

The next time she comes around, it is still dark. The slight stirring of Deborah's body wakes him up and he is next to her in a flash. She suddenly remembers where she is.

'Ravi, tell me the truth. What happened?'

'You took an overdose of sleeping pills by mistake because you hadn't slept for three days in a row. You just need to rest and rest and rest. So go back to sleep now.'

'Don't tell my mom.'

'I haven't.'

'Shit!'

'Don't worry, Debbie. It's not that shitty.'

Even in the darkness, he can see her smile and her eyes close.

She is up again. This time she stays still. She doesn't want to wake Ravi up. She lies awake for a few minutes, letting her eyes adjust to the darkness. She remembers the time Ravi took her to an expensive Italian restaurant to make peace. She hardly knew him then. She dreams of her house in Norfolk. Her father getting ready to go out; her mother dressed and waiting in the living room; the old Chevy. The trees swish and sway. She and her sister sit inside the Chevy, laughing and giggling.

The flowers arrive first, blossoms in every colour. Then come the people. Mike, Anwar, Anita, Govind, Narayanan and others from the office. They take turns to stay in the hospital when Ravi or Kamala athai go home to change. Are these the same guys who wouldn't even talk to Deborah earlier? Ravi wonders.

'You didn't tell my parents, did you?'

'No.'

'Not even Sophie?'

'No.'

She breaks into a sob. It comes rushing out from deep inside her being. Ravi lets her cry.

'Ravi, I don't think I can take this any more. I tried my best—I promise—I tried my best to like Chennai… but I just can't. I have failed. I'm sorry, Ravi, I let you down…'

Ravi looks at Deborah's pale face, bereft of the sparkle she always had. 'I always told you Chennai wasn't the place for us. You never listened.'

'No… I've been a failure,' she sobs. 'I tried my best.'

'Sleep now… We will leave Chennai soon. You should have listened to me earlier. This place is not for you or for me.'

A strange feeling takes over his being. He feels the urge to visit a temple. Kapaleeshwarar temple at Mylapore. It is time to remind god of his unfulfilled promise.

Luz Corner is packed at this time of day. Cars, auto-rickshaws, cycles and cows jostle for space in the middle of the road. Though Luz Church Road has been widened, vendors, old booksellers and a string of popular shops with fancy names like 'Lakhs and Lakhs', 'Crores and Crores' and 'Millions and Millions' crowd the edges and the pedestrians have no choice but to spill onto the main road. Ravi carefully negotiates Royapettah High Road, crosses Luz Corner and manoeuvres his car into Maada street. He gets down, avoids the cycles coming like arrows in his direction, the urchins selling flowers and camphor, and takes refuge in the temple. The temple is packed. After a darshan of Ganesha, Ravi stands in front of Kapaleeshwarar and closes his eyes in silent prayer. And then, finally, he sees the deepaarathanai as the flame passes in front of the face of the resplendent goddess Karpagambal.

Kamala athai shifts into the house as soon as she hears that Deborah is in hospital. Ravi converts the library into a makeshift bedroom for her. She oversees the kitchen and sends home-cooked food to Deborah in the hospital. Less salt, less spice, and easily digestible. Idlis are the best, she says, since they are steamed. Deborah eats what she is given. Kamala athai visits the hospital every morning and Ravi gets to go home, change, and attend office for a few hours. When he returns to the hospital in the evening, he sees a familiar sight. Kamala athai's crutches are propped against the wall and she is sitting with one eye on the sleeping Deborah. She holds a prayer book in her hands and reads her shlokams softly. That's what Amma used to do whenever any of her children fell sick. She smeared holy ash on the forehead of the sick child and sat in one corner of that room reciting shlokams. Now, Kamala athai has takens over that role, except that she doesn't smear holy ash across Deborah's forehead.

27

As the house-that-Deborah-chose finally goes to rest, the sounds of the night take over. The rare car passing by, honking at an empty road; the lone dog barking at an invisible cat; the tapping of the watchman's stick to keep away an unseen thief.

Appa is unable to sleep.

Since his arrival at the door of Ravi's house, he has peeled away his life, layer by layer. His retirement as CFO and Senior Vice-president of his company; his growing distance from his family; the indifference of his two sons; his attachment to Sundari; Amma's death; his daughter's wedding and the void she left behind; Ravi's betrayal. One by one, he has confronted his emotions, stared them in the face and tried to come to terms with them. All but one. He has never expected his feelings for Jennifer to emerge so suddenly, decades later.

After London, Appa had met Jennifer only once, nearly thirty years later, on one of his business trips to Boston. He learnt that her husband had died several years earlier and her son lived on the west coast with his wife and children. She lived alone now but she was happy. She had always been self-sufficient. They started to write to each other but after a few letters, their exchanges stopped.

When Appa arrived at Ravi's house and saw Deborah, he was, more than ever before, faced with the life he had missed. Perhaps this was why he had been so harsh on Ravi—for aspiring to the life he himself could not have.

He goes to the library, picks up a sheaf of papers, sits down at the desk and starts writing to Jennifer.

You know what my father was like—a very strict man. To a young boy, an almost tyrannical figure. My mother died when I was barely three. In a couple of years, my father remarried. The family found a young woman, Sundari, for him to marry. Sundari had a dosham—a fatal flaw—in her horoscope and to neutralize it, she was given in marriage to a widower—my father.

While Appa and his two sisters were siblings from the first wife, there were two girls and two boys from the second wife—all of whom looked at their father in awe and dread.

It was my father who purchased the land and built the house on Vedaranyam Street. It was near his clinic. With a large family to support, the house was designed to be big and spacious. My stepmother brought up my two sisters and me as her own children. In due course, my own mother became a distant memory and my stepmother meant everything to me.

Appa never lived in any house other than the one on Vedaranyam Street. His childhood, school days and even his Presidency College days were spent at Vedaranyam Street. His sisters and stepsisters married and left. Appa was a brilliant student and soon landed a prestigious job in a British company. Two years after he got the job, he married a fair, good-looking girl. They continued to live at Vedaranyam Street. Only, this time they were shifted to the rooms upstairs to give them privacy. His father died and soon his stepmother died too. After her death, Appa christened the house Sundari.

Sundari—the House of Inner Beauty.

He continues writing.

It might seem strange to you that I have never stayed at any house other than my own. I never imagined I would have to leave Sundari one day. But now in Ravi's house, when I am listening to the Suprabhatham *in the morning or taking a walk in the garden or browsing through the books in the library, I realize I am not missing Sundari as much as I ought to. Except for a suitcase of clothes and some important papers, everything that could remind me of my life has been left behind at Vedaranyam Street. I know I am obsessed about getting back Sundari, but, you see, I spent my whole life there. For me Sundari symbolizes a happy childhood, a happy marriage, a happy family—and the wonderful memories of my few months with you in London. My wife's death shattered my world. Now I am losing Sundari too.*

Kamala athai remembers what Appa told her about Deborah soon after the incident. 'Deborah was amazing. I was amazed at how she single-handedly went after my sons that afternoon. It took guts.'

Kamala athai makes up her mind: she will speak to Anand and Arjun. What they had done was unacceptable. If Amma were alive, they wouldn't have dared do such a thing to Appa or to Deborah. Amma would never have let this happen, Kamala athai thinks. Now that Amma was gone, I have to step in. I can't let this go on.

She rings up Sundari to speak to Anand.

Anand's wife picks up the phone. 'One minute, athai—'

'No, Kanti, wait! I have to ask you something—'

'Athai, it is best you speak to Anand directly…'

Kamala athai's admonishments fall on deaf ears. 'It's time Appa faced reality,' Anand says. 'Arjun and I have our own families now. We need to run our household and need all the financial help we can get. But all Appa is interested in is keeping his property intact. Everytime we need money to do something, we have to approach him like a beggar. If he can't trust us and give us money now, when will he ever give it? He is doing all this just to keep us under his thumb, that's all. Athai, why don't you knock some sense into him?'

'Firstly, if you had been more responsible, you would not have to go to Appa like a beggar but stand on your own legs. So it's not all Appa's fault. He doesn't want you both to take the money and squander it. And what about Deborah? You need not have treated her the way you did.'

'Athai, don't talk to me about her. She is the ruin of this family. Since she entered Ravi's life, everything has gone wrong. Our family has been destroyed. Amma died. The brothers are estranged. Appa has left. What's all this? She has come like a curse on the family. Athai, you are wasting time talking to me. I am not the one you should convince. Ravi is. Talk to him.'

That was that. Kamala athai finally calls Jaya. Jaya is the only one left who can try to bring the warring parties together.

The water-tanker comes into the house and pours its contents into the underground sump. Appa stands there like a guard and sees to it that every drop is emptied into it. When we pay three hundred rupees for water, it better be emptied till the last drop, Appa firmly believes. Even if it means collecting the excess water in a large barrel to water the lawns. After all, the grass needs water too. And in Chennai, that is a luxury. A surge in temperature has brought Chennai yet again to the brink of desperation. There is no water in the reservoirs; catchment water storages in Red Hills, Poondi, Chembarampakkam and Cholavaram are all dry. There is no inflow of any 'cusecs'—as the newspapers call it. No 'cusecs' and no 'mcft'. An entire city carries on without a drop of water. Every Chennaivaasi decides that he will pack up and leave one day, but that day never comes. What comes with monotonous regularity is acute water shortage. Earlier, it was for three months in the year. Then four. Then six. Now it is all year round. Earlier, every politician pledged to solve it and never did. Now they no longer bother.

Every year, Tamil politicians go to Karnataka, and sometimes Andhra, to ask for water. They are almost always refused. There is trading of charges and much bloodletting. The Tamils close ranks. The Tamil dailies are full of it. The Centre usually has to intervene to restore peace, but the Tamil cities remain dry for another year. Thus a waterless cycle continues.

Appa stands outside till the last drop is emptied. They now have water for the next five days. His presence in the house comes in handy and he feels glad he can be of some help. Even if it is just emptying the contents of the water-tanker.

'Appa, if you decide to partition the house, we will fight it at court,' Anand had said. 'Otherwise, we are considering selling our shares to the real-estate don Karim Basha. You remember him, don't you? He's the one I collaborated with for a movie venture and lost a few lakhs. The movie may have bombed but Basha is still a crorepati. He is willing to buy out our share in exchange for separate flats for Arjun and me in the heart of Chennai. It is his way of making up for the loss we suffered earlier.'

It was a threat, Appa knew that. But he was not going to back down. Anand and Arjun knew Appa would not want to share the house with a Muslim. He would have to relent and let them stay on till they made the ancestral property their own.

'Karim Basha?' he repeated.

'Yes.'

'The same person who swindled you of lakhs of rupees?'

'Yes.'

'Are you threatening me?'

'Of course not,' Anand laughed. 'Why do you see this as a threat? After all, you're going to partition the property. What does it matter what we do with our share?'

'You could continue to live there. I never said I want to drive you both out, the way you drove me out. You could take your share and buy new flats and rent them out. All I want is a legal recognition of the division of property, not your physical eviction. You got greedy... and now you have landed us in this predicament.'

'There is no predicament. If you partition, it's okay with us. We will take care of ourselves quite well. If you don't want to, then let's sit down and talk. Not in front of that white whore, somewhere else.'

'Shut up, you bastard!' Appa flared up. 'Control your tongue.'

The conversation was going nowhere.

'Karim Basha can buy us out and all of you as well. He will raze Sundari to the ground and build a multi-storied complex. Maybe all of us can benefit from that.'

'I am not about to preside over the destruction of Sundari. I am trying to find a way to preserve Sundari and give you what is legitimately yours.'

Appa could see the house being destroyed. Even as he thought about it, a shudder passed through him. He saw Sundari being broken, brick by brick. Smashing the structure—a building built with mortar and bricks and made impenetrable with the love of its inhabitants. Once the love wears away, it is easier to dismantle. The top storey comes down first and the inner vitals are exposed. It's like chipping away at one's life, bit by bit. Appa could not bear the thought of another structure in its place. Multi-storied apartments? A shopping plaza? Whatever it is, let me not see it in my lifetime, he prayed silently.

Appa's life had now started revolving around Ravi's house. His dak, his pension cheques, bank statements, insurance papers, phone calls, relatives and friends all came here now. He had come with three suitcases and had lived that way all this while. He had not been to Sundari and didn't feel the need to. Why should he? he wondered. For his sons' companionship? To sleep in his own bed? To re-read the books in his library? He had done all that for decades. It occurred to him that he had with him everything he needed to keep himself alive and well, even happy. He was happy in Ravi's house, in spite of the hostility with which Ravi had greeted him.

Appa suddenly realized that Sundari was not the house on Vedaranyam Street. It was a state of mind. How foolish that he never thought of it this way before. He had been chasing a chimera. He remembers Ravi's angry words: 'Can you give me back my home? Can you welcome Deborah and me into that house again—the same house I left five years ago?' Sundari was not a piece of concrete. It was written in the heart.

He could create his own Sundari elsewhere.

Once this realization dawned on Appa, he felt liberated, as though he had finally stumbled upon the happiness he had been seeking. If he had to stay alone, Sundari was certainly not the house he would choose to stay in. All that bound him to Vedaranyam Street was nostalgia. And to keep a house for the sake of nostalgia was a heavy price to pay.

28

He is to meet Anand and Arjun today. They insisted on meeting at their lawyer's chambers. When Appa goes to pick up Vaidyanathan on his way, he finally gets some good news.

'I rang up Karim Basha,' Vaidy says.

'Karim Basha? Why?' Appa asks.

'The question is not why. The question is, what did he say?'

'What?'

'He said something I had suspected all along.'

'What?'

'Something you too should have anticipated.'

'Dai, what the hell did he say?'

'He said that if the whole house is not for sale, he is not interested.'

'Really! That means my sons were bluffing.'

'Exactly.'

'He is still interested in the house—the whole one?'

'I should think so.'

Appa feels lighter. It is time for some hard bargaining.

Chinnamma decides to take matters into her own hands. She can't let Deborah-amma be insulted like this by the brothers. She knows how badly it has affected her. She saw how gentle and loving Ravi was. How bravely Appa dealt with the turn of events. This is a family that needs all the help it can get.

For the second time that month, Chinnamma takes the long bus ride to the slum where she used to live. She knows she will find help there.

'It feels like ages since we made love,' says Ravi, looking at Deborah. She has just come out of the shower and has a large yellow towel wrapped around her.

'Not that long, really,' she laughs.

Ravi swiftly gets up from the bed and walks up to Deborah. She is still combing her hair. He goes behind her, catches her by the shoulders and propels her towards the dressing table till they stand in front of the mirror.

'I want you to see how you look,' he says, biting her ears. Stands of wet hair sting his left cheek.

'Well… how do I look?'

'Tired. Look at your eyes, I've never seen them like this. It's about time I put some life into them.'

'And how's that?'

'Like this…' He puts his arms around her and the towel drops to the floor.

While the couple make love, Chinnamma is wooing Thambi Maarimuthu in her own way.

'Thangachchi Chinnamma,' Thambi Maarimuthu asks after hearing Chinnamma's story, 'why are you so bothered about these Brahmins?'

'Thambi, they may be Brahmins but they are decent people.'

'There you go again, praising them. How do you expect me to help a Brahmin, when I have tried to fight them my whole life?'

'What is this, Thambi? You talk as if Brahmins haven't done anything at all for us. Even an illiterate person like me knows how, during the independence struggle, the English Collector Nash Dorai was shot dead by Tamil Brahmins Vanchi Iyer and Neelekanta Brahmachari, and how Subramania Bharati inspired Tamils to rise against the British and how Rajaji—'

'Thangachchi, you are correct. Hundred per cent. But you don't realize that even as they were fighting for our political independence from the British, they were continuing the oppression of the lower castes in our own society, keeping us enslaved. That's why a pure Brahmin like Dr Ambedkar converted to Buddhism and led thousands, thousands of his followers to do so. Thousands, not one or two…'

'But he was a north Indian, Thambi.'

'Brahmins are the same, the same everywhere. Look at what happened in Meenakshipuram. After that incident where several Dalits converted to Islam to escape oppression by Hindus, many are looking to Islam to bring them out of their misery. Don't you also remember how, when I was a child, that Brahmin had me beaten up by the police by falsely implicating me in a robbery at his house, when he knew it was someone else? Just because the robber was a Brahmin. Do you also remember how—'

'Enough, Thambi, you have started talking like a politician. All I want is some help and I have come to you for that.'

'I have never refused help, never refused anyone, thangachchi, least of all you. You know that. But to help Brahmins… that goes against my philosophy.'

'I understand your doctor is Dr Krishnan. Isn't he a Brahmin?'

'Dr Krishnan is different. He not only treats me but gives free service to this whole kuppam.'

'All the more reason why you should not waste time cursing the Brahmins. They are human beings like you and me. That's why I have come to you. Thambi, I need your help. These people—Iyer or no Iyer—have treated me very well and they mean a lot to me. Now, when they need help, I could think of no one but you. If you can help, say so. If not, tell me right now and I will leave.'

'Now, now, thangachchi, you are getting angry for nothing. Don't worry. If you feel so strongly, I'll help. What do I get in return?'

Chinnamma looks at him. His eyes are smiling.

'Nothing. I have nothing to give. If I were younger, I would have given you a good fuck.'

His laughter rings through the house. Chinnamma laughs too and for a brief moment, they can hardly control themselves; he is almost in tears.

'All right, ask anything you want,' he says, waving his hands. 'If I can do it, I will.'

'That's all I wanted to hear,' says Chinnamma with quiet satisfaction. He listens patiently as she explains.

'Leave it to me,' he says finally. 'I'll find a way out of this.'

Just as she is leaving, he asks casually, 'By the way, thangachchi, you said the white amma of the house is American. Will she do what you have just said you won't give me?'

Thambi laughs again.

Deborah resumes her evening walks. She always preferred to go for walks late in the evening. The fast-descending darkness gave her cover and anonymity. She wasn't too keen on night walks since the roads were usually pitch dark. Most street lights didn't work either due to stolen or broken lamps or just plain neglect. But anonymity for Deborah was an illusion. Many people from the colony bumped into her whenever she set out for a stroll.

'How are you, Deborah?'

Do I know you?

'Good.'

'You look like you are in a rush!'

Yes, I'm trying to put as much distance as possible between us.

'Yes, I am a bit.'

'Ravi is not with you today?'

No, he is hiding under my skirt after seeing you miles away.

'No, he is still at work.'

'At this hour? Poor boy, he is working so hard.'

At least he has work to do, not like you, attacking unsuspecting walkers.

'Yes, see you later.'

But now she walks with Appa, who is delighted to find a new walking companion. He changes his walks from morning to evening to suit her routine. And they end up chatting about everything under the sun.

While Chinnamma stands wooing Thambi Maarimuthu, Appa, his two sons and their lawyers sit swatting mosquitoes in the high court.

The mosquitoes of Chennai are of a special breed. It is widely speculated that they are the direct mutant descendants of ancient blood-sucking vampires. They suck blood from all Chennaivaasis. Even the thick-skinned buffaloes, standing on all the important road dividers of Chennai and blocking traffic, can be seen swishing their tails in vain to keep the mosquitoes at bay.

Appa is happy to emerge from his sons' lawyer's chamber. Even the large fan inside couldn't keep the mosquitoes out. It had been a difficult meeting, but not a hopeless one. Appa had conveyed to his sons that he was willing to sell the entire house. Let's sell the house and divide it into five parts, he advised. Karim Basha can take it. It's a good idea to negotiate with him. You two can even keep the property if you buy the three of us out, Appa volunteered. The house is an anachronism in this day and age when the whole concept of the joint family has practically vanished, he said dispassionately. In any case, it was becoming a white elephant—too expensive to maintain.

The two brothers had not quite expected this. Appa willing to sell the house? They had come prepared to browbeat Appa into letting them stay in the house for the foreseeable future, either through threat, procrastination or litigation or all three together. Instead, Appa said, 'I'm willing to make a deal with Karim Basha or anyone else who is interested in the property.'

Arjun and Anand retreated in disarray.

Appa knew his victory was momentary. If they backed out of the sale option, he had no choice but to start litigation. That would effectively ensure that the property didn't come into his hands—at least not in his lifetime.

As Appa comes out of the high court, he notices the

sculpture of Manuneethi Cholan—the famous Chola King known for his sense of justice and fair play.

Appa explains his dilemma to Deborah.

'I don't know what to do,' Appa confesses.

'I guess you've already thought of speaking to Karim Basha.'

'Speak to Karim Basha? That wily Muslim? Never! Not after the way he swindled my son out of lakhs of rupees.'

'But he didn't exactly swindle Anand. It was probably Anand's fault as well,' she points out.

'But with what face shall I meet Basha? What do I tell him?'

'You never know, Appa. You may find out something you didn't know before. After all, all you know now is what Anand has told you…'

'I can't go to Triplicane and meet a Muslim film financier. What will people say? They'll laugh at me—a Brahmin going to a Muslim, and to beg for what?'

'You don't have to beg for anything. All you need to do is talk to him about the house. You can call him here if you like.'

'Here?' he asks incredulously. 'That's far worse.'

'Appa, I think you need to go that extra mile—Muslim or no Muslim. Cut through the cobwebs and meet the guy.'

Appa sighs. 'Is this what my life has come to after all these years?'

'It could have been worse. Ravi could have eloped with a Muslim girl!'

They both laugh.

…I know time is running out and I may never return to my house again. All my memories are buried within its walls. Like the Mughal king walled up the two sons of Guru Gobind Singh alive,

*I have walled up my memories inside Sundari. And I will probably
have to leave them behind for good. But when I tell myself that I will
never see this house again, I feel a strange calm. I can't quite explain
it. It is as if I am looking forward to a new life beyond those walls.
Why don't I feel any loss after having lived in Sundari all my life,
with my wife, my children and relatives? Is the house worth so little
that I can shake it away like an autumn leaf? It can't be. Now my
sons have gone their way and I am left only with memories. Yet I
feel young, I feel as though I am living life again, this time beyond
the walls of Sundari. What more an old man can discover, I don't
know. I don't know what I want to do but I know I can do it if I
want to and that is enough. When I see the photo of my wife by the
bed, I know what I am leaving behind. I can't take her where I am
going. I can only wait until I join her!*

*Is this because of Deborah? I'm not sure. It seems that she is the
only person who understands me. I confide in her and she is mature
enough to understand me. Strange, isn't it, that I seek comfort from
an American? I find her a soothing influence even on Ravi. Maybe
her presence has something to do with my upbeat mood these days. It
is all too complex for my understanding.*

Appa puts down the pen. It is dusk and he can see thick
clouds stretch across the sky. He reads what he has written
and smiles. Jennifer would understand, he thinks. She always
did.

One day, after some hesitation, he brings out a weather-
beaten leather-bound book. It is a photo album.

'This is all I could think of bringing with me from
Sundari,' he tells Deborah.

One look at the black-and-white photos mounted on the
grey cardboard leaves and Deborah realizes she has seen
them before. Amma had showed her the same album one
day. She had taken Deborah to the bedroom, closed the

door and warned her, 'Appa will kill me if he knows I have brought this album here. He is very possessive about his photo albums, especially this one.'

Rows of friends and relatives in veshtis, pants and saris in white and grey stare out of photograph after photograph. Appa gleefully points to his impish Flying Standard, framed between Amma and himself. 'This is in front of my college—Presidency College. One of the best colleges in those days. And that is one of the best cars I ever had.'

The Flying Standard has been photographed in various places—at a wedding janavasam, at a family picnic, with unidentifiable kids sitting on its roof, in the garage and in front of the massive Nandi at Chamundi Hills.

Then comes Sundari, photographed from different angles.

'The house was built by my grandfather, actually. He started it and my father added his bit—the garage and a couple more rooms to the first floor. I extended the kitchen and built another room at the back. I converted the cow stables—we had to sell the cows at some point; it wasn't feasible to have cows at home any more—into store rooms, a bathroom and a resting room for the servants and the watchman.

'I was born in that house, you know,' Appa continues. 'And it was always full of people. In fact, at one point, the house became so crowded—with ammanjis, mannis and friends—that I toyed with the idea of converting the outhouse in one corner of the land into a regular office where I could work and read in peace. I had it painted and even moved in some furniture. But at the end of the day, I was a little too comfortable in my own bedroom with the study-cum-library close by.' My favourite room in Sundari was the puja room. I created a parallel world there. Panchaloha idols, pictures, lamps, flowers, tins containing vibhuthi and kunkumam from all over India. I see that you and Ravi have your own niche for puja.'

'Actually, Jews don't need a puja room,' Deborah explained.

'Really? Then the Torah you have kept there...'

'We just have to face Jerusalem and pray. In India, we face west. In the States, east. Prayers are integral to our existence just like they are for you. For Shabbat, we light two candles and have a cup of wine and some fruit.'

'That seems simple enough.'

'Appa, we TamBrams and Jews share more than you think. We both want to preserve our traditions. Puja, religion, prayers and philosophy are just the beginning. My parents wanted me to be a little Einstein! Studies, books, classes, more studies, then music, painting classes... they made me do all that and more. All this just to ensure I know where I come from, where I belong and what makes me different from the others.'

His bluff had been called. Vaidyanathan called Appa and told him the two brothers were not willing to sell the property nor were they willing to partition it. 'Your sons are not going to negotiate. You have no choice but to go to court. That will mean no decision in your lifetime. You can kiss goodbye to the property unless you come to some kind of compromise with your sons,' Vaidyanathan advised. 'You can't even sell your share at a good price now that your two sons legally have two-fifths of the building in their possession. They will procrastinate and frustrate your attempts to sell it.'

29

'Where is Deborah?' Ravi asks as he enters the house. Padma is clearing away some tumblers from the drawing room. Appa must have finished his coffee.

'Amma is on the terrace,' Padma says.

'Terrace? What is she doing there?'

'Flying a kite, ayyah.'

'Kite? Has she gone mad or what! Who is with her?'

'Periayyah. And Kamala-amma.'

'Appa? What the…' He runs up to the terrace and is greeted by a strange sight.

Appa holds the thread in his right hand and rolls the ball of thread with his left. He looks up at the kite, high up in the sky, barely moving. Deborah gazes in wonder at the ease with which Appa has hoisted the kite up even though there is hardly any wind to assist him at this time of day.

The kite-flying season is Appa's favourite, partly because he is so good at flying kites. When he was a little boy, the gardener taught him everything he knew about kites and Appa learnt to get any type of kite up in the air with deftness. When he hears the rustle of the kite cutting, wheezing and rasping through the wind, Appa's heart soars. The gardener taught him how to make his own kite, sometimes from newspaper, sometimes from coloured sheets of paper. The thread was treated with a finely ground paste of crushed glass and the maanja was ready. As his kite went up, the thread wrestled and tugged at the threads of the other kites in the sky, till they all went taut and, just as suddenly, got detached from their masters. The children on the street would run after them and salvage them for themselves.

After the birth of Anand, Appa had given it up.

'Here, hold this,' Appa says and gives the thread to Deborah. 'Just concentrate on the sensation on your fingertips. It will tug at your heart and soon you will soar as high as the kite itself.'

A little tug and she can feel the force of the wind against the kite. 'Yes... I can feel it.'

'Not so soon. It will slowly take over your whole body.'

She waits and feels the sensation envelop her being.

'It's a pity none of my children showed any passion for kite flying.'

'Maybe you never wanted to teach them,' Kamala athai speaks for the first time. 'Maybe you never wanted to get caught flying kites when they were around! If only you had asked them to... they may have turned out different.'

... Would you believe I actually taught my future daughter-in-law to fly a kite? At this age! My wife would have died of shame if she had seen me running around the terrace, tugging at the thread like a child. And, for a moment, I was. I was back in another era, with my gardener and my friends from the cheri... trying to compete, snipe and cut and bring down each other's kites. I could feel myself levitate and my heart soar. I have not felt like that for a long time...

It is Navarathri again and the house is quiet. The bustle
that Appa is normally used to is missing. No children and
adults go around arranging the Kondapalli and Mysore dolls.
Appa does his puja every one of the ten days. Sometimes his
prayers last till lunch time, but he is in no hurry.

Navarathri was a big occasion at Sundari. Everyone in the house
pitched in. First my mother, until she died. Then my wife took over
and soon became the centre of all action during Navarathri. My
wife was like a lion tamer, cracking the whip on the servants to take
out something from the loft or the outhouse. Those who came to stay
during Navarathri became addicted to the festivities and could not
resist contributing in some way to the kolu. The Mysore dolls came
out first. They had been given to her by my mother. They are not even
available these days—the artists have passed on. My wife had them
taken out from huge trunks in the outhouse. With the dolls came
wigs, costume jewellery, decoration items, large background props like
paintings of mountains on canvas—my favourite was that of Mount
Kailash since it could be used as a backdrop to almost any heavenly
scene during the kolu—and the inevitable kalasam. Mysore dolls are
made of very light wood and each part of the doll was dismantled
and stored, so we had to assemble them one by one.The theme for
the Navarathri kolu was decided at least two months ahead. They
usually covered themes from the Ramayanam, the Bhagavatham, the
Kanda Puranam and mythological stories. For some odd reason, we
rarely chose stories from the Mahabaratha, whether by design or by
accident, I'm not sure. To make sure the themes were authentically
portrayed, my wife read several books my mother had collected over
the years.

A large corner of the drawing room was devoted exclusively to the
grand kolu. The scenes would be decorated until the entire pantheon
of gods seemed to descend on the kolu. When friends and relatives
were invited to come and take betel leaf, betel nut, kunkumam and

*shundal, the visitors were treated to a grand representation of a
mythological scene. Apart from the kolu, four different offerings
were prepared—vadai, payasam, one sweet and one kind of rice.
Lalitha Sahasranamam was recited on each of the ten days to invoke
the goddess.*

*The younger lot—Anand, Arjun and anyone else who was
staying at Sundari at that time—usually invented their own version
of kolu, like mixing water with plaster of Paris in a plastic bucket,
pouring this over white bedsheets, taking it out into the sunshine,
folding the bedsheets into cones by propping them up with wooden
sticks planted firmly on the grass until they dried in the hot sun and
became mountains. These were painted over with poster colours and
placed in one corner of the drawing room; the electric train set was
brought out and the tracks carefully laid, weaving in and out of the
mountains. The children brought in small houses, signals, cars,
people and soon that corner of the drawing room was transformed
into a cross between the Wild West and a village in Thanjavur.*

*By the time Navarathri was over and the Mysore and Kondapalli
dolls were packed up for another year, we felt as though we had
survived a cyclone.*

'Now, I can't see myself being a part of such celebrations
again,' Appa sighs. 'Those days are gone. My daughters-in-law
have no use for them. What am I to do with all these Mysore
dolls? They are invaluable. You can't find them anywhere
now. I can't bring myself to throw them away. Maybe I'll give
them to a museum…'

'Give them to me,' says Deborah.

'You? What will you do with them?'

'Use them for Navarathri.'

'Navarathri!'

'Appa, I promise you I will celebrate Navarathri every year
and I will make sure I use Amma's Mysore dolls.'

Appa's heart leaps with joy.

'You really want them?'

'Of course. I want to continue your family's tradition. It's a lovely practice.'

'Amma would have been so happy today to see this,' Appa says. He has tears in his eyes.

That Friday—a Navarathri holiday—Ravi sees a large eversilver vessel outside the kitchen. A thin youth leans against the back door, smoking a beedi. Padma is in the process of emptying a paathram of cooked rice into the vessel. As soon as the youth sees Ravi, he throws the beedi away and straightens himself. Padma doesn't look up and continues emptying the rice paathram.

'What is this, pa?' Ravi asks the youth.

'Ayyah, this is for the kuppam nearby,' he replies.

'What is?'

'Rice.'

'I can see that. But what's it for?'

'Ayyah, starting this auspicious day, every Friday periayyah will send a vessel of cooked rice to the kuppam nearby,' Padma explains. 'There are fifteen-odd families and periayyah has agreed to contribute one vessel a week for their food, especially for the children.'

'Oh!' Ravi has seen this before, at Vedaranyam Street.

Every morning, at about eleven, Appa and Amma made kanjee and kept it just outside the house. Anyone coming that way was entitled to a cup of kanjee. Usually the beggars got it first, then workers, and then the passers-by. It was a tradition that Appa's parents had started.

When Appa's mother visited the Annapurneswari temple at Cherukunnam in Kerala she discovered that the temple closed for the day only after all those who were in need of food had been fed. In fact, the temple had a practice of leaving a bundle of cooked rice tied to the branch of a tree on the temple premises so that even if a thief were to stray into the temple, he would not go hungry. It inspired Appa's mother to start her own version of feeding the poor.

Gradually the kanjee was substituted with steaming hot pongal and cups of tea. With Amma's death, all this had come to an abrupt halt. Neither Anand nor Arjun nor their wives were interested in continuing the tradition, though they could well afford it.

30

As he drives to Karim Basha's house, Appa isn't sure if he is doing the right thing. After Deborah planted this idea in his mind, he had been tossing it around. Finally he decided that Deborah was indeed right. There is no harm in trying it out. But will Karim Basha yield?

After all, what does Karim Basha have to gain from Appa? Anand owes him money and Karim Basha wants it back. Beyond that, what interest can he have in an old man coming to plead with him?

He drives towards Triplicane or Tiruvallikeni—the sacred lily pond—as it used to be called. Basha lives in a predominantly Muslim street. It is easy to see the difference. Apart from the number of colourful lungis on display, the shops that crowd the street sport names like Rashid Departmental Stores, Basheerullah Kitchenware and Ansari Sports. There is also Karim's Biryani House. As he looks at the restaurant, Appa remembers eating idiyappam biryani at his classmate Irfan's home, made specially for him with vegetables and without mutton. He had thoroughly enjoyed it. He didn't touch anything else since the rest of the food was non-veg. He settled for curd-rice after the biryani. He

had been surprised at the light aromatic spices the Tamil
Muslims used which were so different from the pungent ones
the Hyderabadi Muslims used. Even Brahmins used hotter
spices. Tamil Muslims also used a lot of masi or dried fish,
powdered and mixed with just about any dish.

Speakers from the minaret of the solitary mosque wait
silently, ready for the call for azan.

And suddenly the street comes to life.

Allahu Akbar, the Imam calls the faithful.

'Stop the car on the side for a second,' Appa tells the
driver. 'Let the prayer time finish. Karim Basha would have
gone to pray.'

Ash-hadu alla ilaha illallah.

Several loudspeakers are heard, all over Triplicane. The
sing-song of each voice adds to the din and Appa feels as if
he is in the midst of a Veda patshala.

Ash-hadu anna Muhammadar Rasulullah.

Appa had several Muslim friends in his schooldays and
that age he had never really thought about which religion his
friends belonged to. It didn't really matter. What mattered
was that they could play cricket together, go to the first show
of Gemini Tamil movies in Wellington or Sun, or English
movies in Elphinston or Globe, memorise an extract of
Shakespeare's *Hamlet*. True, there was always a thin line
between the Hindus and Muslims of Madras which neither
crossed. But the bond was stronger in those days. TamBrams
bought their month's provisions from Muslim shopkeepers,
as they found them more trustworthy than their Hindu
counterparts. Appa once visited the Tiruvetteeswarar temple
in Triplicane and learnt that milk, fruits and flowers for the
puja had been donated by Muslims for over a hundred years.
Triplicane was the stronghold of Muslims. The Iyengars

and the Muslims lived in harmony. Muslims and Hindus ate together at the famous Ratna Café.

The first time Appa entered Triplicane was to see a movie in Imperial Cinema on Triplicane High Road. He and his friends walked all the way to the cinema and after a satisfying evening went home by tram.

Hayya alas salah. Hasten to prayer.

But things have gone wrong recently and Appa is not quite sure when it all started. In the early eighties, thousands of Dalits in the Meenakshipuram village in Kanyakumari were converted to Islam. They even changed the name of their village to Rehmatnagar. The same thing happened in Tirunelveli, Ramanathapuram and Thanjavur. The media was busy trying to sway public opinion one way or the other. It exposed Hinduism and its drawbacks. But it also helped fuel fundamentalist sentiments. Then Babri Masjid was destroyed. It was a defining moment for Islamic militancy. Money started pouring in from countries that thought of themselves as defenders of Islam and the schism between Muslims and Hindus grew wider.

Appa isn't sure what his Muslim friends think of religion and politics now. Such topics are carefully avoided. Gone is the lively banter about Vinayaka Chaturthi processions going through Muslim areas or Eid processions going through Brahmin areas or whether Muslims should have a uniform civil code. Anything that smacks of religious slur became an issue. The younger generation are growing up thinking that Muslims are indeed different from Hindus even if they live on the same street, speak the same language, wear the same clothes and eat the same food. Playing cricket with Muslim friends without bothering about their individual beliefs is a distant memory. It is, therefore, with great misgiving that Appa goes to the home of Karim Basha.

Hayya alal falah.
Allahu Akbar.
La ilaha illallah.

The house is grand and old, with colonial-style pillars and high ceilings. Karim Basha is standing on the porch when Appa's car pulls up. Appa is surprised to see Basha waiting for him.

'Salaam alaikum,' Karim Basha greets him warmly as Appa steps out of the car.

'Alaikum salaam wa rahmatullahi wa barakatuh,' Appa replies.

'Your pronunciation is impeccable,' Karim Basha says in surprise.

They shake hands.

'My physics teacher in school taught me some parts of Al Quran Al Kareem,' Appa feels the need to explain. 'His hobby was comparative study of religion. It was strange that a man of science taught us the value of religion. But that was how it was. Anyway, let me not bore you with my stories.'

'No, no, it isn't boring at all. I always knew I was going to meet a scholar when I met you. You have proved it!'

They are led into the house through the verandah, shielded from the scorching sun by several cane and bamboo thattis. In the drawing room, it is distinctly cooler.

Karim Basha's house is not as opulent as Appa imagined it would be. It is an old house, much like Sundari. His children and grandchildren must be living here all together, Appa guesses. It hardly looks like the house belongs to someone who dabbles in Tamil cinema, real estate and many other business ventures. The furniture is minimal and of good quality. There are no photographs or portraits; instead, paintings of landscapes hug the walls. There is a small silk prayer mat in the far corner of the room.

As they settle down on the cane sofa, a servant comes with a tumbler of water, places it in front of Appa and goes away silently.

'You have a simple and austere house,' Appa can't help observing.

'Thank you,' says Karim Basha.

'With your background in film and real estate...'

Karim Basha laughs. 'You are not the first person to think this way. In fact, many of my acquaintances think I dine with stars and politicians daily. But sir, at the end of the day, I am a reserved person. I have my own circle of friends. The greatest joy I get is from being with my children and grandchildren. What could give greater satisfaction?'

Appa nods in agreement. Even if they are like my sons, he thinks.

A phone rings somewhere inside the house and when the servant comes out, Karim Basha asks him to attend to all telephone calls and not interrupt them.

They exchange stories. Silly of me to have thought that Karim Basha will come walking down a grand stairway into a room filled with chandeliers and crystals, Appa thinks. Karim Basha tells him how he started out as a poor boy near Parry's Corner struggling to make ends meet. And Appa realizes that sitting in front of him is a self-made man, humble and self-confident.

Karim Basha's wife brings them coffee. Appa realizes that she does not normally come out to greet strangers and is touched by her gesture. She is wearing a black burqa but her veil is thrown back over her head. She greets Appa with a 'salaam alaikum', puts the tray down on the table and leaves.

With the coffee warming his insides, it is time to talk about Anand. Appa asks Karim Basha how much money his son owes him. Karim Basha tells him. Appa winces at the amount. It is much more than he had anticipated. But things start to fall in place now. Anand has no way of paying off Karim Basha, except by holding onto the house in the hope of getting something out of it.

'Sir, it is not my intention to harass anyone in your family,' Karim Basha interjects before Appa can speak. 'You have come all this way, no doubt, to clear things up. When a father goes so for the sake of his son, I know how it feels. I understand your situation. So let me tell you that the money can be returned whenever you are ready. It can be months or years, and I am not going to press for its return unless you are ready to do so. I don't need it now. Please take your time. That's the least I can do.'

'Karimji, your gesture is indeed magnanimous. I came here with a completely different image of you and now I find you are truly noble. Your name itself signifies your personality. But I didn't come here to ask you to postpone the payment of my son's debt.'

'I know a self-respecting Brahmin like yourself would never ask that. But I want you to know that I, on my part, will not embarrass you or your son in any way. Sir, when your son first came to me, I tried to dissuade him from getting into this field. I tried to convince him that this is an area where the risks are enormous and for a newcomer it can be suicide. But he was persistent, so I gave him the loan. Now I wish I had refused him. Somehow, I feel personally responsible for his predicament and this is why I want you to take all the time you need to repay the debt.'

'Karimji, I am grateful for your consideration. I wish there were more people in this world like you. But what I came here for is just the opposite!'

'I don't understand.'

'I want you to ask Anand for immediate repayment of the debt.'

Karim Basha looks confused. 'I don't understand.'

'Well, I heard from Anand that you are interested in buying my house on Vedaranyam Street.'

'Yes, I thought it was for sale. I wouldn't dream of taking advantage of you in any way.'

'Are you still interested in it?'

'Of course, sir. It is prime property and my company can match the highest bid any day.'

'Then we have a common interest. I wish to sell it and you want to buy it. But there is a hitch. That is where I need your help. The property is a joint one. It cannot be sold unless Anand also agrees. Every one of my children has agreed except Anand. Once he agrees, we can plan its sale.'

'But how will my asking Anand to return his debts help?'

'If you demand it now, he will have no option but to agree to sell the house and settle the debt from the proceeds.'

Karim Basha nods, still looking bewildered.

'And one more favour, Karimji…' Appa adds. 'Please keep this entirely between us.'

31

Shitting on someone's head isn't Jaya's idea of fun. In fact, she doesn't think much of it. But then, Jaya isn't a Chennai crow.

Chennai crows sit on heads and shit on them. The heads are round, smooth and black, and that suits them perfectly. When they get tired of circling around the beach, they come back to rest their wings on these heads and shit again. If you look up at the dark granite statues dotting the Marina beach, you will see a crown of white around their heads. White dried crow shit looks fine on top of Avvaiyar. She is an old woman and meant to have grey hair. In fact, a young Avvaiyar with dark black hair during the November rainy season is transformed into an old greying Avvaiyar in summer when she serves as a pit stop for Chennai crows. But one has second thoughts after seeing the discolouration of the poet Bharathi's turban or noticing that the lovely mane on the poet Thiruvalluvar's head has become turgid or seeing the addition of some unexpected grey hair to the bald head of Mahatma Gandhi. But this time the heads of Avvaiyar, Bharati, Thiruvalluvar and Gandhi are black and shining. The rains have washed the crows' marks away.

Jaya and Kamala athai sit with their backs to the Gandhi statue. The sea is some distance away and they can hear the waves crashing against the shore.There is the usual crowd. Even the threat of rain doesn't bother them. They don't believe it can rain in Chennai this time of the year. There is a brisk breeze and Jaya's hair flies in different directions. It is getting dark. A huge black cloud floats across the sea, moving inland. Remnants of the early morning downpour, Jaya assumes, and doesn't give it another thought.

Evening is for the elders, their grandchildren, even their children. It is not for the youth or for lovers. The lovers come in the late mornings and early afternoons to hide behind fishing boats, holding hands. Some do more. Come evening and the lovers are replaced with parents and grandparents, veshtis and saris flapping in the sea breeze, sitting on the sand eating sundal, murukku or milagu vadai while the children make sandcastles.

The coastline is full of people trying to wade in or get their feet wet. The waves are strong and rough this evening. The men hitch up their veshtis and wrap them around their waists like bath towels. Their hairy legs are wet. Their shirts billow in the breeze. The women refuse to hitch up their saris and end up with wet saris from the knee below.

Jaya sits still. She is barely looking at the crowd or the sea. What she has heard from Kamala athai saddens her. She had not realized it was this bad. The way her brothers had treated Deborah was unacceptable. Staying in Bangalore, she was insulated from all this. She didn't belong to her parents' house any longer, even her gothram had changed after marriage, but she knows it is upto her to set things right.

The cloud cover has grown thicker and it is fairly dark.

As Jaya and Kamala athai sit watching the clouds spread across the beach, Deborah can see them too, from inside her car. The clouds look ominous, bearing the promise of rain to wash away the dust from the skies and grime from the streets. But it does not rain. It is merely a threat. Chennaivaasis are used to such empty threats.

Deborah drives into her lane and sees them milling around. Four or five men dressed in khakis and veshtis. An unusual sight in these parts, she thinks, and keeps driving. Late evening is not a time for strangers to congregate, that too on this lane. It belongs to one of the better localities of the city and isn't the preferred option for hanging out. They are probably completing their work at a nearby house. Just then, one of them walks up to the car and stops in front of it. She brakes hard. Before she knows what is happening, the others have surrounded the car. One of them gestures for her to lower the window. She sits frozen, her hands on the wheel. The glass is still raised, but she knows they can break it. When she doesn't respond, the man pulls out a knife. The others begin knocking at the other windows.

She reaches for her handbag, lying on the front seat next to her. Her hand gropes inside and finds what she is looking for. She draws it out and gets a firm grip.

It is a pistol.

Jaya's car passes through Nungambakkam High Road. It is jam-packed even at this time of day, long before the rush hour. Cars, auto-rickshaws, buses and motorcycles fight for space on the two lanes. The bus stops make it worse. Appa used to tell Jaya stories of a time when there were hardly any houses on this road. A few palaces like the Wanaparthy Palace, palaces of the Rani of Vijayanagaram and Raja of

Chellapalli dot the area. As a schoolboy, when Appa walked down this road at night with his friends after an evening show near Gemini, they used to sing or speak loudly to scare ghosts and thieves away. Such was the desolate state of Nungambakkam High Road. Now, Jaya waits patiently as the car inches forward behind a green Pallavan Transport bus and a large white Ambassador.

Jaya's mind is not on the road. The chat with Kamala athai has put things in perspective. Her family is in danger of breaking up.

As the car enters the gate of Sundari, Jaya looks at her old home—she hasn't seen it for some time, certainly not after her father left. She thought the house without Appa would be unimaginable, but it looms large as always. As she looks at it, there is a strange feeling inside her. Nothing seems to have changed but she knows that in fundamental ways, something has.

The goondas have surrounded the car. Deborah looks at the knife gleaming against the closed window. She grips the pistol firmly with both hands and raises it till it is aimed straight between the eyes of the person nearest to her. Her hands are surprisingly steady.

For a moment he freezes. His knife is still held against the window, but she can see his grip slacken. Then there is a shout and the others push him aside. 'Run, Vasu, run,' they shout. She can hear the dull shout through the raised glass. She watches them flee.

When she is sure they have actually vanished, she takes a deep breath and looks down at her weapon. She couldn't have fired even if she wanted to. It is a toy pistol, a perfect replica but still a toy. She had bought it at a toy store for an eventuality like this. For the first time, her hand trembles.

Her palm is moist. She drops the gun in her lap and presses the accelerator.

She is safe.

When she reaches home, Chinnamma is still there.

It is time for Chinnamma to visit Thambi Maarimuthu again.

She has heard Deborah out—Deborah doesn't want to tell Ravi about it lest he does something rash. 'It's the brothers,' Chinnamma declares. 'You leave it to me, amma, I'll handle it. I know who has done this.'

'You do!'

'Yes. Amma, I come from a different strata of society. So we know what these things are.'

'Who is it?'

'Not now. I will check and tell you in good time, amma.'

'We have to do something, Chinnamma…'

'We will do something. But don't tell anyone yet.'

It is strange how Chinnamma has become a conduit between one strata of society and another. Even stranger that Deborah should be seeking her help. She wonders if Ravi even knows about this other side of Chennai. A dark and unforgiving side where life goes on behind the shadowy recesses of buildings, behind the comfort of slums and cheris, behind the colour of money changing hands, behind the four walls of self-appointed Chennai dons and behind the veneer of progress, prosperity and modernity. Chinnamma had been brought up in one and graduated to the other. Deborah had tried to bring her out of a life of despair and given her something to live for in her old age. Little did she think that Chinnamma would one day straddle the divide in Chennai society with ease.

Appa decides to eat out. With Sundari slowly but surely slipping away, shouldn't he get used to eating out and not being a 'burden'? Even if he can't cook, at least he can eat out. He remembers the Udupi restaurants he used to visit when he was in college. They were hygienic, tasty and inexpensive. He asks the driver to take him to the nearest one. The driver looks at Appa as if he has lost his mind but quietly obliges. It has been a long time since Appa has been to one. Twenty years, maybe more. He remembers the one near Mowbrays Road. It's close to where Tennis Krishnan lives, he remembers but is unable to find it. The driver knows that there isn't one there any more and quietly guides him to another location. Appa's eyes gleam.

The restaurant is small but full, like all Udupi restaurants. The customers look curiously at Appa as he enters. They seem to sense that he doesn't belong here with his expensive veshti, silk jibba and obvious hesitation. He looks around and, finding an empty corner, sits down on a steel chair in front of an empty steel table. The waiter, whose lungi is clumsily tied around his waist, realizes that this is a different type of customer he is dealing with, and quickly lets the lungi down to cover his legs out of respect for this new customer. He places a tumbler of water in front of him and asks him what he wants. Appa makes a mental note not to drink the water. He feels like he is back in college. He asks the waiter what is available and listens with undisguised happiness to the familiar list of items. He can picture Vaidy and others sitting in the heat, sweating, swearing, gobbling up idlis and dosas till they could barely get up. Waking up from the Udupi dream, he realizes that the waiter is impatiently waiting for him to order. He orders a masala dosa and coffee.

It is hot inside, and he is already drenched in sweat. The fan above simply circulates the hot air. It's just as well, he tells himself. If I have to live alone, I'll have to come to Udupi periodically. I have to get used to this heat. The dosa arrives. He likes the sambhar but the chutney is too hot. He is forced to drink the water.

Appa comes home triumphantly. Already he feels that he is less of a burden. After a few more days of eating out, he will become almost independent. He smiles at the thought.

Deborah is surprised to hear that he has already eaten.

It is well past midnight when Appa wakes up with mild diarrhoea.

The water hadn't been boiled.

'Appa, athai, Anand and Arjun were threatened by goondas,' says an agitated Jaya.

'Goondas!'

'Yes, and they told them to keep their hands off the property or else.'

'Oh!'

'I think something is really wrong here.'

'Are you sure Anand and Arjun weren't lying?'

'I don't think so. And they think one of you did it—not Appa, of course…'

'That leaves only Ravi. Don't be silly, Jaya, what's wrong with you?' Kamala athai exclaims.

'Or Deborah…' Jaya says.

'Are you mad?' says Appa.

'Well, they are just speculating, and why not? Anyone could have a motive.'

'Jaya, calm down. You are getting carried away. Goondas don't need a motive to act. It's terrible that they have been threatened and we have to find out who did it, but—'

'They say someone called Maarimuthu did it, or his boys.'

'Maarimuthu?' Appa mulls over the name. 'Never heard of him...'

'He is a well-known goonda in this area, I believe.'

'How do those two know that he is the one who did it? Do they know him? Since they seem to know him well, perhaps they should ask him themselves!'

'I don't know, Appa.'

'Let's not come to hasty conclusions. Can we discuss this and figure out what to do?'

Thambi Maarimuthu confesses that it is he who has struck a deal with the two brothers.

'Thangachchi, they came to me. I said yes. They offered me a good price. After all, all they wanted me to do was to ask some of my boys to frighten that white woman. But those idiots!' He guffaws. 'Little did they realize that she was carrying a gun. A gun! When she pulled it out, they ran... ran for their lives. Like dogs! With their tails between their legs. Hah! But who allowed her to keep a gun? Does she have a licence?'

Chinnamma shrugs. 'She must be having. She is a foreigner, remember.'

'Anyway, she scared the shit out of my boys.'

'But I asked you not to harm her or this family,' Chinnamma says, annoyed. 'Why did you do this? It was the brothers I wanted you to put the fear of god into...'

'Yes, I did that too, just as you wanted.' He had sent his men to the brothers. But they had struck a deal with him instead.

'Then what happened?' Chinnamma asks. 'Why did you do this to the white woman?'

'Thangachchi, in the end, all of them, all of them come to me for help. Outside, they talk about goondas and shout loudly from the rooftops that they are pious and pure. But given a chance, one chance, they all do what everyone wants to do—take revenge, use people like us to settle their scores. Then they go back to their existence as if nothing happened.'

'Thambi, I didn't come to you for another lecture. Why did you do it?'

'Thangachchi, don't take it personally. I told you it doesn't matter to me who wins. When they fight between themselves, I will help any side as long as they pay me well. Let them kill themselves. All the better. We will be rid of some more Brahmins.'

'So you struck a deal with them? Did you want to kidnap the white woman? Is that why you sent your—'

'Thangachchi, how can you say such a thing? I told you, it was just to frighten her. I swear… I swear I instructed my boys not to harm her.'

'Sometimes I don't know what to believe.'

'I swear I—'

'What's your price?' she asks.

Thambi Maarimuthu is surprised at the suddenness of the question.

'For what?'

'For you to stop supporting the two brothers.'

'I have no price when it comes to you, thangachchi,' he says smoothly.

'I have had enough of this thangachchi business. Name your price.'

'Thangachchi, you really think badly of me.'

'No, I'm being practical. I thought you would help me and leave the family alone. I was happy that you promised to get me those photos. But money seems to speak more strongly than my pleas.'

'No, no. You think wrongly of me. Your words hurt me. Since I promised to put the fear of Maarimuthu into the brothers, I thought there was no harm in helping the brothers out and earning some money on the side as well. After all, they just wanted my boys to threaten the white woman. Believe me, I had no intention of harming her.'

'No, it's more than that. You have no respect for my words. You are just letting yourself be used by them. All for some extra money. If it's a question of money, then I can also pay you, trust me.'

'You mean that white woman will pay me… pay me to stop these brothers from harassing them?'

'It doesn't matter who pays. What's the price?'

Thambi Maarimuthu keeps quiet.

'You really think I sell my soul, don't you?' he says after a while.

'If I did, I would not have come to you. There are others I can turn to but until now, I thought you were the most honourable of them all. Still, if you have taken money, I need to know how much they gave you. I can speak your language too, you know.'

Thambi's eyes flash for a moment. No one else would dare speak to him in this manner. But Chinnamma is different.

'I cannot do business with you, thangachchi,' he sighs. 'But I can do business with them. That's why—'

'Then what is it that you want? For you to do such a thing…'

'Frankly, thangachchi, I just sent my boys to threaten them like we agreed. But I soon realized that it was a fight for the house. That was what it was all about. In which case, I am interested in the house too, thangachchi. That's why

I felt there was no harm in playing both sides and see what comes up...'

'You are just a petty double-crosser, that's what you are!' Chinnamma cries out. 'Just a petty—'

'Thangachchi, stop right there. It's not my intention to double-cross anyone, oh no. But in the end, they are all the same, all the same. They use us to settle their scores. By day, they are all honourable men. By night, they are like any of us. That's why I have lost all respect—'

'They can do whatever they want,' she stops him midway. 'But how the hell can you double-cross me? Now I know your game. All this hobnobbing with politicians has ruined you. I thought you had some morality left but obviously I was wrong.'

'Thangachchi, that's enough.' His voice hardens.

'Don't try and stop me.' Her voice shakes with indignation. 'You are just another third-rate human being. I should have known earlier. You are not the boy who grew up in my hut. You are not the person people used to come to for help from this cheri. To think I treated you like my son!' She heads for the door.

'Thangachchi, thangachchi—wait, stop. Wait!' He runs after her.

But Chinnamma is already weaving her way through the cheri.

'Don't be absurd. I'd never do such a thing in my life,' Ravi says.

Appa, Kamala athai, Deborah, Ravi and Jaya sit around the drawing room.

'But it did happen... Anand isn't lying. Maarimuthu's men did it.'

'I am glad they did. It's a pity they didn't get thrashed!'
They all look at Ravi, aghast.

'Ravi!' exclaims Kamala athai. 'You can't speak like this!'

'Why not? Believe me, athai, if I wanted to hurt my brothers, I would have left no stone unturned to do so. Anyway, it's about time they realized they can't get away with everything. They need to be taught a lesson. And there is no one in this family to teach them that. I initially planned to file an FIR with the police for the assault on Deborah. But the more I thought of it—and Deborah also dissuaded me—I thought it best to avoid this kind of publicity for the family. I didn't do a thing after that. Why descend to the same level as my brothers and have a street fight? And expose this great joint family of ours in Chennai? That's why I didn't do it. And I never will. Now at least you understand, Jaya.'

There is silence. 'Ravi, it's not that I don't believe you...' Jaya begins.

'By the way, Jaya,' Appa says. 'It is not just we who are interested in the house. Many are. Some of them are people Anand and Arjun know well. And their dealings are not entirely clean. Don't take everything Anand says as god's word. Who knows why it happened?'

Jaya wonders whether Deborah could have had a hand in it. Deborah sits silently throughout the conversation, wondering whether Ravi did indeed have a hand in it. Appa wonders whether Karim Basha had a hand in it. Kamala athai shakes her head, wondering what to do to make the family come together.

32

Deepavali is just days away.

Appa's plan hasn't worked yet. He is prepared to wait. After all, he needs to give Karim Basha some time. Appa continues to live in Ravi's house. He has not been kicked out yet. That in itself is an achievement. He lives from one day to the next, fearing banishment. He had never intended to stay as long as Deepavali.

I must give them something nice for Deepavali, he resolves. New clothes, of course; perhaps a portable CD player too. Ravi and Deborah hardly listen to music and this may help them start listening to some Karnatic music. In any case, Appa's old tape recorder conked out a few days ago. This makes him restless. He cannot play his *Suprabhatham* every morning or listen to MS or Semmangudi.

Venkatramaiyer is ready to see Appa. Appa has to ask him about the house. How long must he endure this? He takes Deborah with him.

Deborah enters a real astrologer's house for the first time.

'So she is the one!' Venkatramaiyer says as soon as he sees Deborah. 'She looks like Goddess Mahalakshmi herself. I told

Mami that she should get used to the idea of an American daughter-in-law. Poor lady, she died before it could happen.' Turning to Deborah, he says in English, 'She was one of the most pious and blessed women you could ever have hoped for as a mother-in-law. She was a great lady.'

Three cups of hot coffee are produced and placed before them. Venkatramaiyer picks up Appa's horoscope and says, 'I have studied it. The house will go out of your hands. That's something you cannot stop. The shani patch is ending. However, there's no need for you to lament the loss of your house. It has served you and your family well.'

'I don't mind it going out of my hands, but does this mean that my sons will litigate and cheat me out of it?'

'No, there will be no litigation. That much I can tell you.'

'No litigation? How can that be?'

'I don't see litigation. I see your separation from the property. But no litigation. No court cases in your horoscope. There will be estrangement but no litigation.'

'That has already happened,' Appa says and his face darkens.

'The property will leave your hands and that will be the end of it, at least as far as your family is concerned. It may come back to you in a different way later, I don't know exactly how.'

'Everything points to litigation,' Appa says quietly. 'Why should my sons pass on the opportunity to file a case and prolong it endlessly?'

'Circumstances may arise.'

Appa nods, not quite believing him. Maybe these 'circumstances' have something to do with Karim Basha. He needs to give Karim Basha time—that much is clear.

The kitchen is stifling. The exhaust is on but it does nothing to quell the heat of Chennai. Deborah struggles with the book propped up in front of her; her hands are immersed in a mound of baking powder and flour. Carefully, she adds the flour to a mixture of oil, salt, spices and some cinnamon and ginger. She has avoided mixing eggs since Appa will not be able to eat it then.

It is Rosh Hashanah—the Jewish new year. Rosh Hashanah without eggs or meat. She never bothered about celebrating it in the past, except to look forward to staying back at home that day and licking the honey syrup clean off the spoon, sometimes forgetting that it was still hot. Now she is excited about it. It is funny how she feels a lot more Jewish than ever before.

She is making Tayglach—the sweet honey-boiled crunchy dough. She will have a formal Rosh Hashanah meal and has invited some of her Jewish friends from the US Consulate.

From the corner of her eye, Deborah keeps a watch on the honey syrup boiling on the burner. It is the traditional syrup of honey, lemon juice, water and sugar. Her fingers work furiously at mixing the flour and baking powder with the oil and spices. The dough becomes sticky. She rolls it out, cuts it into strips and drops them into the boiling syrup.

Just when the last of the pieces goes into the boiling syrup, the telephone rings. She quickly puts the burner to simmer and picks up the cordless handset lying on top of the fridge. It is her mother, calling from Norfolk.

When the doorbell rings, Chinnamma opens the door to find a stranger standing in the verandah. He is dark, wears a T-shirt and trousers, sports a thick moustache and has a thin gold chain around his neck.

'I've got a note from Thambi Maarimuthu for you,' he says.

'I don't know him,' she says and is about to withdraw when he pleads, 'Amma, please read the note.' She takes the note from him.

'Who is it?' She hears Appa's voice from the bedroom upstairs.

'No one, periayyah,' she says, going to the verandah and closing the door behind her.

She opens the note.

Thangachchi, you have misunderstood me. Your words hurt me. I am not the third-rate street rat that you think I am. Please meet me just once. I will agree to whatever you say. How can I not? You have been my mother, father and friend all rolled into one. When I misbehave, is this how my mother treats me? Please come now with Babu, who has delivered this letter to you. He is my man and is trustworthy. He will bring you here. Thambi.

'Keep stirring and add more water if required. Don't forget to add the nuts and fruits after about forty or fifty minutes of boiling,' her mother reminds her.

Deborah holds the cordless between her left ear and shoulder and stirs the syrup.

'Yup, got it.'

'Wait till it becomes golden brown before you remove it to cool.'

'Okay.'

'Have you kept the aluminium foil ready to spread it out?'

'Yes,' Deborah lies. She has forgotten.

'It's a pity you can't serve fish. You could have made steamed ginger fish with mullet or bass. But make sure you have figs, apples, pomegranate and carrots on the table. And some round challah or oatmeal challah would be ideal.'

'Yes, but I don't have that here. I'll make do with something close to it. There are pretty good hotels here.'

'Darling, are you also planning to bake the honey cake?'

'Mom, I have enough problems getting the Tayglach done.'

'No Tzimmes?'

'Mom, you know how I hated that even when I lived there! I'm just thankful nobody forces me to cook yezhukari kozhambu here.'

'What's that?'

'Never mind!'

'Well, if you are happy, I am!'

'Yes, I am happy.'

'*Ketiva ve-chatima tovah*, darling,' her mother wishes her. 'Your dad will go to the brook behind our house tomorrow, to recite prayers and throw some bread and cast off his sins.'

'I'll bet you've forced him to.'

Her mother chuckles. 'Well, when judgement is given on Rosh Hashanah, I do want him to get into the good books and live at least another year as my husband and as your father! If he doesn't take it seriously, I have threatened to blow the shofar into his ear!'

When Chinnamma gets into the car with Babu, she finds Thambi Maarimuthu sitting inside. 'Thangachchi, I have behaved badly. I'm sorry,' he says as soon as he sees her. Babu drives them to a quiet street nearby and parks the car in the shade.

'Thambi, now that you have given me your point of view time and again, listen to me. I am not here to score points against you. In this Brahmin family, some gross injustice has been done. All I asked you was to correct this injustice. I may be an old illiterate lady, but I have one piece of advice for you: when it comes to taking sides, don't be neutral about right and wrong; make a choice. I don't want to see you—a person I have known since you were this high—go down that way. Money will come and go. But don't dehumanize yourself by going after it without morality. You cannot buy right and wrong with money. But enough of this lecture. You know what to do.'

'Whatever you say… Just don't ask me to love Brahmins, that's all.'

'Do as I tell you and don't interfere with this family again. What you tell the brothers is your problem. In fact, if you put the fear of god into them, even better. Make sure the two brothers don't mess with this family again. Shake them up. What is your price?'

'Thangachchi, there's no price for you.'

'No, work is work. You should tell me your price.'

'I have already done what you want.' He hands over an envelope to her. 'See for yourself. It has all the photos of that paapaan, in all the compromising poses you want. He was caught red-handed by the police some time earlier when he was in his car with that whore. When I show him this he will immediately agree. He cannot afford this scandal. None of them can. I don't have to use anyone or make any threats, nothing. This will take care of it.'

'You will be compensated for this, Thambi, I assure you.'

'Don't raise this money business again, not again. If I can't do this for you, who can I do it for? Thangachchi, I just want you to know that in the end everyone is the same… the same whether you call him a paapaan or chettiar or nadar.'

'Okay, you have made your point. This sounds more like the Thambi I know. I want the family to get their share and not get cheated.'

'Thangachchi, you drive a hard bargain. I wish you worked for me, instead of those boys of mine who run away at the sight of a gun.'

'I'm already with you. When did I ever leave the cheri?'

'I know, thangachchi. You will always be one of us. But I never imagined it would come to this one day, that I would have to support paapaans.'

'Brahmins or non-Brahmins, do the right thing, Thambi. That's what matters in the end.'

'I shall stick to our deal, thangachchi. And if I do, will I get to go to bed with that white woman?'

'Never. Don't even dream of it, Thambi.'

'Deborah-amma, it's the brothers all right,' Chinnamma confirms. 'They will be taken care of by my friend, don't worry. They will negotiate with you soon, just watch.'

'What is your friend going to do?'

'He has something which Arjun saar would not like to be made public.'

'Like a photo?'

'Yes.'

'Blackmail?'

'Yes. Don't worry, nothing will go wrong. Nobody will be hurt. Sometimes one has to descend to the level of those one fights.'

'Your friend… is his name Maarimuthu?'

Chinnamma sucks in her breath. 'Amma! How do you know?'

33

'Don't we have to give Appa something for Deepavali?' Deborah asks Ravi.

'Why do we have to pamper him? He can buy his own clothes.'

'We have to give him something. I heard from Kamala athai that he has bought something for us.'

'So? Tit for tat?'

'Ravi!'

'Okay, do what you have to do,' he shrugs.

'We have only two days left. We have to think of a present soon.'

'All he wears is a veshti. A few faded shirts. Some torn banians. Maybe we can buy him a few torn banians to make him feel that we love him.'

'Let's get him a veshti,' she says, ignoring him. 'I'll be down in fifteen minutes.'

Choosing a veshti is not an easy job, Ravi quickly realizes. He is familiar with a shop in Mambalam where he used to tag along with Appa as a child. The traffic is bad at this time. In Mambalam, it's bad all the time.

'Do you want a Paththara veshti or Eerettu?' the shopkeeper asks.

'What's the difference?'

'Paththara is for those who want to wear the veshti in the traditional pancha kachcham way. Eerettu is for a slightly relaxed fit,' he smiles.

'Eerettu sounds good,' Deborah says, trying not to look lost.

'Of course, we also have Onbathu anju but I would still go for the Eerettu,' the shopkeeper says helpfully. 'Do you want a Mayil Kan veshti or a Rudraksha Pattu?'

The only time Ravi wore a Mayil Kan was during his poonal ceremony. It was the same veshti that Appa's father and Appa had worn at their own poonal ceremonies. The broad silk zari had been rough on the skin around the waist and left red marks by the time the ceremony was over.

'I prefer a Mayil Kan,' Ravi says confidently.

'You could take a nine-count Mayil Kan,' the shopkeeper says. 'I have some colourful zari to go with it.'

'I thought there were only two traditional colours for zari?'

'These days, we make the borders in several colours to attract customers, including violet. Tell me, saar, who wants to wear a veshti these days? They are reserved for special occasions. Business is not good, saar.' He shakes his head. 'So we are forced to make innovations like different coloured borders and try and cut costs as well. We have tested zari, which is even brighter than the original silk zari but the price of the veshti is much cheaper. We try all sorts, saar.'

'Well, I prefer a traditional green border in silk zari. Appa has many in red.'

'Fine, saar. No problem.'

He brings out a lovely Mayil Kan with green border. Appa is taken care of for Deepavali.

There are enough fireworks being sold on the pavement to blow up Chennai twice over. All the pavement shops are selling firecrackers of every brand and type: Jil Jil Maynee sparkler boxes with a picture of a buxom circus trapeze woman on the cover, wheels and tharai chakkarams of varying diameters, flower pots, rockets, Lakshmi vedi, 100-wala garlands, 5000-wala garlands and atom bombs. Even Mouse brand firecrackers.

Appa had insisted on bringing Deborah to Parry's Corner to buy fireworks. 'It's the best place for fireworks in Chennai. I have always bought my fireworks here,' he tells her proudly.

There is a group of people holding placards at the street corner. Their faces are not visible in the milling crowd but the placards are hoisted high above their heads. The writing is in Tamil.

'What do they say?' Deborah asks Appa.

'It says, "Save children's lives. Don't buy fireworks."'

'What do they mean?'

'They are probably referring to Sivakasi, where most of these fireworks have been made. They are usually made by children.'

'So why isn't it being stopped?'

'Don't ask me,' he shrugs. 'I am only here to buy fireworks, not to support child labour.'

'Okay, but this is inhuman.'

'Yes, but this is all part of a campaign by non-Hindus. There was even a newspaper article this morning saying fireworks should be banned because they pollute the air!'

'Shouldn't it be, if it really is harmful?'

'And deprive millions of Hindus that one day in the year when they can burst crackers and bombs and celebrate? Generations have done it before and nothing has happened!

I haven't heard of a single person dying of smoke from fireworks lit on Deepavali. Bah! All this propaganda by Christian missionaries… just gone beyond the limit…'

Appa and Deborah walk around and pick up some pattasu.

It is Deepavali.

Appa is awake at four-thirty. After he has taken a bath and put on his new Mayil Kan veshti, he pulls out a single firecracker from one of the boxes—Ganesha Fireworks, it says auspiciously—and goes to the garden. It is a ritual that Amma followed every year. She lit the first firecracker of Deepavali morning. The children came out later to start theirs. But she always fired the first one. Appa decides to take over that role for old time's sake. He trots off to the far corner of the compound wall, to avoid waking up Ravi and Deborah. He carefully lights the fuse. The firecracker goes off—and wakes them up anyway.

Appa sits outside and watches Ravi and Deborah burst crackers. The neighbours have also started theirs. The sky is filled with a rush of crackers and rockets. Appa holds an oosi pattasu in his hand. It is a small string of crackers loosely tied together. He holds the fuse to a candle and throws the lit cracker into the air. It crackles and sparkles for several seconds before it descends slowly, fizzling out like an extinguished cigar.

He looks at Ravi scurrying towards the crackers and running back. Deborah is wearing the salwar set he has bought her. Venkatramaiyer was right. She looks like an ivory carving of Goddess Mahalakshmi. She is a bit more circumspect about the fireworks but is enjoying herself nevertheless. Some young boys and girls—relatives of Padma—join Ravi and Deborah. They sport new clothes, hold a long fiery sparkling maththapu each and stand waiting for their turn to light the rockets. Each rocket is placed carefully inside a glass beer bottle and lit up. It zooms up. Sometimes it goes diagonally, and one of them narrowly misses Appa. He laughs but Ravi is not amused. He admonishes the youngsters and they try to be more careful the next few times. In a short while, they have forgotten, and start sending the rockets in different directions.

Kamala athai joins them too, and later Appa's 'walking' friends come by to wish him. Appa looks around. The house is full. The cook Padma is running in and out of the kitchen, barely able to cater to the demand for coffee. Chinnamma is helping her, but standing several feet away from the kitchen door. Padma had woken up at four and made the sweets: Mysore pak and badaam halwa. The murukku and cheedai were made the previous day.

Mike joins them with his girlfriend Annie. They are wearing new clothes too. Swarnam comes in with her husband. Her daughter Chitra has been stitched a red silk paavadai with gold zari border. Her mother has made her wear a pearl necklace and a gold uddiyanam, which is a little too big for Chitra's waist. Appa looks around. He sees a house full of people, a bustling home where people walk in and out as if it is their own, not for a moment thinking they will not be welcome. There is laughter, joy, warmth being spread around.

It is Sundari.

Wherever I live becomes my Sundari, he realizes in wonder.

And thus, in the midst of Deepavali, Appa finds Sundari. It never left him. In fact, it is Sundari because of his presence. He is Sundari.

In the evening, Anand calls Appa to say that they are willing to partition the house and sell it.

34

As silence descends over the house the next day and Padma retires for an afternoon nap, Appa trots into the library after a sumptuous lunch. Ravi and Deborah are at work. The million pieces of paper strewn all over the porch and driveway from the fireworks have been swept away by Chinnamma.

Appa takes his coffee into the library and settles down. He had conveyed the good news to Vaidyanathan in the morning. Vaidy was extremely surprised. I have never seen anyone throw away a winning case and settle for a compromise, he says again and again. You are lucky. What was aimed at your head has taken only your headgear. He would meet the brothers soon and get the partition deed signed. 'Dai Vaidy,' Appa had reminded him, 'please remove the words "in view of the internal family quarrels amongst the family members, the members are not able to continue their joint enjoyment of the properties belonging to the family…" from the deed.'

There is a knock and Deborah enters.

'You? Here? I thought you had a full day today after all the festivities yesterday.'

'Yes, I do. But I wanted to speak to you.'

'What is it?'

She comes in and locks the door behind her. She takes off her dark glasses, draws up a chair next to Appa's and sits down. 'I have something to tell you.'

'What is it?'

'I have a confession to make.'

Appa looks at her, confused.

'Appa, I have wronged you.' She covers her face with her palms and starts sobbing.

'Why? What happened?' Appa gets up and puts a hand on her shoulder.

She looks up and her face is streaked with tears.

'Appa, I have done something terrible. I hope you can forgive me.'

'Of course, but what happened?'

'You know your sons have agreed to the partition and sale.'

'Yes.'

'It was I who made them agree.'

'What's wrong with that?'

'I had them blackmailed. It was I who gave the go-ahead to have Arjun blackmailed. Appa, please forgive me. I acted like a common criminal,' she cries. 'I was just trying to do what's best for us.'

'Well... I should have guessed! I was wondering how Anand convinced Arjun. I knew Karim Basha would tackle Anand, but I kept racking my brains on how Arjun could be brought around.'

'I'm really sorry. I shouldn't have taken what Arjun said so personally. In a fit of madness—'

'In a fit of sanity, I should say. I took care of Anand and you took care of Arjun,' Appa smiles suddenly. 'In fact, Anand told me yesterday that Karim Basha had wanted his money back and tried to pressurise him to sell his share in the house. Anand said he resisted and told him that he wouldn't do it. But he also said Arjun was blackmailed by Maarimuthu's boys. That seemed to clinch the matter. They decided the best course of action was to agree to the sale to preserve their honour—or whatever is left of it.' Appa smiles warmly at her. 'We did this together, you and I.'

Appa leaves for Vedaranyam Street to wrap up the partition and to find a buyer.

He is not excited about returning to Sundari. But he has to, for the sake of his sons. He knows things will never be the same between him and his two sons. Once that bond was broken, it was impossible to get it back. Even so, he is surprised that, in the face of the disintegration of the family, they didn't make the slightest effort to save their relationships. Perhaps it was Appa who sowed the seeds of his estrangement by shunning Ravi and showing Anand and Arjun that human relationships weren't as sacred as they had been taught to believe. It was only a matter of time before Appa himself was turned out by his children.

He leaves Ravi's house, taking with him his audio cassettes, four suitcases, one handbag, his bedding and the holdall. He leaves behind the two framed photos of Gayathri and Hanuman in the puja room. He leaves behind the two stainless steel vessels and forgets to take a torn banian.

He also leaves behind a house where his absence is finally noticed.

'The old man wasn't too bad after all,' Ravi tells Debbie a few days later.

'I miss him,' she says simply.

'Well, that's overdoing it, but I'm glad he came here and we sorted things out.'

'Yeah, but I miss him. For once we were like a family, not two individuals figuring out which way to go.'

'And here I thought you would be happy to have your privacy back. At least we can start eating non-veg food again. I'm starved.'

No one is prepared for the events that start moving at a blinding pace. Karim Basha is the highest bidder for Sundari and all of them are consulted by Appa about the price. The deal goes through. Ravi gets a sizeable chunk of money—much more than he had anticipated. His brothers are promised two flats at reduced cost after the house is demolished and an apartment complex built. Appa extracts one important written commitment from Karim Basha. The new housing complex is to be named Sundari. Jaya gets another apartment in her name in the same complex. Ravi is the only one who has opted to take money instead. The last thing he wants is an apartment in the same complex as his brothers.

Appa opts to take money too. That is a surprise. Why money? Doesn't he need a home?

'Will he stay with Arjun or Anand?' Ravi wonders.

'Neither.'

'Debbie, parents in India don't live alone. Not in Chennai, anyway. He'll have to stay with either one of them.'

'Not necessary. He won't be happy with Anand or Arjun.'

'Exactly. So who is he going to live with?'

'With us.'

Ravi looks at her to see if she is joking.

'Joke? Ha, ha.'

'No.'

'Yes.'

'No. I don't mind if he moves in here.'

'I do.'

'I wouldn't.'

'What's wrong with you? A brief interlude is okay. But living with him permanently?'

'So what? Don't you think we are emotionally better off now than before he came into our lives?' she asks.

'Just because we have faced our past doesn't make us emotionally closer.'

'It does.'

'Maybe a little. That still doesn't mean we can start living with him.'

'Who knows? I am sure we can. Remember what it was like when we were in the States? American life is unforgiving because we isolate ourselves. I have seen quite a bit of Chennai. When your father came into our lives, many others came in too. It was so natural, as though they had always belonged to us. That's really something. In a way, they took us for granted. But they did it because we belonged to them as much as they belonged to us. That's what makes us part of a family. That's what was lacking in our life here in Chennai for the two years that we were alone. Now that we finally belong, let's not throw it away.'

'But before we think about Appa, maybe we should give a thought to whether we ourselves should continue to stay in Chennai. Now that my family is effectively splintered, I really have no reason to stay here at all, Debbie. Maybe we should go back to the US, get married and settle down there, like Bala did. Let's have a Washington wedding.'

'No, I want a Chennai wedding and we will stay here.'

'Let's at least have a Chennai–Jewish wedding. I bet Chennai hasn't seen one in several decades. Just make sure you don't serve any of that inedible Jewish food.'

'In which case, we have to import some Rabbis.'

'Yes, from Cochin, speaking Malayalam or Yiddish. They will have us married in a language neither of us can understand.'

'Under the Special Marriages Act of 1954.'

'So you have read the law, have you?'

Deborah has changed. Gone are the days when she tried to drown her loneliness in work, or hide her foreignness in the darkness of a Chennai evening. She has made up her mind about where she wants her home to be.

Chennai.

Epilogue

More than a month passes.

The deed is done.

Appa is all packed and set to bid a final goodbye to Sundari.

'Don't leave the house during Rahukalam,' the priest says.

'How does it matter? A tragedy is about to befall—I am leaving my only home… and here you are talking about Rahukalam.'

'Yes, it is very sad. But your departure is also the beginning of a new journey, don't forget!'

Yet another joint family in Chennai vanishes.

But Appa isn't grieving the loss. He looks cheerful. He looks younger too and Ravi thinks it is because of his haircut. Deborah thinks it is because he is genuinely happy with the turn of events. Ravi cannot imagine how anyone could be happy about selling one's ancestral house. Especially since Appa spent his entire life there. He wouldn't know how to start living in a smaller place. Even the thought of a smaller place would distress him.

But he is still cheerful. And they don't have a clue about what he plans to do next.

'Ravi, Deborah,' he says, 'what I say will come as a bit of a surprise to you. But I've decided to visit America for a few weeks next month.'

'America?' they echo.

Appa smiles. 'I told you it will surprise you. Yes, America. Even a person like me needs a change once in a while!'

'Of course,' says Deborah quickly.

'I finally have some money to spend on myself. My duties are over, even if you two are still unmarried. You're independent people with minds of your own. You will be fine without me.'

Deborah laughs. 'What are the places you are visiting?'

'I am off to Boston,' says Appa.

'Why Boston?' Ravi interrupts. 'Anyway, Gopal is there and I can easily ask him to put you up. By the way, Appa, don't go about throwing away your partition money. I can ask several people in the US to put you up and you can have a holiday in any part of the US for as long as you want.'

Appa looks at them. He bends down and adjusts the fold of his veshti. He pours another mouthful of hot coffee from the stainless steel tumbler and enjoys the warm sensation streaming through his body. There is stillness in the air as Ravi and Deborah wait for Appa to speak.

From a corner of the ceiling, a gecko chirps. Ravi looks up. There it is, transfixed on the ceiling, looking down at the three of them. He notes the direction from where the chirping comes. I must look this up in my book of Tamil customs, he tells himself. But he remembers reading the last time that this position of the gecko could mean that someone close is about to leave…

Portends loss of relatives?

'Do you both have some time to spare or are you rushing off to dinner?'

'No, we have time.'

'Ravi, I don't quite know where to start but this is a journey I have to make. It happened a long time ago, long before I got married. I remember the evening my father and I left Madras to go to Dhanushkodi. The train was called Boat Mail…'

Acknowledgements

I would like to thank my Publisher and Chief Editor V.K. Karthika for her faith in this book. If not for her infectious enthusiasm, unwavering support and tweaking of the narration at the right places, this book wouldn't have happened.

My editor Neelini Sarkar nurtured the manuscript like a child. It was not only a rewarding experience for me to work closely with her on the manuscript, but her insights and suggestions have enriched the text and the story.

My uncle Baranidaran's nod to my writing abilities means a lot to me. His writings, plays and literary works in Tamil have convinced me of the virtue of remaining true in letter and in spirit to the Chennai ethos and milieu.

My niece Avanija Sundaramurti shared her expertise in the publishing trade to assist me in this process.

It was with Arup Dutta that I shared my first draft. His critical, no-nonsense eye helped put things in perspective.

My parents Kalpakam and Srinivasamurti stepped in with some course corrections whenever the book started to stray from authenticity.

My sister Mathangi has remained a strong supporter of my writing over the years and has backed me whole-heartedly.

My children Bhavani and Vishwajit remain fans of my writing – which is no mean feat.